TERROR AT 3AM

When PTSD Turns Deadly

A novel by

Duane D. Wilson

1

Author's Note:

A series of haunting and unforgettable rapes and murders plagued California between 1976 and 1986. These unsolved crimes inspired the following novel and contain many of the *modus operandi* of the actual crime series.

For information on that series of crimes, see: http://ear-ons.com/

The crimes were committed before DNA was available – with the exception of some 1986 killings in Southern California. Still at large, the rapist- turned- killer has never been identified.

It is hoped the telling of this story will draw attention to the need for significant rehabilitation programs for our veterans who struggle with post-traumatic stress disorder.

PTSD victims often suffer from destroyed lives, damaged families and, sometimes, suicide. When PTSD evolves to engender assaultive and murderous tactics familiar from military training, and when conventional investigative methods are unable to stop the crimes . . . the human suffering is tragic.

This is such a story.

All characters in the novel are fictional.

Duane D. Wilson

This novel is dedicated to
Don Richard
A friend who died much too young
A friend who generously inspired others

1

Sacramento County, 1977

In the darkness and fog, his form blended into the night. He could not see them, but he sensed his unit's presence on his right and left flanks. It was up to him to hold the center. As he waited for the order to move forward and attack, the old familiar feelings of fear, mixed with excitement, washed over his body. Such danger had become an aphrodisiac for him.

Then he heard it, his signal to attack sounding from a distant Amtrak whistle. He rose from the grass and vaulted the six-foot cinderblock wall, crouching in the target's backyard . . . waiting. He knew the time: 3:00 a.m. Now, the floor plan of his victim's home, memorized during a reconnaissance mission two days prior, dominated his thinking. Consistent with his training, the entry point to the back bedroom, an unlocked window, waited for him. This was zero hour. No turning back. All thoughts of his unit vanished. He acted alone.

Tonight's target was another Sacramento woman. She was tall, slender, with long dark hair. A profile that drew him as a moth to a light.

As he approached the back of the house, the ex-soldier struggled against recurring visions of olive-skinned women lying naked, eyes pleading, their ravaged bodies screaming. For a moment he remembered when he hated those missions with the sights, sounds and smell of death. In due time, hatred turned to pleasure and he understood well the

6

importance of brutality: It separated the strong from the weak.

Pulling on surgical gloves and pushing open the unlocked window, he lifted his lean body into the house with the ease of a gymnast. Silent, motionless, the intruder waited and listened before removing his clothes, folding them into a neat pile by the open window.

Confident all was quiet, he reached into his backpack and took out a mask. Like a skilled actor, he pulled it over his face, making a slight adjustment for his eyes, he removed a chrome-plated pistol and a flashlight, slung the backpack over his left shoulder and began his silent creep through the house.

A faint glow from a hall night-light lit a path as he counted each step to the kitchen where he sliced the telephone cord. Fifteen steps down the hallway, he found two people asleep in the master bedroom.

His victims lay quiet and vulnerable in their slumber. For a moment, he fought the old distraction, the visions of screaming women, and he forced the images from his mind. *Focus on the mission. Focus. Focus. Focus.* He leaned down, pointed the flashlight, pausing momentarily, savoring the power, the control. And then . . . light!

Before sleep could find its way into her weary spirit, Beth Heatherton lay awake in bed, listening to the faint snoring of the man next to her. His name was Ron, and she berated herself for not asking his last name before bringing him home. At the time, his name was not important. She didn't need a name; she needed sex. In truth, she needed to be held; she craved touch. This was the first time in more than three years she'd made love to a man other than Hal. Only five days ago her Hal, marriage, and life ever after played prominently in her mind.

She had been so ready for marriage. Now a nauseating void remained as she felt herself recalling the fateful Friday evening when Hal invited her to dinner. She anticipated the perfect atmosphere for the long-awaited proposal. For months, she'd used all her feminine wiles to move him toward the topic of marriage. She recalled Hal's redundant responses: 'Hang on honey, you know I'm snowed under at work. We've got plenty of time.' He always sounded convincing and she had tried to respect his work pressures and the extra time his job demanded. After all, for three years they'd enjoyed each other's company with dinner dates every weekend and even one memorable week flying to Italy, renting a car and exploring the Amalfi coast. She felt sure Friday night would be her reward.

He must have a ring, she assured herself, thrilled with the thought of it. Shockingly, following dinner and her suggestion for a bottle of Mondavi reserve, instead of a proposal, Hal calmly announced their relationship was over. His explanation, devoid of emotion, burned into her memory. 'I've met another woman and I'm serious about her.' No pleading, no questioning, could sway this new Hal. He had already moved on. Even now, days later, Beth still could not think clearly.

Girlfriends encouraged her, 'Get over it . . . find another man. When Hal knows you're with someone else, he'll come running back.' Well, here she was with another man in her bed and all she felt was loss. Even the sex left a void. She missed Hal. Why wasn't he here holding her? Suddenly, a light exploded in her face and she heard her own screams.

Then the gruff order: *'Shut up, bitch.'*

2

Detective Susan Allen finished her daily run at exactly 5:30 a.m. on a cool morning in early January. She poured a cup of coffee and settled onto the couch, wishing she could remain there for the rest of the day. The tensions of investigating a serial rapist hung heavy on her mind and she ached for the women victims. Their stories repulsed and angered her.

Frequently, she found her days ending with a sense of unease she'd never before experienced. While running relaxed her body, nothing stopped her constant doubts about the rape investigation. Who could help her sort through these doubts? More and more she felt isolated.

Allen knew she was an anomaly; a woman appointed as a detective in a major police department in the 1970s was not the rule. In fact, the roster of female patrol officers in Sacramento was quite small.

On the job, she'd endured the stigma of being hired more for her beauty than for the serious professional she modeled. The sexist jokes and snide remarks were a frequent occurrence. And, when she made detective the rumors circulated it was because she 'was sleeping her way to the top'. Nothing was further from the truth.

In fact, she refused to date anyone in law enforcement. As a result, Susan kept her own counsel. Especially this morning the reality of her isolation was leading her to a clarity she'd not yet voiced: This serial rape investigation is seriously flawed and no one in the department is facing that fact.

On the surface it appeared everyone was doing their job, but twenty one rapes, all in a small subdivision east of town? 'This shouldn't happen,' she thought in the pre-dawn light of her apartment: 'What are we doing wrong? What about Weaver's recent drinking? Why did the brass wait until there had been fifteen rapes before assigning their only female detective to the case? Why can't I figure this out?' Susan was still wrestling with questions when the phone rang.

Not surprisingly, the dispatcher reported another attack. The victim taken to ER only minutes earlier. Susan walked to the bathroom and turned on the shower. As it warmed, she couldn't stop thinking that only an hour earlier she had been jogging on the deserted Sacramento streets. Had anyone seen her? She shivered as she stepped into the warm, welcoming water.

The ringing broke through Bud Weaver's sleep-deprived brain. He rolled over and after a several tries found the telephone. The bedside clock read 5:53 A.M. as the portly, fifty-two-year old investigator cursed aloud, 'Damn.' A meeting last night with internal affairs had lasted well past midnight and writing a report on the rape investigation took another hour. He knew this phone call could only mean another rape.

'Homicide, Weaver.' Even at home he answered the phone as if he were on duty.

'I didn't expect J. Edgar Hoover although the phone rang long enough to wake the dead,' the graveyard dispatcher chuckled.

'I'm in no mood for jokes,' Weaver growled.

'Sorry to wake you, but duty calls.'

'Where is it this time?'

'Just haul your old bones out of bed and get down to the emergency ward at City Memorial. A nurse named Mary Gonzalez will give you the vitals on the woman they just brought in. Apparently she's in bad shape. The victim's male friend seems to be okay. He's waiting there to talk with you.'

'Call Allen and tell her to swing by. Might as well use one car. Save the county money.'

'Already have. She'll be pulling up soon. Call in when you get to ER. I'll have a case number ready for you.'

Weaver sat on the edge of the bed and rubbed his thighs. The muscles felt tight. Sighing deeply, he walked to the closet, pulled on yesterday's pants, a clean shirt from a dry cleaner bag and headed for the bathroom. He splashed cold water on his face and fleetingly used a toothbrush. He'd managed four, maybe five passes with an electric razor when he heard a car stop in front of his house. The detective walked into the living room and gave a quick blink of the porch light to let Allen know he was awake.

Black Jack, nicknamed BJ by an ex-wife, meowed from the kitchen doorway. 'Damned cat,' Weaver mumbled, walking back to the kitchen. He reached into a grocery bag, still sitting on the counter where he'd left it two days earlier: paper towels, a box of crackers, three cans of chili and nine cans of cat food. He searched for one labelled 'seafood', popped it open, and began to scoop the contents into BJ's dish.

The cat brushed his leg with persistent meows. 'Yeah, yeah, I'm on it,' the detective grumbled, somewhat apologetically, as he paused to stroke the soft fur, finding a brief moment of satisfaction.

Quickly slipping on his shoes, he was out the door. It would be noon before he noticed one black sock and the other brown. These were the moments when regrets about divorcing his last wife entered his mind.

'Get me to some coffee,' Weaver directed within seconds of tossing his briefcase into the back seat and settling into the unmarked squad car.

'Look for the thermos and cup behind your seat. I figured you'd need some, and what is a woman good for but taking care of a man?' Susan Allen responded with a cynicism now a regular part of their rapport. She focused on her driving and pretended not to notice Weaver pull a small, silver flask from his pocket. In the time they'd worked together, Allen had been careful not to disclose her true feelings about Weaver's professional lapses, but this morning her mind flashed again to his drinking. Was it just stress? Nevertheless, she kept silent, knowing the burden was hers to make their partnership work.

'Maybe this one will be where he left his billfold at the scene, or the woman recognized the bastard as her husband's barber,' Weaver said.

'Fat chance,' Allen responded. 'And, did you see last night's news? Gun sales are going through the roof. It scares me to think how much fear there is in this city, innocent people might be killed by a gun in the wrong . . .'

13

'Hell, I'm more worried that someone won't have a gun. This guy needs to be shot,' Weaver cut her off.

'But, Bud, think about it. The terror this rapist is generating could cause someone to shoot his own son coming home from a late night. All of Rancho is on the verge of mass hysteria,' she countered.

'Too much damned publicity,' he grunted.

As she drove, Allen thought ahead, reviewing strategy for approaching the newest victim. This morning's investigation would bring her face-to-face with her seventh rape victim, another woman deeply damaged and desperately in need of understanding. Today, Allen wondered if she was emotionally up to the task.

They drove easily through the light early morning traffic, arriving at the hospital emergency entrance just as a 6:30 a.m. news alert began. Allen parked the patrol car in a bay marked 'police only' while blocking Weaver's reach to turn off the car's AM radio.

'I don't wanna hear any god-dammed news,' Weaver barked.

Allen turned to face the lead detective, her voice firm, 'Bud . . . I do.'

The Sacramento rapist led the morning news.

3

Weaver exited the squad car with a sigh, weary even before the day began. Clutching his briefcase, he walked several paces ahead of Allen who carried only a note pad. They both knew the routine. Allen would interview the female victim, Weaver the male witness.

Despite the early hour, many of the ER waiting room chairs were filled. Weaver scanned the room and immediately focused on one man who sat with his head bowed, hands clenched. The detective approached with an open badge just as the man looked up and blurted, 'Officer, officer, I'm . . . I'm Ron Willard. Are you here about Beth?'

'She the rape victim?' Weaver asked, unaware all eyes in the room focused on him.

'Yes, she . . . we were both attacked.'

'I'm Detective Weaver from the Sheriff's Department and I need to ask you a few questions. But, let's not talk here. Follow me,' he said, moving brusquely back to the hallway.

Willard followed to a small conference room adjacent to the ER. Before sitting down, Ron stammered, 'I . . . I can't remember much it . . . it was just terrible and I . . . .'

'Hold it. Slow down. Let's start at the beginning. First, let me start the tape. Sit down. This is gonna take some time.' With that Weaver opened his briefcase and removed a small tape recorder. He pushed 'start' and held up his left hand, signaling Ron to remain quiet.

Using a reporter's formal tone, the officer began, 'This is detective Weaver, Sacramento County Sheriff's Department, the date is January 4th, 1976, City Memorial Hospital, Sacramento, California, 0643 hours, interviewing Ron . . . what's your last name, address and phone number. Home and work?'

'Wil . . . Willard. Ron Willard,' the witness said as he shakily delivered the rest of his information into the recorder.

The pace of Weaver's approach seemed to settle Ron a bit. He quit shaking and asked Weaver if he could smoke.

'Yeah, go ahead.' Weaver continued, 'What's your lady's name?'

'Beth'

'Her last name. Does Beth have a last name?'

'Heath . . . I think, or something like that. But, longer . . . Harthton maybe. I'm not sure. I don't really know her that well.'

'Close enough. I'll get the spelling later. Present during the rape of Beth H. in the early morning hours.' Weaver leaned back, looked directly at Willard, 'We need every detail you can remember. When and where did you first get together with Beth? Talk about the people around you, especially anyone watching Beth or following her before you talk about what happened later.'

Immediately Weaver's thoughts began to wander as he wished for more coffee and aspirin. Willard coughed, bringing the detective back into focus. 'What's this about not really knowing her?'

'I know it sounds weird, but I had only met her a few times. She hung out at the Barrel Club where I

16

often go after work. She was usually with a guy named Hal. I only knew their first names. Last night she was there alone and she acted differently. Came on to me. Know what I mean?' Willard explained.

'You mean she was there alone, so you moved on her. Anyone else move on her?'

'No, it wasn't like that. I was having a drink at the bar and she came in and sat right down next to me. You can ask Brent. I bought her a drink. It went on from there. I didn't see anyone else paying any attention to her. My back was to the room.'

'Who's Brent?' Weaver asked.

'The bartender. I don't know his last name.'

'Is he the regular bartender?'

'Yeah.' Willard said.

'Did she say why she was so friendly all of a sudden?'

'Not right off, but later she told me she and her boyfriend had a falling out.'

'Any details?' Weaver asked.

'Not really. Something about another woman, I think she said. Maybe his secretary.'

'Did you ever look around?'

'No, we had two, maybe three drinks. Then we decided to go to her place and have some wine.'

'Her idea or yours?'

Willard hesitated, 'I . . . I suggested it, but she agreed right off.'

'What about when you left? Did you notice anybody paying attention to her?'

'No, mostly just regulars, guys and women I see around all the time.'

17

'Can you give me any names? They might have been more observant than you.'

'Just some first names: Dan, Trixie, Phyllis, Greg . . . Carl maybe.'

'You're not big with last names are you?'

Willard shook his head, 'It's not that kind of place. We just go there to unwind, relax, play a little pool . . . .'

'And get laid?'

'Yeah . . . sometimes.'

'What time did you arrive at the Barrel Club, what time did Beth show up and what time did the two of you leave? Start with leaving work.'

'I clocked out around five thirty, maybe a quarter to six. I work at Coastal Cutting Tools, about five blocks from the club. I was on my second drink when Beth came in, so it must have been around 6:15, 6:20. We left around 8:00 maybe a little earlier.'

'How did you get to her place?'

'We drove our own cars. I followed her in mine.'

'This the first time you'd ever been to her house?'

'Yeah, like I said, this was the first time.'

'How come you didn't go to your place?' Weaver snapped, keeping the questions going quickly.

Williard blushed and said, 'I . . . I've got a lady friend that drops around unexpectedly sometimes. I didn't want to be interrupted.'

'And she wasn't afraid her boyfriend would drop by her pad?'

'No, she said they broke up.'

'Did you see anyone following you from the bar?'

18

'No, but after three or four drinks I was pretty much just looking straight ahead, focused on my driving. Know what I mean?'

'I get the picture,' Weaver smiled. 'Did you notice anyone hanging around the neighborhood when you got to her house?'

'No. Seemed like a quiet area.'

'What time did you get there?'

'It only took about ten, maybe fifteen minutes.'

'Everything went as planned until you unexpectedly had company. Is that right? Weaver asked.

'Yeah, we talked, drank a little wine, went to bed, made love, fell asleep. Next thing I knew I woke up to her screaming and a light in my face.'

Weaver noticed Ron's lips starting to tremble. 'Did you think about trying to jump the guy?

Willard shook his head, 'No, no way. I saw a gun, and the way he talked, I just knew he'd kill us unless we did as he said. And . . . and that mask, oh my God . . . it was unbelievable.'

'Walk me through what happened. Give me a sequence if you can,' Weaver interjected.

'It was strange. He knew Beth's name. I think he even called me Hal, but everything is fuzzy.' Ron paused, put his elbow on the table, rubbed his eyes and continued. 'He turned on the light and shoved me over on my stomach; then he ordered me to put my hands behind my back. He told Beth to tie me up. She tried and fumbled. I think she had shoe laces. He shoved her off the bed and tied my hands. Tight.' Willard stopped talking and rubbed his left wrist,

19

obviously swollen. 'That's when Beth tried to shoot him.'

'She did *what*?' Weaver asked, incredulous.

'Somehow she had a gun pointed at him. He just laughed. I heard a couple of clicks, but the gun didn't fire. She dropped the gun and started to cry, begging him to leave.'

'Gutsy broad. Where'd she get the gun?'

'I don't know for sure. Under her pillow?'

'Damn.' Weaver shook his head in disbelief, 'What happened next?'

'He ordered us to get up and walk into the kitchen. When we got there, he pushed me down on my face. I thought he was gonna kill me.' Willard began to shake again.

'Easy now,' Weaver said slowly, 'take a couple deep breaths.'

Ron wiped at his eyes with the back of his hand, steadied himself and continued, 'He tied my ankles and jerked my feet up . . . almost to my hands. I felt like a calf in a rodeo. He made Beth put dishes on my back, then said if he heard them fall off he'd put a bullet in my head. I didn't dare move. I could hardly breathe, I . . .'

'Did he tie Beth?' Weaver interrupted.

Willard hesitated, 'I think so. I couldn't see after that because he took her away. But, later when she cut me loose, I saw cord burns on her wrists and ankles.'

'Describe his voice?' Weaver continued.

Willard leaned back, hesitated and mumbled, 'He talked low. Hard to understand.'

'Speak up!' Weaver said motioning at the tape recorder. 'OK, then what?'

20

'I didn't know for sure when he left because he would disappear, then suddenly come back. He kept making threats. Finally, when he hadn't returned for a long time, Beth got free and cut me loose. The phone was dead, so I pulled on my pants and ran to the neighbors . . . asked them to call the police.'

'You never saw his face?'

'No . . . like I told you, he had on a ski cap pulled over his head and I could see only his eyes,' Willard said.

'Did you see any hair?'

'Only arm hair. Kinda blondish . . . and thick.'

Weaver leaned back in his chair, studying the young man. After a short silence he asked, 'How tall was he?'

'He seemed a little shorter than I and I'm six feet one. But he was very muscular. Shit . . . the guy was naked.'

'Anything you noticed about his privates?'

'I can't remember. I don't want to remember,' Willard sighed, lowering his eyes and staring at the table top.

'Can you estimate his weight?'

'I dunno, maybe 170, 180 something like that.'

'Anything familiar about him . . . anything at all?' Weaver asked in a tone indicating the questioning was about over.

'No. It was all so unreal. I'm having trouble thinking . . . remembering. I'm really worried about Beth. Is she going to be alright? I could see she was bleeding.'

'Don't know,' Weaver said sharply. 'The doctors are with her. She probably won't have much to do with men for some time. I'll leave you this note pad and pen. You write down everything you remember. Details are important.

I'll pick it up from you tomorrow. You're free to go. Be available by phone. You think of anything before then, you call me pronto . . . got it?'

Not waiting for an answer, the detective turned off the tape recorder, dropped his business card on the table, closed his briefcase and then, as an afterthought, asked, 'Did you hear him leave the house?'

'No. I heard nothing.'

Weaver found Allen talking to a nurse. As he approached, she broke off conversation and waited for him to join her. Silently, they walked through the emergency entrance out into the parking lot. Allen was first to speak, 'Did you get anything new?'

'Not a damn thing from him other than our victim is promiscuous, but nothing new on the rapist. Sounds pretty much samo-samo.'

'He didn't mention the bananas?'

'Bananas?'

'That's what the rapist used; both vaginally and rectally. It was either the bananas or something else that tore up her up. She's in surgery.'

'Damn, isn't he a creative son-of-a-bitch. She gonna be alright?' Weaver asked.

'Hopefully, but it'll be tomorrow before I can talk to her. She's lost blood and was out of her head when she arrived at the hospital. There is no way she could handle questions. I got a call from the guys at the scene. They found a .25 caliber automatic on the floor of the bedroom. Got real excited, then ran a check and discovered the gun was hers. One strange thing: The firing pin was filed off.'

'That's right. Willard said she tried to shoot the bastard. The fucker must'a followed his pattern and prowled the house prior to this morning, located the gun and disarmed it. That's why he laughed when she threatened him with the gun. Any mention of prints?'

'Lots of prints. I don't hold much hope on that front. I'm sure he wore gloves like he always does.'

Weaver nodded, 'Let's grab some breakfast. Gonna be another long day.'

4

The red brick Criminal Justice Building at Sacramento City College faced a tree-lined quad, resembling the cozy campus of an Ivy League school. Students and faculty alike spent many hours enjoying the California sunshine on the vast lawn, except today, a windy winter morning.

Roger Blomberg, chairman of the Administration of Justice Department, stood and moved from his desk to the window. The sun's light was fading from the western sky as he glanced at his watch: 4:34 p.m. 'My appointment may be a no show,' he thought, just as his secretary, Beverly, rang the intercom, 'Roger, your four-thirty called earlier to say he might be a little late. Sorry, I forgot to tell you.'

'Not a problem . . . in fact, I think I see him coming now,' he said, watching a well-dressed man in his late twenties, briefcase in hand, approaching the building. He walked with intensity, then stopped abruptly to smooth his dark, curly hair.

'Help him relax a bit, okay? He appears a touch uptight,' Blomberg said.

'Of course, I'll tell him he's just meeting an old hippie,' she responded.

Accustomed to this enjoyable banter, Blomberg paid no attention to her remark and was pleased to see his soon-to-be teaching intern relaxed as he walked into the office.

Beverly delivered two cups of coffee and the men settled in for a chat about Connors' undergraduate and graduate work, his reasons for coming to

Sacramento and his desire to learn about the inner workings of the criminal mind.

After going over the outline of the sexual deviancy course Connors would be teaching, Blomberg asked, 'Where does your interest in teaching the class come from?'

'Well,' Connors paused, 'that's a key question for me, because, quite honestly, I bring some family history to the table when I talk about sexual deviancy.'

Blomberg leaned forward, an obvious show of concern on his face.

'Don't worry. I'm not speaking about me, personally,' Connors added quickly.

'Then what . . . ?'

'The short of the story concerns my sister's daughter who was kidnapped, raped and killed when she was only 10 years old. Our family never recovered from the tragedy and the realities we discovered continue to haunt us,' the young professor's voice grew soft.

'Realities?'

'The most alarming was the fact the killer lived only a few houses from my sister, and he had a history of stalking young girls.'

'Was he registered with the authorities as a sex offender?' the professor asked.

'Yeah. The Boulder PD messed up. They should have been notified since he had also spent time in a county lock up for stalking a young girl. But the paperwork was never processed and no one, not even a nearby elementary school, was alerted.'

The professor shook his head, 'I'm so sorry. You have experienced an unbelievable tragedy.'

25

Connors continued, 'I decided to begin studying criminal justice based on this experience. Then it became clear to me that understanding the 'criminal mind' would be helpful in averting tragedies like my niece's death and, ideally, in apprehending sexual predators.'

'Has this become a crusade of yours, to improve the system?'

Connors quickly reassured, 'You mean can I remain objective? Don't worry, I'm not a zealot, just motivated to understand these offenders.'

The direct response put Blomberg at ease. The last thing he needed was to bring someone on board who carried a personal vendetta. 'Do you see yourself working in law enforcement?'

'Not directly. But, I do see myself working with law enforcement,' Connors responded.

The professor sat back in his chair, his left hand stroking his beard. Both men remained silent until Connors spoke, 'I see your local paper is doing some heavy coverage on the rapes happening here in Sacramento.' Pointing to the newspaper on the professor's desk.

'Have you been following this story?' Blomberg asked, 'The reporters are dubbing him the EAR, short for. . .'

'East Area Rapist,' Connors finished his sentence. 'And, yes I spent the morning reading today's paper, including the editorial which was critical of your Sheriff's Department. I also happened to overhear some talk in a coffee shop on Freeport Boulevard about the rapes'.

'Oh?'

'From the perspective I got this morning, there are lots of folks who are afraid to go out at night and are sleeping with their lights on. And the waitress told me many of her friends are buying guns. What's going on with the police? Has there been any progress?' Connors queried.

Blomberg shook his head, 'Not much from what I hear. I believe the slow progress is a result of how the sheriff's department is conducting the investigation. You're right, this guy is not your typical rapist. Actually, he's a trained terrorist.'

Connors looked again at the newspaper and scanned the headline:

Twenty-second Rape & City Nears Hysteria; Sheriff's Dept. Offers No New Information; Sister of First Victim Speaks Out

Before asking, 'Did I hear you say terrorist?'

'I did,' the professor spoke emphatically. 'And, the Sheriff's department continues to investigate this case as a conventional rape series.'

'Terrorist is a loaded term. What's your reasoning?' Connors asked.

Blomberg glanced at his watch. 'I'm afraid I'm out of time right now, but we should plan to get together over dinner and I can answer that and fill you in on what I know. In fact, this case might be of value to you. It may provide insight into the mind of a sex offender; and, questions about the series are sure to come up in your class. Are you free tonight? Is your fiancé in town with you?'

Connors looked down and then up, 'Yes and no. I am free tonight and no my fiancé is not here with me. Actually, our engagement has been called off.'

The professor sensed he'd touched a nerve in his young protégé and quickly moved on. 'Let's plan to meet for dinner at 7:30 tonight at the *Amigo*. On your way out ask Beverly for directions. This may work well, especially since my suspect in this series will be in your class on Monday morning.' The professor stood and extended a handshake.

Connors also stood, momentarily taken aback by this last statement. Before he could ask for clarification his new mentor had gathered his coat, picked up some papers and was moving towards the door.

When Connors arrived at the restaurant, he was surprised by both the size of the Thursday night crowd and the noise level. He wove his way through the tables to where Blomberg was sitting. In the few hours since they last talked, Connors' growing sense of concern troubled him. 'Was it the department chair's criticism of the police or was it his remark about a rape suspect taking his class?' He wasn't sure.

'Have any trouble finding the place?' Blomberg asked.

'No, your secretary's directions were excellent.'

The two men could not have been more different. Connors, a stocky, youthful 29-year-old with classic features, the kind women would describe as preppy and handsome, contrasted strongly with Blomberg. The younger man appeared traditional and conservative; the older was California casual. Connors dressed sharply in a button-down shirt, pressed khaki pants, sports coat, tie and polished loafers. The professor in his late fifties, tall and lanky, wore a full beard and shoulder length hair. His Levis were faded and a V-neck sweater showed signs of wear. 'I should have told you this is a laid back establishment,' Blomberg smiled.

Connors laughed. 'I've always been one to overdress. Good breeding my mother would say.' He loosened and then removed his tie, stuffing it into his jacket pocket. 'That does feel better.'

'I took a chance and ordered beer for you, I hope you like *Tecate*,' Blomberg asked as a waitress approached their table carrying two bottles and chilled glasses.

For a few minutes conversation stopped as they sipped their beer and listened to a lively Mariachi band.

The professor was the first to break the silence, 'I think we covered most of the details about your course this afternoon. Unless you have questions.'

'I feel comfortable with the course and I'll have a final outline on your desk Monday morning. But, I have to admit, I've been wondering what you meant about a rape suspect being in my class?' Connors tried to sound casual.

'Sorry, I shouldn't have left you hanging.' Blomberg chuckled. 'His name is Tyrus Brock. I noticed his name on your class roster, so unless he changes his mind, you'll see him in class.'

'What makes you think he's the rapist?'

'I'll explain, but let's order. It's been a long day and I missed lunch.'

With two Mexican platters and a side of guacamole on order, the professor continued, 'This

Brock should be no problem for you. I'm sure he will keep a low profile.'

When the food arrived, the professor began relating, between bites, what had been happening in Sacramento. 'Like I said earlier, I believe this man is basically a terrorist. It's not that sex doesn't play a role in the rapes. It obviously does. I'm sure many psychologists could theorize he had a domineering mother and a weak father. Of course, that description probably describes half of the male population. Thankfully few become rapists.'

'Don't most experts say rape is actually rage against women?' Connors interjected.

'True, but I've got a strong sense something else is overriding his sexual problems and hatred of women. This rapist brutalizes men as well. He often deliberately selects couples. That's where the terrorist part comes in.'

The professor stopped, letting Connors absorb the information. Blomberg lowered his voice, 'To commit so many rapes in such a short period of time and not get caught requires planning skills and an unusual attention to detail, characteristics most rapists don't possess.'

'You're saying this guy actually plans his attacks?

'Absolutely. Most rapists are opportunists, and before long they make mistakes. That's why they get caught. This guy is short on mistakes. Since there are no schools for a would-be-rapist, he received his training somewhere. And I have been concerned for some time about the mental stability of some Vietnam veterans I've had as students. Some with obvious emotional problems. Wounds you cannot see.'

'How did you conclude this Brock is the rapist?' Connors asked.

'Suspected rapist,' the professor clarified. 'Actually, he was handed to me.'

'How's that?'

'I helped an ex-con named David Moran write a grant proposal for a campus program named Vesta. The program uses education to rehabilitate paroled convicts. Moran interviews inmates who are within six months of their parole date and selects those who can handle college work. Initially, we excluded drug and sex offenders. Also, anyone with a history of violent acts. But, the courts in their sovereign wisdom ruled we couldn't exclude anyone on the basis of a parolee's criminal history.

Before long Brock got into the program. Apparently, he'd served several years as a Special Forces soldier in Viet Nam. He was discharged after being convicted of rape and then did time in Folsom Prison, enrolling into the Vesta program shortly before the Sacramento rape series began. It wasn't long before Moran noticed Brock was never on campus the morning after a rape was reported.'

'Let me get this straight you think this Brock got his training in the military?'

Bromberg nodded, 'Exactly. It would be interesting to see if he actually engaged in combat while in Nam and what the nature of his assignment was. This rapist gives every indication of being trained in guerrilla warfare.

Most of the houses he chooses are next to open areas, empty lots or parks. He also prowls and gains information about the occupants prior to the night of

31

the rape. Just like armies when they scout ahead to gather information. Sounds like military training to me. In addition, Brock fits the rapist's physical description.'

'Haven't you turned his name in to the police?'

'Believe me, I have.' Blomberg assured. 'The *Sacramento Union*, the evening paper, established a 'Secret Witness' program with a reward of twenty thousand dollars for information leading to the arrest and conviction of the rapist.

Moran wanted the money but didn't want his fellow cons to know he'd fingered Brock. He asked me to get the reward and then split it with him. I called Brock's name in and later even talked to several detectives, including the lead investigator, a detective named Weaver.'

'Did the police say they checked him out?' Connors asked.

'Yes, they insist he's been eliminated as a suspect, Blomberg said. 'However, I have little faith in their investigative abilities. My educated bet is Moran is right and the police are wrong. I'm thinking you could dig around the edges of the case a bit and then offer your observations to the mix.'

'By digging around the edges, you want me to see what I can find out about this Brock guy?' Connors asked, finding the entire topic a little overwhelming.

'Something like that. It just came to me while I was talking with you this afternoon. Most of what you would be doing would be dealing with official agencies, so it shouldn't be dangerous.' Blomberg said as he took a long drink of water.

Then he continued, 'As far as I know, the Sheriff's Department is trying to use evidence collected from the crime scenes; and since there is virtually no evidence, they are getting nowhere. I think a better approach would be to match a suspect's personality and background with the known modus operandi of the rapist. If they find a suspect who matches his physical description and has served in either the Army or Marines, they should put him under 24-hour surveillance.'

The waitress returned to fill their water glasses, and Connors waited until they were alone again before responding. 'This sounds interesting, but in all honesty I need time to think about it.'

'Sure, I understand. Mull it over, and we can talk again on Monday. If you decide to take the task on, I'll help you all I can.'

As he left the restaurant, Connors cautioned his racing mind to slow down. What was he getting into? He had come to Sacramento to teach a class, not investigate a suspected rapist. Even so, he couldn't deny the case sounded compelling. What if the professor was right? Theory had its place, but the chance to do hands-on research was an opportunity he found difficult to resist. Still, this was research on a violent man, and hadn't Blomberg said at one point that he expected the rapist to begin killing?

As he drove from the parking lot, Connors couldn't decide if what he felt was excitement or fear.

5

Detective Weaver sat at his desk in what passed for an office. Actually, it was a small alcove off the main squad room, crammed with several detectives' desks. His, a three-by-four battleship grey, sat directly inside the entrance.

From this position he caught the noise from both the squad room and the constant ringing of telephones, as well as conversation from the other detectives. The alcove had no window, only a large bulletin board hanging on one wall, plastered with notes, messages, case numbers, fading family pictures and an outdated 1976 calendar.

Weaver loathed spending time at his desk, but a case summary had to be in Captain Phillips' hands soon. A scheduled press conference at 4:30 meant Phillips wanted the report by 3:30. 'Damned brass,' Weaver mumbled to himself, 'always concerned with paperwork and looking good for the press.'

Never comfortable behind a typewriter, especially with his growing girth turning to fat, Weaver's large frame made deskwork aggravating. As a patrolman and even when working vice he'd managed to keep his weight reasonable. Now, after seven years of stress dealing with homicides and sex offenses, as well as his age and his third divorce, both his body and his spirit were redefined.

'God, I need a drink,' he thought, 'what I wouldn't give for a nice neat homicide, not some crazy rapist with every damned reporter in town wanting to know why we haven't caught the bastard.'

Just as the report started to come together, Allen approached his desk and Weaver was immediately distracted. He could not get used to working alongside a fellow officer with a school girl's body, a figure that turned heads. She didn't flaunt but instead carried herself with the poise and dignity of a beautiful woman.

'You writing a report or a treatise?' Allen quipped, seeing him still at the typewriter.

'I woulda been finished an hour ago if you were takin' calls like I asked,' Weaver growled, eyes on the keyboard.

'Taking calls, that's all I've done. I've been on the phone since long before lunch,' she countered.

'Lunch . . . hell, I'd be glad to have time to go to the can. You got anything new?'

'Well, no one called to confess, if that's what you mean except your favorite lady. She said she talked with you earlier and didn't like your attitude.'

'Yeah, that would be Sandi Willis. She keeps harping on that Brock guy. He musta got her drunk and plunked her good, and now she wants him to rot in prison. Maybe we should put her together with that arrogant Blomberg. Can you imagine a commie and a lesbian? They'd make quite a pair,' Weaver managed a quick laugh.

'How come this professor is such a burr under your saddle?' Allen asked, sitting down in the one available chair, crossing her long legs.

'Aw, he's a fuckin' poor excuse for an ex- cop. Worked too long in Berkeley and the hippies got to him. He's always spoutin' off . . . got theories up the ying-yang. Gives all the damned liberals ammunition.

35

He's nothin' but trouble. And, the crazy jerk is dying to be sheriff.'

Allen decided to change the subject. 'Don't forget we have to brief the detectives on which suspects to contact if a rape is called in. Our new guy, Sheridan, is bugging me about his assignment.'

'He probably wants to know which broad to alert. If he would just forget the pussy, he'd make a half-assed cop someday,' Weaver said, shifting his weight in his chair.

Allen had learned during her first year as a deputy to ignore such remarks, crass as they were. 'Do you really think it's worth the effort to send detectives to a suspect's house immediately after a victim calls in a rape? Calls are usually more than an hour after the rapist has left the scene. It ties up a lot of manpower. And, so far, we've gained nothing from it.'

Weaver's gruffness began to escalate, 'It certainly has worked in other cases. How else are we gonna eliminate suspects? The lab guys can't figure out the blood types.'

Allen countered, 'I just keep thinking this rapist has time to get home. Wouldn't it be better to assign the guys to surveillance.'

'Watching what?' Weaver snorted

'Watching the homes of prime suspects . . . maybe the bike path.'

'I'm not gonna put anyone out there all night counting bikes and joggers,' Weavers said curtly. 'Let me finish this report for Phillips.'

'Speaking of the Captain, he told me he wants a detailed memo for the graveyard shift. He wants it to emphasize high priority areas where we think the rapist may hit. Says he feels the patrol deputies need more guidance,' Allen said, retreating toward the squad room.

'Hell, we could give 'em the bastard's address, and it wouldn't help catch this guy. He has to drive to and from each and every rape and the deputies haven't even made a field interrogation card on him. No, just give'em the same memo as last week. If Phillips wants more detail, let him figure out what to write.'

Allen stopped, 'You have no faith in the uniforms.'

'Why should I? This pervert is running circles around them.'

'What does that say about us? We haven't exactly looked like Sherlock on this case.' She couldn't resist the dig. With twenty two known rapes, Allen's concerns about their investigative approach continued to haunt her. So far, Weaver's years of expertise had yielded nothing; and, she was growing irritated with her back seat role.

'We'll get him. It's just a matter of time. He'll fuck up and make a mistake. Then we'll nab him,' Weaver spoke with confidence. 'Now get the hell out of here, and let me finish this damn report. Phillips will be here any minute.'

Within moments he was interrupted again when Sergeant Howell of internal affairs rapped on his desk. Weaver slammed the typewriter carriage, 'What?' he barked.

'Sounds like you got a little problem with the lady,' Howell almost whispered, glancing over his shoulder towards the direction Allen was walking

'Nothin' I can't handle.' Weaver responded.

'You sure about that?' the grizzled sergeant said, leaning down into Weaver's face.

Weaver turned away, 'Yeah, but, between her and that damned Phillips, you guys are makin' it harder than hell on me.'

'Phillips knows nothing and just make sure *she* doesn't either,' Howell said softly. 'And, we can't give you much more time.' He turned and walked away leaving Weaver angry.

Susan sighed and walked through the adjoining squad room, sat down at her desk and stared out the window. Two things caught her eye: the rapidly changing sky, turning from bland grey to dusty rose, and a city bus, with open doors waiting for passengers just below her second floor window. Several women boarded and she wondered about them. 'Where did they live? Did they think about safety? Did they live in fear? Did darkness frighten them?'

'I need a break,' she muttered to herself. She'd call her friend Anne to see if the two might get together. Too many weeks had passed since she'd hung out with a girlfriend and Anne was a true confidante. The detective remembered distinctly Anne's reaction to Susan's divorce: 'You'll be in pain now, that's for sure. But one day you will find a true soul mate and be happier than you ever were with Jeff. Anytime you need to talk, just give me a call.'

Well, tonight was the night for a girlfriend call. But first, Susan wanted to review some files. No matter what Weaver said she continued to have a growing sense of fear and the fear centered on two questions: What if the rapist begins to kill his victims? And, why can't I figure out why our investigation is failing?

6

Day one as a college professor found Scott Connors exasperated. The class roster listed 47; and 63 students showed up. After explaining he would do his best to accommodate as many as possible, he called roll:

'Angelino.'

'Here.'

'Avery.'

'Here.'

'Backus.'

'Here'

'Brock.'

'Here,' Tyrus Brock responded, a half-smile faintly crossing his face.

Connors felt a chill climb his spine as he looked into the eyes of a handsome, collegiate-looking man, someone who definitely did not look like a rapist.

Avoiding hesitation, the professor completed the roll call. With this preliminary task behind him, he pressed on, despite a distinct sense of unease knowing Blomberg's suspect sat directly in front of him.

Connors purposely kept his first lecture short, focusing mainly on class requirements and general theories of criminal causation. He took care to remain objective in his remarks. There would be plenty of time for controversial positions in the weeks ahead.

Not surprisingly, 20 minutes into the lecture, he was interrupted with a question about the local rape series. A student in the back of the room asked, 'Professor Connors, would knowing why a person commits rape be of any value in catching the East Area Rapist?'

He paused a moment before responding, 'Hopefully, throughout the class we will be able to explore some of the ways understanding the mental health of a criminal and their life experiences can play a role in the investigation and apprehension of criminals.' His response sounded stiff, and he noted Brock, the alleged suspect, remained indifferent as Connors continued, 'I will admit, I know little about your current rape series. I've only been in Sacramento a few days.'

Connors continued his agenda for the sexual deviancy class, going over the syllabus and discussing other particulars. The time passed quickly and with the students dismissed, he hurried toward the Criminal Justice building to check in with his department chair. They met in the hallway.

'Good morning,' Blomberg greeted him, 'I'm afraid I'm on my way to another meeting, but it looks like you survived your first class. How'd it go?'

Connors turned and continued to walk, matching his professor's pace, 'Very well, lots of students. Your man showed up right on time.'

'Yes, my guess is you will find Brock very punctual. What's your read?'

'Other than he's clean cut, I could tell nothing. He showed no emotion, even when a question about the EAR came up.' Connors said.

'That's been my impression of him. Did you decide whether or not you want to take this on?' Blomberg asked.

'Yes, I'm intrigued. And since I'm only teaching one class, I should have extra time. Can you give me some names to get me started?'

'Absolutely.' The professor stopped, reached into his briefcase and pulled out a single sheet.

'The first name is David Moran, head of the Vesta Program, and I took the liberty of anticipating your interest and called him. He can meet with you tonight at seven. Do you mind going to his house?'

'No . . . not at all,' Connors said, trying not to show surprise at the plans already laid out for him. Obviously, the professor had anticipated he would be interested in going further with this investigation.

'Good, just keep in mind he is a little unusual, so don't let that throw you. I included an address and a map. I've listed two others and their phone numbers.'

'What do you mean Moran is unusual?' Connors asked.

Blomberg grinned. 'Remember he's the ex-con who gave me Brock's name. By unusual . . . well, he's like no ex-con I ever met. You'll have to see for yourself.' And with that he turned into the Dean's office, leaving Connors holding the paper listing three names: David Moran, Vesta; Jeff Baker, Department of Justice (DOJ); Charlene Mathews, Women's Crisis Center.

'Well, for better or worse, I'm in this now,' Connors muttered to himself.

Connors was surprised as he pulled up to Moran's address. The house was near the center of town in a long row of Victorians. How does an ex-con live in this upscale neighborhood, he wondered. But,

42

as he walked up to the house he saw a 'B' after the number and realized the house was divided into flats. Moran lived in the middle one.

One knock and the door opened, revealing an attractive black woman. 'You must be Mr. Connors. Please come in, David is expecting you.' He followed her into a well-furnished living room where a fire burned in a brick fireplace. Both the woman and the room gave Connors a warm feeling, which disappeared as soon as Moran stood up to greet him.

A foreboding figure, Moran stood at least 6' 4', thin and big boned. He looked to be in his middle thirties. His long face, bushy black eyebrows, coal black hair, and a cold smile gave Connors pause. The effect was striking, prompting Connors to think of a river boat gambler. Connors noted his big hands, but the handshake itself was weak.

Surprisingly, Moran spoke in a friendly manner, 'Pleasure to meet you. Have a seat,' he said motioning toward a large leather chair. 'Well, as you know, I'm Moran and this is my lady, Melody.'

'I hope Professor Blomberg explained why I'm here.'

'Yeah, he did,' he answered. 'You're lookin' for information on Tyrus Brock.'

An awkward silence followed before Connors responded, 'I'm from Phoenix and in Sacramento to teach a class on sexual deviancy. I guess he thought gaining information about this rape series would be helpful in my research. He asked me to, 'dig around the edges' as he put it.'

Moran's tone hardened, 'I gave that information to him, not to broadcast it. Apparently he trusts you,

43

but I don't. How do I know you don't have a big mouth?'

Melody broke in, 'Would you gentlemen like some coffee?' The interjection of her question made the scene almost surreal to Connors.

'I would love a cup of decaf,' Connors responded. Moran nodded and Melody left the room. 'I can assure you, I will keep our conversation in strict confidence,' Connors replied, speaking firmly, forcing himself to look directly into Moran's eyes. 'I don't know anyone in Sacramento and in a few months I will be returning to Phoenix. I give you my word: no one will know I even talked with you.'

Moran seemed to relax, but only for a moment. He leaned close to Connors and lowered his voice, 'Look kid, let's get one thing straight. I told Blomberg I would split the reward with him 50-50. If he wants to split his share with you that's all right by me, but I still get my half.'

Immediately, two things were clear to Connors: Moran was not involved out of civic duty, and by lowering his voice, it was obvious he did not want Melody to know about the money arrangement.

'You can relax, I'm in this because I'm writing a master's thesis for Arizona State. The professor and I did not discuss money. All I want is some insight into why men rape.' Again, he locked eyes with Moran, determined not to be intimidated.

Moran leaned back and looked toward the fire. 'What makes you think you can nail this guy? The fuckin' cops can't catch him. A college kid like you will be dead quick if you mess with Brock.'

44

'At this point I have no illusions of confronting the guy. All I plan to do is gather information about who he is and why he might be the rapist. If I come up with information that would help the police, I suppose I would share it with them, but that's not why I'm doing this,' Connors replied keeping his voice firm, his words measured.

'You keep my name out of it, understand?' Moran's tone, again, left no doubt about his parameters.

'I assure you I will not tell anyone about this meeting or any other contact I may have with you.'

Connors' promise seemed to appease him. Melody entered the room with two cups of coffee, and Connors was able to ingratiate himself to her with a few questions. In doing so, he gave himself time to figure out how to proceed with Moran. She chatted openly about her own college plans and how she met Moran while hosting at a popular Sacramento nightclub. She was so pleasant Connors wished he'd come to visit her.

The ex-con broke into their casual conversation, 'What do you want to know about Brock?'

'Why do you think he is the East Area Rapist?' Connors moved right to the point.

'First, I don't think, *I know*.' Moran's emphasis was clear as he continued, 'I've been around criminals all of my life. Hell, I've been a criminal all my life. This Vesta rehab gig is my first straight job. My father was a criminal, so were both my uncles. I've served time in juve' lockups, county jails and state prison. I've worked with criminals and I've lived with criminals.

45

I knew Brock was bad news when I first interviewed him in the joint. I didn't want him in my program then, and I don't want him in it now. But, a fuckin' judge said keeping perverts out is discrimination. I had to take him. I got no time for perverts. To me there is no difference between a rapist and a pimp. The bastards hang together in the joint.' Moran paused and sipped his coffee. With eyes now glued to the fire, the ex-con seemed to momentarily distance himself; then he continued, 'Don't get me wrong. I like to fuck. Just ask Melody.'

Connors felt himself blush. This definitely was not conversation he would ever use around a woman and he could not look at Melody.

Suddenly, Moran's attitude changed, sharpened, 'But I don't truck with kid fuckers or guys who force women. Soon as I found out he was a rapist I would've quit talkin' to him, but the punk lied. Said he went down for manslaughter. A bar fight . . . I think he said. So, I interviewed him. Then, when I went to the man and found out the prick had a rape jacket, I was fried. Turned him down. No way I was gonna let him in my program.'

Connors interrupted, 'But he got in!'

'Yeah, next thing I know I'm called into court before some judge, who wouldn't know a crook if one pissed on him, askin' me why I turned Brock down. I told him we're running this program at a college with thousands of dizzy broads running around, mini-skirts up to their asses and we didn't need no perverts. The judge said the shrink's reports on Brock showed he had found religion, was a minister to other prisoners and was rehabilitated. Of course, that's all bullshit. These bastards use Jesus to get an early release. I've used God myself and would've used Buddha. That Brock, he fooled the judge and now I'm stuck with the fucker.'

'So, you don't like the guy, but does that make him a rapist?' Connors challenged.

'No, course not. But, it caused me to watch him closer than the others. In my program we have 35 ex-cons, so he's just one of many. But after about the fourth or fifth rape, I began noticing he wasn't reporting into the office the day after. So I go back to his file and that causes me to remember him braggin' about being in the Special Forces and having medals and all that shit from Nam.'

'You know he has a military background?' Connors asked.

'Yeah, claimed he did four tours in Nam. Seems proud of it. Claimed to be in some kind of special unit . . . forget what he called it. This could all be bullshit. None of that kind of talk impresses me. But, when they quoted Blomberg in the papers saying this rapist may have military experience, I put that together with him not showing up at school the day after a rape. Plus he fits the physical description.'

'You keep attendance records?'

'Yeah. All the cons have to sign in every morning. But it's more than just that with Brock. This guy has big problems. I've seen it in lots of guys who go down for violent crimes. It's a feeling you get just bein' around them. Take me; all I ever did was steal. I like nice things and good-looking broads and both take money. For me, I thought stealing was easy, so I stole. But these rape guys and baby fuckers, they do it for

47

something inside themselves. They don't give a shit for money. They got to satisfy an itch.'

'And Brock fits that mold?' Connors asked.

'Hell yes he does! I got several women counselors who work with these jerks. Most of the broads are world-savers. They feel sorry for these cons and fall for their jive. I try to explain it to them but they can't seem to learn. Brock dresses sharp; he's polite to the ladies. Several of them tried to lay him. He won't have any of it. Turned down good-looking bitches. Ain't no normal guy gonna walk away from hot pussy.'

'So, he's a rapist who still has sex problems. What else have you observed that points toward him being the rapist?' Connors pressed.

'Well, for one he brags about cops he knows. Sounds like a cop wannabe. And, the word around the office is that his wife is a lesbian. Now why would a normal guy marry a lesbian? And this Christian shit. He brags about preaching at some church in the city. It's all a front. The guy is more jive ass than the pimps I knew in the joint. He lies about lies and never blinks an eye. I tell you straight, the guy is slicker than snail shit.'

Connors couldn't help but be amused by the metaphors. 'Have you ever talked to him about his family?'

'Naw. Never says nothin' about family.'

'Does he ever talk about his military experiences?'

'Only that he hates slopes. Won't have nothin' to do with Asian students. Blacks or Mexicans either. Seems to be a flat out racist. I talked to him a couple of times about using the 'nigger' word in the office. We got lots of brothers in our program, and they don't want a white guy saying it. And you notice all the ladies this man rapes have been white bread? He don't touch no sister.'

'Have you ever seen him confronted by a black student?'

'No one confronts Brock, not even me. He can look daggers and you see trouble. Brocks not a man you cross.'

'So you believe he has the potential for violence?'

'Believe me, man, I know. I've looked in the eyes of too many killers to miss where he's coming from. Killing for him is like swatting flies. He may be just raping now, but before long someone is going to cross him and wind up dead. No, this guy doesn't just have potential, this guy is already a killer and when you study his eyes you know it. That's why, so far, his victims are still alive. The first one that don't read the message is gonna wind up on a slab.'

Connors could feel the gravity of Moran's words. This information was more instructional than any the young professor had encountered in the sterile classrooms of the university. Even the stories he heard working as a bartender didn't have the edge of Moran's ramblings.

Connors probed further, 'Since Blomberg turned Brock's name in to the police and you're convinced he is the rapist, why haven't the police been able to catch him?'

'Look, I don't hold much stock in the pigs. No police investigation ever nailed me. They caught me because the guys I was workin' with went State to get themselves a lighter sentence. One of the problems of being a criminal is that you have to work with other criminals and you can't trust the bastards.'

"What about Brock?'

This guy works alone. There's no one to squeal on him. And remember he went to criminal college for three years,' Moran snickered.

By this time, Connors understood Blomberg's characterization of Moran. 'Unusual' didn't begin to describe him. 'Are you referring to the three years he spent in prison?'

'Hell yes! What do you think inmates talk about in lock up? They talk about how they got caught and what they're gonna do better next time. That Brock, he's a smart one.'

'You're saying Brock's immediate arrest and incarceration after returning from Vietnam was his classroom?' Connors asked.

'Damned right. If you think prison rehabs anyone, you really are green! Nothin' prison ever did for me kept me straight. My bet is he listened real well in the joint and learned a lot. No, this guy is sharp. They can have his name, address and telephone number and still not catch him. Foolin' with Brock is a death wish. A bookish kid like you is no match.'

Connors sensed Moran had spoken all he would. The evening's social call had turned into a serious primer on criminals, namely one Tyrus Brock. And, if only half of what Moran said about Brock was true, he was indeed dangerous.

7

A solid night's sleep behind her, Susan Allen reported to the office at 7:45 a.m., relieved there had been no rape call. A couple of hours with Ann the evening before had helped clear her head and she felt good. Yet, despite a positive start to her day, the female detective still kept thinking about her last conversation with Weaver and the tension building between them. Why was her superior so resistant to her ideas?

Once at her desk, Susan found the quiet morning offered a perfect excuse to linger over a bagel and coffee while reviewing crime reports from the previous day, as well as the tip file on the rape series. At 10:00 a.m. she carried the file into Weaver and dropped it on his desk. Weaver, working intently on a grid map of the city, looked up, surprised by her action. 'What the hell? What's this about?'

'This is our tip file. I've just spent a couple of hours reviewing it and getting it organized. The yellow labels are where people expressed suspicion of Tyrus Brock. Count them, at least four callers. I'm beginning to have second thoughts.'

'Second thoughts about what?' Weaver grunted. 'The only second thoughts I'm having is all the publicity we're giving this fuckin' rapist. Why'n the world are we holdin' a press conference seems like every damned day? This pervert feeds off the publicity. He loves it.'

'I don't particularly like the publicity either, but I was referring to Brock as a suspect. I know you've eliminated him, but I looked over this file, and it's not just that professor who's suspicious of him. Sure, Blomberg was the first, but obviously there are others.'

'I don't need no tip file,' Weaver interrupted, 'I know his name comes up often, but he absolutely has been eliminated.

'But see for yourself. Others have called in, a correctional officer from Folsom and a records guy from DOJ. That seems like a lot of people who are suspicious of Brock,' Allen responded, shaking her head at her boss' bull-headed reaction to the statistical strength of the tip file.

Weaver responded firmly, 'Dammit. Long before you were on the case, City PD eliminated Brock. He's an ex-soldier! And we have sent our guys to his house after a reported rape and found him home, car in the driveway with a cold engine. That's good enough for me.'

'But there's no mention of how City PD eliminated him. And, we don't know the exact time the rapist leaves the scene. He might have time to get home before someone can get to his house and question him. I've had a bad feeling about this case ever since I was assigned. It's been over a month and I haven't heard of a single thing city police contributed. What would it hurt to have another look at Brock?'

'Allen, you just don't understand. The only reason we got so much manpower tied up on this damned case is the publicity. Every time this guy pulls a rape, the city goes crazy. You should spend your time on real suspects, not second guessin' my work.'

'I'm not second guessing, just raising an issue which concerns me,' Susan responded, not quite sure how to proceed. She wanted to say to her superior, 'Thirty years in the department and this is how you analyze data?' She knew better and held her tongue.

'Allen, there's a lot you don't know. We don't give a rat's ass about Brock. He's been arrested on a 314 and it wouldn't surprise me if parole is pushing him to get the hell out of Sacramento,' Weaver responded.

Allen's eyes widened, 'Indecent exposure. That raises a red flag for me. And, when Brock leaves . . . .'

'Then this whole damn thing will go away, and we can get back to real police work,' Weaver snapped.

'Stopping rapes is not real police work?' Allen challenged, her voice charged with betrayal. 'And, if he's the rapist, what's to stop him from raping women wherever he goes?'

'Then it'll be some other city's problem, not ours. C'mon Allen, we gotta keep this in perspective. This rapist hasn't killed anyone and look at how many deputies we got tied up chasin' all over the county listenin' to hysterical women,' Weaver demanded, his face flushed.

'Okay, okay, you don't need to get upset. But, I still think we should take another look, a studied look, at Brock.' Allen was determined to get the last word as she turned to leave the room.

'Hold it. Don't you walk out of here, you want to stay on this case! You follow my orders,' Weaver snapped.

'Fine, forget it,' Susan responded, realizing their impasse, 'I'm going over to talk with the lab guys. We need clarity on blood. So far they've identified several different foreign blood types from the rape scenes, yet we know there's only one rapist. It's time for an explanation.'

'Good, that's something productive. You go work on that.'

With Allen gone, Weaver muttered to himself, 'Just what we get havin' a woman on this case. Whatever happened to the old days? Sure the hell wouldn't be stressing over a few rapes. And they call this progress?'

Suddenly, Howell appeared, his voice lowered, 'Bud, sounds like you're still having trouble with Allen. You gotta keep her in line.'

Weaver turned in his chair, 'Fuck you. She's all talk. Don't be blaming me for her. Wasn't my call. But, I'll handle her.'

'Just see that you do,' Howell said.

8

Darlene Grant, parole agent for the California Department of Corrections, felt overwhelmed.

Three parole revocation hearings in the past two weeks, four violent-prone parolees needing interviews, and paperwork associated with her caseload of 124 was clearly wearing her down. A classic case of too much responsibility and too few resources.

Both of her in-boxes were full. Stacks of files cluttered the floor. She sighed and pulled a box labeled November 1976 over to her desk. 'I can't believe I'm so far behind. How am I ever going to catch up?' she wondered aloud.

She laid a slender file on her desk and read the name: Brock, Tyrus. The first page listed his crime and a prison release date of July 6, 1976; then, she found a report from his assigned therapist, Dr. Ron Bevins. Quickly browsing through the first two pages, she noted Brock had been on time, cooperative, pleasant, seemed to be doing well in college and was looking forward to marriage.

She stopped abruptly halfway down page three where she found Bevins handwritten entry:

See attached written statement by Tyrus Brock regarding an experience while a special forces soldier serving in Vietnam. His crimes occurred within days of his return to San Diego and appear to be the result of post-combat stress. This does concern me. I'm seeing more vets with obvious mental health issues. Vietnam must have been hell for a lot of them. I will be exploring this possibility with Brock in subsequent sessions. But, even if this is true, with his enrollment in college and pending marriage, his prospects are strong for a successful transition to civilian life.

I asked him to write about his most traumatic experience. Notice the sophisticated writing style, indicating an intelligent mind and evidence of a good education. Although his narrative does digress at one point, I am not labeling it clinical. I believe requiring Brock to journal his experiences will provide a release for suppressed anger and guilt. Next session is scheduled for February 3, 1977.

Grant immediately moved to the copy of the narrative. The writing was cramped, but neat. She began to make notes as she read, and found herself quickly sucked into the parolee's words, written in a stream of consciousness:

I'm haunted by one memory worse than any other from Nam. I don't think it'll ever go away and I hate how it makes me feel. Always, I see the face of the little girl with eyes like deep liquid pools. The bullet entered square between those dark eyes. I still see that small hole. One very small hole . . . one explosion that destroyed a tiny skull. Day after day, after day, after day her eyes continue to stare through me. Sights and sounds of that failed mission ebb and flow in my memory. The whole operation was a disaster. Someone gave the unit wrong coordinates, the wrong building. Thirteen women and eight children left dead in the first light of dawn. Shoot anything that wiggles.

'Forget it, mistakes happen,' the fucking Captain said. 'When we have a target, we go in shooting. To

56

hesitate, even a second is death.' There is no way I can forget. I see my mother's eyes, hazel with dark rims. Her fair skin. I remember her fair skin. Soft and smooth and translucent. She loved me. I know she did until . . . we used to sit on the porch swing singing 'Beautiful Savior.' She taught me harmony. He ruined it. I could see in her eyes he had ruined it. No more songs only tears. No more laughing. I ain't a cry baby. Beat me, beat me, you fucker beat me!

The parole officer sat for several minutes thinking, before re-reading Dr. Bevin's summary:

Based on Mr. Brock's willingness to be open and discuss his emotions, I believe I can recommend limited supervision as it appears his crimes were directly related to combat stress. If there is a change, I will notify you immediately.

Grant leaned back in her chair, pushed her glasses up onto her forehead and dropped the report back on the desk. Truthfully, she'd never read a reflective piece quite like this. The Vietnam connection? A child's eyes? His mother's eyes? 'Another messed up ex-soldier,' she said aloud. For an instant she questioned Dr. Bevin's summation, but then quickly dismissed her doubts; the doctor was highly respected, no one doubted his counsel. With that, she picked up the Dictaphone and began her report: 'Tyrus Brock, DOJ number B-4183573, reported to his therapist Dr. Bevins, as scheduled. His criminal problems apparently stem from combat stress during his service in Vietnam. Reports to date give every indication he is amendable to treatment. He will be placed on limited supervision. No home *visits required at this time. Brock does not appear to be a threat to the public.'*

9

The rapist drove with deliberate caution, stopping completely at each stop sign, careful to signal at every turn on a cold and blustery January night.

Perfect, he thought, wind always makes an approach safer. As he drove past the front of his primary target, 31105 Zinfandel Way, he nodded, approvingly. No strange cars in the driveway or on the street.

This target had been a long time developing. For weeks he'd struggled with images of pre-adolescent girls. He thought of his first such encounter in a small village, near rice fields, the chaos of war all around. He remembered the noise, screams and smell of artillery fire pelting his senses . . . she looked into his eyes, stunned and frightened. She was his first, he found her, and then he took her. He owned her. The encounter had never left his mind. Tonight it gave him impetus.

For weeks he'd hoped for just the right age and appearance, wanting a girl no younger than ten and no older than twelve, with long hair and big eyes. Two days ago he had found Amy, a near perfect eleven-year-old, while searching through her family's picture album. Tonight was the night when the demons inside him would find calm. First the power, then control, finally release . . . for at least a few days.

He shifted his Volkswagen bug down to second and swung around the block. As he passed the empty lot behind Amy's house he cut the engine and glided to a stop. Any apprehension he felt earlier in the day was gone. He thought of Nam and found relief in the pattern. The closer to the target, the more anxiety yielded to calm. Tonight would be no different. His reconnaissance skill had located the ideal target and prepared an entry point. There was no reason to delay. Memories of countless hours of training and constant drilling always paid off. Know your enemy and he is yours. Kill or be killed. There are two kinds of soldiers: The quick and the dead.

He felt his power rising.

Before leaving the car, he opened his backpack, retrieved a penlight, and began to check the contents. He pulled out the chrome-plated Smith and Wesson to make sure all six cylinders held live rounds. He thought of the cons in Folsom, all their bullshit about automatics, but they were idiots when it came to guns. He wanted nothing to do with automatics. The chance of a jam or malfunction was rare, but it was not worth the risk. He needed a foolproof handgun, hence the revolver. In addition, automatics scattered shell casings all over. 'I'll be damned if I'll leave any evidence behind, except what I choose to leave.'

He checked the remaining items: six pieces of nylon cord, ski mask, extra tennis shoes, two condoms, hooded black sweatshirt, two pair of surgical gloves, black jogging pants, a syringe containing blood and, of course, the knife. Sure, the bowie knife was too long for effective combat, but he savored the psychological effect. Satisfied, he zipped the backpack and stepped out of the car.

The night was dark with just a sliver of moon hidden behind large storm clouds. It beckoned him and he moved with ease toward his target. 'Darkness is a friend', he thought, use it wisely. Deep in the shadows he stripped. He folded his clothes carefully and placed them under a bush. With his backpack slung over his left shoulder and using his right arm, he vaulted the wood wall behind the house.

Inside the yard, he crouched, ignoring the chilling wind. Still and silent. He did not move until he heard a distant train whistle.

Now. *Forward!*

The early hour and the thought of another rape made Allen noticeably irritated. She could not help losing patience as Weaver accidentally tipped his flask and spilled whiskey on the car seat. 'Damn Bud. Can't you hit the cup? I don't want the car smelling like booze,' she chastised him.

The lead detective reminded Allen of her mother's drinking problems. Ever since her father's death, whenever stress or tension entered their house, out came the liquor. She thought back to the hours her mother spent anesthetizing herself with alcohol, hours spent alone detached from the family. 'Can't project my issues on Weaver,' she admonished herself silently.

Allen struggled to regain her focus. She knew the stress of this case was having an effect on him. He wore it on his face. The truth was she felt frustrated and not in the mood for his annoying habits. Originally, Allen planned to take the day off, as this was her fourteenth straight shift without a break. Having to adjust her plans when the rape call came in at daybreak, left her less than cheerful.

'Cut me some slack,' Weaver responded. 'I was out late last night, and I mean to tell you it was a bad night. Lost a shit-load at poker,' he said, nursing the still-steaming cup of coffee. 'God, why can't these calls come in at nine or ten, not six fuckin' a.m. Suppose this guy deliberately sets it up so we get jacked out of bed?'

'It would help if you knocked off the booze,' Allen said, unable to bottle her feelings, firm in her resolve to raise the drinking issue.

'Hell, Allen, you know I work better this way. One shot of the snake that bit me and I'll be razor sharp,' Weaver snapped. He took another big swig of the doctored coffee.

Although unconvinced, Allen decided to let it go and moved on. 'It sounds worse than the others. This guy is a nightmare and the violence is escalating just like the shrinks said it would. According to dispatch there are three victims: An eleven-year-old girl, a badly injured mother and a traumatized father who has broken down completely. Apparently, he has already been admitted to the psych ward.'

Weaver shook his head, took another drink of coffee, and asked, 'Where's the little girl?'

'When I got the call, she was still at the house. The mother, however, was found unconscious and has been transported to ER. Apparently, Sgt. Roberts has the crime scene secured. Maybe that means the little girl is not hurt. Dispatch mentioned that the grandparents will be at there when we arrive.'

'For Christ sake, that will really make things difficult, just what we don't need, some old geezers screwing up the crime scene, makin' it impossible to talk with the victims.'

'I think they said the grandfather is an attorney,' Allen said, knowing Weaver's disdain for lawyers.

'God, can it get any worse? I may need more than one shot for this one. Drive a little slower.'

Suddenly there was static and then the police radio blared, '550 – 52'

'Turn down that volume,' Weaver barked as he reached for the mike. '52'

'52 . . . report to Hartford Memorial. Sergeant Roberts just called and said the eleven year old daughter started hemorrhaging and both female victims are now at the hospital.'

'Fuck,' spat Weaver.

'Crime scene people won't be able to get to the house until after eight,' the dispatcher continued.

'What, can't those fairies get the hell out of bed like the rest of us?'

The dispatcher, ignoring Weaver's remark, continued, 'It will be Evans and McAllister.'

'Okay, okay, has Lieutenant Creighton talked to his uniforms? Anybody report activity near the scene any time after midnight?'

'Sorry, Creighton said to pass onto you, nothing at this time. He's expanding the neighborhood check, but so far not even a barking dog.'

'Shit,' Weaver said as he slammed down the mike. 'Allen have you ever seen the like? Does this guy fly to and from his crime scenes? God, we've doubled patrols on the whole east side and nobody saw crap.'

Allen turned the car around and headed toward the hospital, changing the subject, 'God Bud, do you realize if he raped this little girl and the mother, this would put his victim count at twenty four. Will this be his youngest victim?'

Weaver refilled his coffee cup, skipping the whiskey. 'No, second or third case before you were assigned, he diddled a fourteen year old. But, if this one is only eleven and he's injured her, it will be a first.'

As they entered the emergency room, Weaver gave direction. 'Usual stuff, I'll try to track down the man of the house, although the shrinks probably already have him so doped up he will be of no value. Leave word with the nurses where you are.'

The charge nurse recognized Allen immediately. 'The mother is in room 2 A. Her name is Sandra. We don't have a last name yet. The little girl is in surgery.'

'Where's the old man?' Weaver asked.

'He's in psych on the second floor. Dr. Nelson is with him.'

Allen found Sandra with a nurse seated beside her, holding her hand and stroking her forehead. 'Sandra, I'm detective Allen of the Sheriff's Department, do you feel strong enough to answer a few questions?'

Rising, the nurse answered, 'Sandra feels she can give you a brief statement, but I need a word with you in the hall first.'

After closing the door behind them, the nurse spoke softly, 'I just wanted to advise you she has not been told her daughter was seriously injured in the assault. Sandra was unconscious when brought in and still thinks her daughter is home. The doctors want to wait until the little girl is out of surgery and Sandra has regained some strength.'

'Certainly, I understand. I'll only ask a few questions now and complete the interview tomorrow,' the detective responded.

'The doctor has completed his exam and collected samples. I'll see if I can get you a preliminary report before you leave. Please let Sandra know I'll come back in as soon as you are finished.'

The nurse impressed Allen with her gentle nature and her ability to bond so quickly with the victim. A troubling thought, one she had experienced before, flashed through her mind. 'Why is it nurses, who deal with trauma every day stay kind and warm while police officers, who also deal with trauma, become cynical and cold?' She wondered if the answer had to do with nurses helping heal while police merely find the wounds and chaos. It was a question for which she had no answer.

As Allen sat down by the bed, Sandra smiled weakly, 'Thank God you're a woman . . . I was afraid they would send a man. I don't think I could look at a man now, let alone speak to one . . . ,' her voice faded.

'I'm sorry to have to ask you to talk about this right now, but we need to stop this evil man and you may be able to help us.'

Allen stroked the woman's hand, sensing an overwhelming wave of compassion. The detective knew she needed to rein in emotions; they were useless during questioning, but she felt a tightening in her throat and sat silent for a moment until it eased.

Sandra spoke first, 'I'll do my best . . . they gave me a shot of something and I'm feeling very tired.' Suddenly, Sandra's composure broke and she began to weep, 'Why me? Why did this happen to me? What did I do?'

Again, Allen waited. She knew Sandra needed these tears and would, no doubt, for a long time. 'I wish I had the answer for you. We think this was the same rapist who has hit several times in the east area of town. He seems to pick houses at random. I do know the more we can learn about this man, the better our chance of finding him before he hurts other women.'

Sandra's sobs continued. Finally, she was able to bring herself under control, 'I'll . . . I'll try.' But the tears welled up again; the pain in her face harshly evident. 'John and I were asleep. Amy was asleep in her room. There . . . there was a bright light in my eyes,' she turned her head, tears flowing down her face, her lower lip quivering. 'I screamed and he . . . he hit me . . . I was stunned . . . then he said, 'Quiet Sandra or you'll die'.' Her sobs started again, 'He . . . he knew my name . . . he knew my name . . . why me? Why did he do this to me?'

For the first time Allen noticed a large bruise spreading over the left side of the victim's cheek. 'Did you recognize his voice?'

'No . . . no . . . it was real strange . . . hoarse, forced like laryngitis. He kept saying he owned me.' She lay for several minutes crying quietly. Opening her eyes, looking at Allen through the tears, she continued, 'He . . . knew my name . . . my husband's name . . . my sister's name. Oh, God, what happened to Amy . . . where's Amy? I need to see Amy . . . bring Amy to me please . . . please I need to see Amy.'

Allen realized there was no reason to continue and rang for help. In a moment the nurse was back. 'I'll need to wait until tomorrow to talk with her,' the detective said.

'That will work better,' the nurse whispered.

Allen quietly left the room, picked up the initial lab reports and headed toward the second floor psych ward, her mind and spirit reeling from Sandra's broken state.

'That was quick, how'd it go?' Weaver greeted her.

'Difficult. Very difficult. I'll have to wait until tomorrow and see if she can talk. Emotionally she's in bad shape. Let's head over to the crime scene.'

Allen drove with her eyes fixed on the road, silent.

Finally, Weaver spoke, 'I couldn't talk to the father, but I did talk briefly with the shrink.'

'And?'

'He had to dope Wallace. That's their last name. Seems the bastard tortured his daughter right in front of him. He had no hard information on the kid, but from what Wallace related to him, she must be in a bad way.'

Allen sighed deeply, 'The mother didn't know about her daughter's assault.'

'Did she give you anything that might help us?'

'Not really. Other than he knew her name, her sister and husband's name.'

They drove in silence.

10

Connors woke early, walked into his small kitchen to start the coffee, then to the porch for the *Sacramento BEE*. It was Valentine's Day, and the front page displayed a banner of red hearts. He felt a sudden, unexpected sadness. On this day, a year ago, in Phoenix, he had proposed to Laurie. By now they would have been married . . . if only. Connors didn't want to think about the *'if only'*. Too much energy and too few answers.

There was so much about the relationship he missed, but there had also been conflict, especially toward the end. And, worst of all, he knew it was his fault.

Haunted by his niece's death, he just could not let himself get close to anyone. Too much guilt. He had tried to change, adapt, to understand Laurie's whims, to bond with her. She was beautiful and brilliant, yet so unpredictable. She'd turn on him, telling him he was aloof . . . unreachable. He never understood this, especially with their lovemaking being so intense. He didn't miss their fights, yet this morning he felt lonely.

Soon, a headline distracted him, *'Marine Colonel Blasts Government Vietnam Policy.'* Turning to the story, he read: *'Yesterday, retired military officer Colonel Gordon R. Rutledge gave a scathing account of government decisions during the Vietnam War. He spoke to the Rosemont Rotary Club at their weekly meeting and surprised the audience with a list of government blunders.'*

As he read the story, Connors muttered out loud, 'This guy sure has guts, and I need to talk to him about Vietnam. If he will criticize the government in a public meeting, he might be just as frank in discussing the effect of the war on individual soldiers. Who could possibly be a better source about post-war trauma than a colonel with experience in Vietnam?'

Connors glanced at the clock, 7:55 a.m. Not too early to phone a military man. He found the colonel's name in the telephone book and, after only two rings, Rutledge answered. Connors introduced himself, saying he was a writer working on a feature story about the war. Somewhat surprisingly, the colonel sounded like he welcomed the invitation to meet and discuss his recent speech. They agreed to meet at 11:00 a.m.

Connors walked into the coffee shop early and found a table. Precisely on the hour, he glanced up and spotted Rutledge, a tall, straight-backed man with short hair and a distinct military gait. After the initial introductions, Connors started the conversation by inquiring how Rutledge was enjoying retirement.

'Not worth a damn, to be honest. I'm driving both myself and my wife crazy.'

'How long have you been retired?' Connors queried.

'A little over two years, and if I don't find something to do soon, I may have to re-enlist.'

Connors relaxed a bit when he realized the man had a sense of humor. 'When did you decide to go public with your criticism of the war?'

'Actually, I've given that speech several times, but this is the first time the press picked up on it. I feel strongly about the issues. And, I believe it very American to speak out when one believes our government has erred, especially when those errors led to the death of thousands of young men. Probably means I won't be running for Congress.'

Connors smiled, growing more and more comfortable with the colonel, especially his dry humor. 'Colonel, I'm very interested in the problems Vietnam vets are having adjusting to civilian life post discharge. What is your thinking on this topic?' he paused briefly, 'I'm trying to compare their adjustment with World War II soldiers.'

Taking a big swallow of coffee and signaling to the waitress for more, Rutledge replied, 'Interesting you should take that approach. Not too many people are making such a comparison.'

'Do you believe it is a worthwhile subject to explore?'

Nodding, the colonel leaned back in his chair, obviously thinking. Connors waited patiently, unsure of where the colonel would go with the question.

Finally, Rutledge spoke, 'Well, there are several major differences. In WWII, most soldiers were returned to the states by ship and had many days, even weeks, to decompress. They talked over their experiences with other soldiers who shared some of the same battles. It gave them time to put their experiences in perspective.

Also, they knew they were returning to a country supportive of the war. WWII veterans were treated like heroes. It's always concerned me that Vietnam veterans flew home to the states within hours of their last battle. No time to decompress. As you know, these soldiers found a hostile public. For years the topic of Vietnam has created divisions within the country. The whole war was mishandled.'

Connors had obviously struck a hot spot with Rutledge; he pressed on, 'So you might expect Vietnam vets to have a difficult adjustment to civilian life? What programs have the military set up to address this problem?'

'I can't speak for the Army, but the Marine Corps has a program at Camp Pendleton to decompress Marines and soldiers assigned to Special Forces, as well as any line personnel who display obvious adjustment problems. Still, the military continues to have a monumental task to understand the full psychosocial effect of combat.' The colonel paused, 'But there is an additional factor, one rarely considered, which concerns me.'

'And that is?'

'Their training. It's different now than the training given to soldiers in WWII or even the Korean War.'

'Different, in what way?'

It seemed to please Rutledge to have found an audience for a topic he obviously had considered many times before this conversation. He began again, enthused, 'Studies after WWII found only twenty five to thirty percent of frontline soldiers actually fired their weapons during battles. This came as a shock to military brass and certainly wasn't publicized. Lots of time and money was spent finding the reasons behind the low firing rate. It came down to the training. In WWII, training was brief and fast. The big need was to get soldiers ready for battle in the shortest possible time. Not much thought was given to training content. Unfortunately, men, who psychologically could not fire at another human being, were sent into battle. Eventually, the training was changed.'

'How so?' Connors asked.

'Killing machines.'

'Killing machines?'

The Colonel nodded, 'We needed men who were conditioned to kill. Without going into a lot of detail, soldiers are now trained to have instant and automatic responses. The modern soldier is trained to shoot and *kill*. Quick response seems to eliminate the thoughts that historically caused soldiers to see the enemy as real people.'

'Did it work?'

'Preliminary studies indicate it has been very successful. In Korea, the firing rate was up to almost fifty percent, and this led to even more refined methods of training. It looks like the firing rate in Vietnam was above ninety percent. Combined with improved weaponry and ammunition, the average rifle squad's firing power is now significantly stronger than during WWII.'

Connors found the colonel's discourse intriguing. Training men to kill, combined with the soldiers' rapid return to civilian life, could seriously affect their ability to adjust. His thoughts drifted momentarily to Brock. 'So, today's soldiers could encounter more difficulty with re-entry,' the young professor queried with a statement.

Colonel Rutledge picked up the thought, 'Yes, this has been bothering me for some time and is why I was surprised when you said you were writing an article on this very re-entry problem. Our soldiers needed debriefing and treatment in many cases, plain and simple. Most get nothing.'

Connors continued, 'On the phone, I asked you about Special Forces. Were there any differences in their training compared to regular line units?'

The colonel took a long time before responding, forcing Connors to wonder if the question was somehow inappropriate. Finally, Rutledge nodded, 'Yes, their training is even more intense. But with Special Forces there was and is an additional problem.'

'What's that?' Connor asked.

'In WWII, the forces were organized and trained quickly. As a result, the units were made up of a variety of personality types. Many of the men were older and already experienced. Since 1960, the men selected for Special Forces have been, for the most part, young, single, and chosen for the simple reason they were loners, men who did not bond with other men. I'm sure the shrinks have a fancy label for it, but they are men I found to be cold and lacking in people skills.'

Connors leaned forward, 'Does the military see this as a problem?'

'Like I said, the Marines do have the re-entry program at Camp Pendleton, but I don't think there has been time to evaluate how effective it has been. The Army has nothing to my knowledge, and none of the services have admitted publicly there is a problem.'

Connors pressed the point, 'So, your concern is that men might be coming back into society who have been trained to kill and who have,' he paused, searching for the right words . . . 'been de-humanized. Could these soldiers be a danger to civilians?'

Rutledge shook his head, 'Well, I don't know if they would necessarily be a danger, although I suppose that could happen, but they will certainly have adjustment problems. I think this is what we are beginning to see. For instance, I'm not sure these men would make the best husbands and family men . . . at least not before they conquered their demons.'

'Would there be a difference in the re-entry stresses of a regular soldiers and those assigned to Special Forces?' Connors asked.

The Colonel's response again came measured, 'Any soldier who has seen battle is scarred. Odds are, a Special Forces soldier would have more and deeper scars. And, of course, due to this training, if they did become criminals, they would be . . . shall we say, extremely dangerous.'

Connors pushed further. 'Could you give me an example of assignments which would have the potential to seriously affect, perhaps irreparably, the psyche of a young Special Forces soldier?'

'Probably not without compromising state secrets; I can't discuss specific operations. Even though I've become an opponent of the government's policy in Vietnam, I'm still a Marine.

But, let me tell you a short story and maybe answer your question.' Rutledge paused, took a long drink of coffee, and continued, 'During WWII, both sides used bombing of civilian populations with the idea it would break the morale of the people. After the war studies revealed that bombing by itself, rather than lowering or destroying morale, actually increased the morale of the people.

However, these same studies also revealed that face-to-face destruction, where people witnessed the enemy killing and torturing their families and neighbors, did destroy morale. Ever since the beginning of Vietnam, both the Army and the Marines used this knowledge in an attempt to destroy the spirit of the Viet Cong. But I'm afraid I can't go any further in explaining what this means.'

Now it was Connors' turn to pause. He found himself overwhelmed with so much information gained in one short hour over a casual cup of coffee with a Marine Colonel.

He felt a sense of awe at the commentary of this old warhorse. And since he had first heard Brock served in some kind of Special Forces unit, Connors had sensed there might be a significant connection between Brock's war experiences and the rapes. It seemed the colonel's words were confirmation.

Connors thanked the officer profusely, had him sign a release for any quotes he might use, and hurried home to write up notes on the conversation. He definitely believed he was onto something big, very big. While not evidence that Brock was the rapist, the information certainly supported Blomberg's theory that the current rapist is well trained in tactics. And, if Brock was the rapist, it would be logical that the police would have a challenge in trying to catch him, especially if they failed to take note of his military training.

With the sense of urgency in Connors' gut now mounting, the young professor realized he needed to call and set up a meeting with Jeff Baker at DOJ, the second contact on his list.

11

Rape days were typically long. It all began with what he called 'collection'. Today he'd chosen Oakland for his destination, a site well away from the missions. Round trip, the journey took four hours, plus time for the collection, necessitating an early start so he could be well-rested for an important night.

Until the collection process was complete, he always found himself battling powerful fears. These inner conflicts were annoying but acceptable. As soon as everything was in place he gained strength and increased his awareness. As a result, the attack strategy worked time and time again, mission after mission.

He arrived on 7th Avenue in Oakland at 10:02 a.m. A perfect spot, he thought, as he fed the parking meter. Parking tickets could be a problem. Always eliminate potential problems.

The morning felt crisp and bright, yet he assumed the opposite posture, stooping over, mussing his hair and pulling baggy pants lower. He began to shuffle down the avenue, past the bars, pawnshops and an occasional painted lady. The wrinkled, soiled clothes gave him a bad feeling and he hated the feeling of being dirty and unkempt, but knew the costume was necessary to blend into the area.

He paused at each alley, looking for the ideal subject. In less than 10 minutes, he'd found his man, a bum sitting with his back against the wall, brown paper bag and bottle next to him on the cement. Even in the shade, he could see the man's droopy jowl, unshaven face and greasy hair.

'How'd you like a twenty dollar bill?' he offered, holding the bill in clear view.

'Wat'cha say?' the grizzled man mumbled, jerking his head up, confused by his unexpected company. 'Whad'ya want?'

'I'm your angel of mercy, ready to give you enough money to buy wine for a week.'

'Money, how much money?' the old man perked up.

'Twenty dollars.'

'Yeah? What for? I . . . I don't do no suckin'.'

'No. No. Nothin' like that. I just need a little blood.'

'Blood? I don't give no blood . . . no good anyway.'

'It's not for the Red Cross. This is for a university study. And, I don't need much. Just a little.'

'And, I get twenty bucks?'

'It's right here,' he said, looking up and down the alley, as he displayed the crisp twenty. The old man grabbed for it. He jerked the bill away. 'Whoa, not until I get the blood.'

'How you gonna get my blood?'

'I have a way. Won't take but a minute; won't hurt at all.' He grabbed the old man's left arm and stretched it out, revealing a dirty forearm. Pushing the sleeve up, he brought the syringe from his pocket, located a vein and inserted the needle. The old man winced as the syringe sucked blood.

'That's it,' he said, dropping the arm, taking care to guard an open, waiting eyeglass case where he set the syringe. Case in hand, he walked briskly to the van.

The Pine Tree Restaurant in Vacaville was a favorite stop. Once parked, he discreetly changed into a clean shirt and pants, thinking only of his mounting hunger. Inside, the hostess offered a wide smile, along with an annoying chatter and sashay as she led him to a window seat. He hated the need to be polite and was glad only when she took his order for steak, eggs over easy and chocolate milk.

It was 3:30 p.m. when he pulled into his driveway, pausing before making the left turn on the tree-lined street. A pack of kids passed his driveway, skipping and hollering at the end of their school day.

'I need some of that energy,' he thought. 'Time for a nap.'

12

Walking toward his desk, Weaver announced boldly to anyone within earshot, 'I'm gonna sleep in the break room tonight. I wanna be here when we book the bastard.'

It was 5:30 p.m., normally the time of day when he began to think about having a scotch on the rocks and something to eat. But not tonight. It was Tuesday and Weaver was announcing a gamble.

'Tonight's the night we nail him', he thought to himself as he reviewed his carefully planned patrol schedule. The patrol commander had objected, but Weaver went right to the top, gaining ten extra deputies, for three square miles, from 11:00 p.m. to 7:00 a.m.

In addition, city police were loaning six of their officers during the same hours. Along with the regular beat officers, a total of twenty-four patrol officers would blanket the area, unheard of for a rape case. 'We're gonna cover this so tight a fuckin' cockroach won't be able to cross a street without getting crushed,' Weaver bragged. 'Any car that turns off Folsom Boulevard onto a side street will be stopped and the driver identified. Period.'

Allen, who had listened while Weaver put his plan together, wasn't buying it. 'Bud, it's just not going to work. Most of the units will be marked cars and this rapist is too good to not notice,' she said. Increasingly aware of her superior's lack of intuitive sense, Allen saw no reason to keep her opinions to herself. A few weeks earlier she would have thought twice about challenging him, but now she felt justified in her boldness.

'Think so? My bet is all he's thinkin' about is getting his rocks off.'

'Getting his rocks off!' Allen leaned forward in her chair, incredulous. 'That's what you think rape is?' She couldn't believe Weaver's assessment of a rapist's motives. 'Rape is more than that. It's a violent crime, committed against innocent and helpless victims. It's about power and control. Welcome to reality Bud!'

Her vehement anger left a bewildered look on Weaver's face. 'Mary . . . Mary mother of Jesus . . . someone's riled up. Okay, have your definition. I just want the bastard caught,' he said.

'And so do I. As a woman, I'm sensitive to how men talk about rape,' Allen snapped.

'Okay. Okay. Calm down. All we need is one of the units to get a field identification card. They got their orders to stop all cars. By tomorrow morning we'll know everyone who was out and about. C'mon in early and watch me book the bastard.'

'Let's hope your plan works. But for the record, Bud, what you need is a good night's sleep, not what you'll get in the break room.' Allen couldn't help noticing her superior's strained, fatigued appearance as she left him setting at his desk.

Weaver shook his head. 'Broads just don't have the stomach for this work,' he thought and turned back to his typing.

'Is she gone?' Sergeant Howell said as he approached Weaver.

'Yeah. She's madder than a wet hen.'

'Forget her for now . . . have you briefed the patrol?'

'Yeah,' the detective reached into his desk, pulled out a stick of gum and stuffed it into his mouth.

'Hope you were careful. We gotta protect Brandt, this Sawyer thing has to be buried,' Howell said.

'They got the message. I told 'em we want this rapist gone. Period. Whatever it takes. . . .'

'Good. It's way past time we put this operation to bed. If this doesn't work out, the old man said he's going to turn it over to Stringer.'

'Shoulda been Stringer's job in the first place.'

'You know why that wasn't possible. Just get it done and you'll be taken care of you.' With that Howell was gone.

The rapist was up, showered and shaved by seven, just in time to watch *Jeopardy* and drink a cold Pepsi. As luck would have it, tonight's game offered a category from which he answered every question correctly: *Religions of the World*. The $500 question: What is the law of lex talionus?   Answer: Old Testament. An eye for an eye.

At 11:30 p.m., he picked out his clothing, selecting dark khaki pants with a dark blue sweatshirt. Next, he spread a city map on the dining room table, careful to review all the streets and parks in tonight's area of operation. He particularly liked the location of the current trap line, three houses within a quarter mile of the American River Parkway. Should there be a problem, he could easily find refuge in the dense trees and brush adjacent to the river. If he needed to float downriver, he was prepared for that as well.

Every one of his plans included at least two escape routes. He took great care to not keep any operational equipment at his house, and, he would check his rape kit once he reached the second vehicle, his VW bug. Tonight the Ford van would remain in his driveway.

He savored the preparation and often remembered how nervous he had been before his first missions in Nam. In time, he grew to find relief in the preparation. Memorizing the routes, the intelligence reports, cleaning and checking all equipment and coordinating with his unit brought focus. Over time, the routine became a catalyst to clear his mind and buoy his confidence. Tonight, working alone, there would be no sloppy seconds. His confidence soared.

At 1:45 a.m. he rode his bike into the lot where he kept the VW bug camouflaged. The abandoned gas station served him well with a couple of other cars always left unattended; he left his VW parked under a drooping eucalyptus branch, tailor made for cover.

The engine started easily, amazingly quiet for a '68, and he drove east on Folsom Blvd. This time of night, while the bars emptied, allowed him to blend smoothly into small episodes of traffic. 'Patrol officers are looking for drunks,' he assured himself.

He noticed two parked patrol cars, side-by-side at the corner of 71st Street, prompting him to check his speed, making sure he was safely within the limit. Several blocks later, well out of the city limits, he saw two more city police cars parked on a side street. 'What the hell are they doing outside their fuckin' jurisdiction', he wondered. Within a couple of minutes, two deputy sheriff patrol cars passed him. He sensed something was wrong. Too many pigs. He made a U-turn reversing his direction and backtracked west on Folsom.

Soon he spotted two more patrol cars, confirming his suspicion – a flood of uniforms. His heart was pumping faster. What to do? He needed to fall back on plan B.

Proceeding north on Howe, he drove to an area close to the American River and found an isolated parking spot near where he kept another bike hidden. Within a minute he was pedaling east along the American River Parkway and easily reached the jump off point to his target by 2:25 a.m. For the next thirty minutes he stood quietly, watching the house and he could not help but smile, 'Stupid pigs, they actually think they can stop me from completing my mission. What fools they are.'

He began to strip off his clothes just as the train whistle blew.

Weaver spent a miserable night. Neither couch in the break room, each with uneven springs, allowed him any real rest. Deputies constantly in and out didn't help. The smell of stale coffee from the coffeemaker heightened his aggravation.

Frustrated, Weaver gave up trying to sleep and returned to his desk cursing every rapist who ever lived. 'If we're going to get the son-of-a-bitch, it'll be in the next couple of hours,' he muttered. He sat at his desk, trying to review case files between periods of nodding off. No phone rang. At 5:45 a.m., he walked a block down to a café, bought a morning paper and several donuts. The phone rang as soon as he returned.

'This is Crowell at dispatch, catch any sleep?'

'What'ya got?' Weaver snapped, ignoring the question.

'Bad news. Sounds like he's at it again. Call just in from a guy who says his wife has been raped.'

'What address?'

'11565 Western Drive. Ambulance is in route.'

'Damn, right smack dab in the middle of an army of cops for Chrissake. Have you heard from any of the guys at the scene?' Weaver barked.

'Not a word.'

For a wistful moment Weaver considered this might not be the EAR, but he knew in his heart it had to be. He sighed, knowing within minutes the press would be calling and the old man would be furious. 'How long', he thought, 'can I take this pressure? If I fail and they called in Stringer, what would that mean for me?'

13

Parole officer Grant was struggling with the wording on a parole violation report when the phone rang. She pushed a stack of files away and fumbled to find the phone. 'Officer Grant, how may I help you?'

'Just the person I need to talk to. This is Dr. Bevins. I'm calling about one of your parolees, Tyrus Brock. Have you had a chance to review my latest report on him?'

'Not a recent one. Sorry, I'm a little snowed under,' she admitted.

'I understand. That's why I'm calling to give you an update.' He spoke quickly, with efficiency. 'In the first report, my preliminary evaluation states Brock's rapes were probably due to combat trauma, but after my last session with him, I'm re-evaluating that assessment. As you know, I have him journaling about issues he finds troubling. I expected another entry about Vietnam; instead, he gave me a rather disturbing incident from his early childhood.

I am particularly concerned because I am seeing a number of returning soldiers exhibiting stress-related problems. Most of them undoubtedly entered the service with seemingly normal emotional health. We haven't considered what combat stress might do to a person who brought mental health problems with him into service. This may be the case with Brock. It could indicate a problem more serious than I first thought. I now strongly recommend you do an in-depth interview.'

'Yes. I understand. Did you send a copy of his journal statement?'

'It's attached to my report dated January 20. Also, he called in sick and missed the last two appointments. There's a definite red flag here and I would recommend you schedule an interview soon. I would like to sit in.'

'No problem. I'll pull your last report right now, and if you have anything additional, give me a call,' Grant said as she began shuffling through one of her in-boxes. 'Oh, one other thing while you're on the line. The war stuff bothers me, too. I'm also getting more and more vets on my caseload, mostly with drug and depression problems. Do you have any additional information on Brock's service record?'

'Good question. I've made several requests for more information, but neither the Army nor the Department of Defense has given me anything additional. They either reply that the information is confidential or ignore the request.'

'Well, thanks for trying. But, if you could probe a little deeper on that angle, I'd appreciate it,' Grant said, knowing the doctor had the best chance to obtain background details.

'Sure, be glad to. Let's stay in touch.'

Grant found Brock's file, buried under half a dozen other case files, and immediately turned to the copy of Brock's journal entry. His neat penmanship and strong sentence structure again impressed Grant, just as they had with his first journal writing. Locating her reading glasses from the top drawer she read:

Why do they keep coming back? Why does my mind do this to me? Why are the memories always with me? If only I could just forget. I need help. I still remember her name even after 24 years. Wanda Clemmons. I was not yet in school, just five years old and I can see myself walking down the old railroad grade that crossed my step-father's farm. The grade was all that was left of a logging railroad spur. The iron tracks had long ago been taken up, and the ties were rotted. I would often walk quietly along the firm grade, looking for ducks, geese, quail, rabbits, and deer. For me, the sense of stealth and the feeling of being in my own private world was special. It was my world and she took it from me. My sisters, my mother, and the old man didn't pay much attention to me and I didn't pay much attention to them. I spent long hours alone. As long as my chores were done and I was in by supper, no one asked or seemed to care where I went. I remember this day so well. I was enjoying the quiet and solitude when suddenly a big, fat girl stepped out from behind a tree and grabbed my hand. I tried to pull away, but I couldn't. 'I'm Wanda, your neighbor, ya wanna play?' I remember thinking she was too big to play and I wasn't used to playing with anyone. But she pulled me down and immediately started stroking my face with one hand and holding me firmly with the other. 'I'll bet you don't know nothin' of sex,' she said in a whispery voice. 'I want to see if you're big enough to get hard and I'll show you how to make me feel good.' I remember not moving . . . not being able to move . . . I lay frozen. She undid my bib overalls and pulled them down to my ankles. I felt so vulnerable and afraid. Something about her control . . . even though it wasn't cold outside, I was shivering all over. 'Don't

be afraid. I won't hurt you. We can both feel good.'
Her hands ran up and down my body. She was fat.
She repulsed me. I didn't know what she was doing,
but I knew it was wrong. She pulled her dress off and
I saw everything. Suddenly, she jumped up and said,
'You're no fun. You're just too small. I can't even feel
you. I remember feeling terrified. I didn't move, as
she stood up and put on her dress. 'You don't tell no
one or I'll say you were foolin' with me. This is a
secret, you hear? I'll get you again when you're
bigger.' With that she was gone. I walked home
slowly. I knew I couldn't tell anyone. And, my
peaceful world would never be the same again. She
took it from me. She took it from me. That bitch . . . .'

Another molestation story. This one in a rural
setting featuring an overpowering teen age girl and a
frightened little boy. She'd heard the story before,
although most of her cases involved the opposite, a
young girl accosted by a male, usually a family
member.

Grant closed the file. Heavy nausea welled up
inside the pit of her stomach. 'Crap,' she muttered.
'Why does this have to happen? Now I have to move
him to high priority. I don't have time for it.'

Brock's case could be serious, no doubt. So were
many others. Adults, usually family members, had
sexually fondled many of the criminals on her
caseload. Girls especially, nearly one in four, carried
the trauma of early molestation. But something about
this story resonated more deeply than any she had
ever encountered. Combined with his military
experiences, this could signal real trouble.

Grant reached for the yellow pad she'd labeled: 'URGENT'. There were already ten items listed. At the bottom of the list she wrote, # 11, schedule Brock. Then as an afterthought, # 12, make appointment for an oil change. The phone rang, and she moved on to another name, another case.

A t 3:30 in the afternoon, Connors arrived at the state DOJ building, an old cannery at 33rd and C Street. The building had only recently been gutted, and, as an economic move, the State created office cubicles with five-foot-tall dividers rather than walls. Connors found the maze of narrow corridors difficult to navigate, especially with cardboard file boxes stacked everywhere. Eventually, he wound his way back to Baker's desk where he was greeted by a gregarious man.

'So you're the young man the professor brags about?' Slightly taller than Connors, Baker was a slender man, in his early 50s, with short gray hair. He motioned Scott towards a chair.

'I'm afraid I haven't done much to brag about, but Blomberg wanted me to meet you. As he probably told you, I'm in Sacramento to teach a class on sexual deviancy, but I'm also here to learn. He wants me to look into the East Area Rape series and thought you might be able to help.'

Baker nodded, 'Sounds like him. He's rather unconventional in his thinking. Most of the local police officials think he's radical, but I've taken two courses from him. I like the way he thinks.'

'How's that?'

Baker looked up from a file he was assembling, 'He thinks, really thinks and his students respond. Nothing conventional about his classes.'

Connors reflected back to his first conversation with the professor. 'He did mention not being popular with the local police. Why is that?'

'It's because of his theory of policing. He wants police departments to de-centralize, wants them to set up neighborhood offices and involve community members in selecting which officers work in their area, stuff like that. He calls it community-based policing. Unfortunately, police officials, especially the local sheriff, see this as far too unconventional. They label him a communist.'

Connors shook his head, 'Excuse me, but isn't smaller government the basic philosophy of conservatives? How can they label someone proposing to reduce the size of a government agency a communist? Isn't it communism that has the government running everything?'

'Exactly. Welcome to the surreal world of criminal justice. Logically, you would think Blomberg's philosophy of policing should be exactly what conservatives like police administrators want. But they see it as losing power. Government agencies don't like change and police administrators hate to give up control. And, they don't like outsiders interfering with their business. I'm sure you understand. Like everything else in society, the criminal justice system is a political animal.'

The statement gave Connors pause, 'I've never thought of it in exactly that light. How does your agency fit in with the local police?'

'We gather information, compile criminal statistics and maintain a crime lab. In addition, we aid small police departments in the investigation of serious crimes.'

'What about this local rapist? Is your agency involved?'

Baker shook his head, 'Not directly, but we are a central repository. Copies of all police reports are sent here and this allows us to collect statistics as well as analyze crime trends and advise police departments in cases that overlap jurisdictions.'

'What happens in that case?' Connors asked.

'Truthfully, not much.'

'What specifically do you do?'

Baker chuckled, 'My job description and title sound impressive but what I actually do is create files. Files that stagnate in our archives. I'm trying to change the system, but it's not easy. The agency is desperately in need of a cross referencing mechanism. What we call files are three by five index cards, very archaic.'

'Really.' Connors was surprised, 'You mean you don't have any computers?'

'Some departments are beginning to use them, but again the files are not connected. And, of course, the top administrators know nothing about computers. They're locked into their old, familiar routines. For example, missing person's files are not connected with our unidentified deceased file. A missing person from San Diego could be found dead in Modesto, but it's unlikely a connection will ever be made,' Baker said.

'Does this same lack of connection happen with sex offenders?'

'More or less. Upon release from prison they're required to register with their local police department. We receive and record that information. If they move from that address, they are, by law, required to physically report to the police department at their new location. Unfortunately, many don't. So we have thousands of registered sex offenders and no one knows where the hell they are.'

'Well, we know for sure there's one in Sacramento,' Connors said quickly. 'Is there any way I can gain access to the police reports?'

'We can only release the records to a person working for an official law enforcement agency.' Baker paused, then continued, 'Now I see what the good professor had in mind. You need access to police reports. Makes sense to me. Let's get you down to personnel so you can apply for an intern position. You'll only need to commit to ten hours a week. Once you're working here, you'll have access to our records.'

Connors felt his Irish grandmother must be working the heavens. In less than an hour, he'd completed another meaningful interview and found an internship that would give him data to help in his investigation.

His elevated mood quickly gave way to a familiar sadness as he walked past three young girls jumping rope. He could tell they were all about the age of his niece when she was killed, and he could see they played without a care in the world, just as it should be.

Despite the promise of spring in the air and the glow from the fading sun, the young professor felt a heaviness come over him, one experienced hundreds of times during the 15 years since her murder.

All children should be able to play without fear, he thought. Within minutes his sadness turned to anger as he considered the terror gripping the people of this city. 'How could this be', he wondered, 'rape, after rape, after rape and still no one arrested?'

He couldn't shake the haunting questions: Was the system so flawed that a highly trained criminal could exploit it and terrorize a community? Could military training and experience create super criminals? Was Brock such a criminal?

15

Professor Blomberg sat at his desk, smoking a pipe yielding the distinct smell of *Borkham Reef,* when Connors entered. The professor waved for him to take a seat, 'Are you enjoying your stay in Sacramento?' he asked.

Connors thought the question odd, especially given the three rapes since his arrival. Then he realized the question was about his personal life. 'Better than I expected. I came here fresh from a broken engagement, unsure how I'd take to a new city. However, between teaching and the rape suspect, I don't have much time to dwell on the past.'

'How are things working out with Baker over at DOJ?' Blomberg changed the topic.

'He's been a great help.'

'Have you found out why Detective Weaver eliminated Brock?'

Connors shook his head, 'Yes and no. In my opinion, Weaver's drawing a hasty conclusion based on illogical reasoning.'

'How's that?'

'After the ninth rape, he sent two detectives to Brock's house at 6:30 a.m. They found his van in the driveway, cold, and Brock at home. The reports consistently indicate the rapist strikes around 3:00 a.m. In the cases I've reviewed, I found the victims all reported the rapist had been gone for some time before they called the police.

Blomberg nodded, 'I see what you mean. But, rumor has it there's confusion over blood types. What's the story there?'

'Yeah, that's a real problem. The city crime lab has come up with several foreign blood types at the scenes, including secretors and non-secretors. These reports suggest there could be three or even four rapists.

But, the MO's so distinctive that there can only be one rapist. We don't know whether it has been sloppy lab work or mistakes made in the field. But, they certainly can't eliminate any suspect on the basis of blood,' Connors emphasized, shaking his head in frustration.

'I'd heard they've found foreign blood at several of the scenes? Does this rapist cut himself deliberately or is he just clumsy?

Connors nodded, 'Good question. I don't recall that aspect being discussed in any of the reports I've read. Could there be more than one rapist?'

Blomberg returned his pipe to a small, mahogany stand on his paper-strewn desk. His ever-ready smile and affable tone switched serious. 'I've been concerned ever since you told me about your interview with the Marine colonel. You've done all you can. Things could easily get out of hand and I think it's time you back off.'

Connors started to speak, but the professor held up his hand and continued, 'I know you've made good progress, but it could get dangerous, especially since you've confirmed Brock served in Nam in Special Forces. It's my recommendation you work with Baker and put together all the information you have in a report. I'll arrange a meeting with Weaver and you turn the information over to him. Ultimately, it's his responsibility.'

'Will he see me? I thought you were on the black list of the Sheriff's Department?' Connors asked, hoping to infuse a little levity.

'With Sheriff Brandt and some deputies yes,' his mentor chuckled, 'Capt. Phillips, Weaver's boss, owes me a favor, in fact a couple of favors. I'll call him and set up a meeting for Monday morning. Can you have a report ready by then?'

'Sure. I'd like to meet Weaver and get a read on him, but I don't agree about me dropping out. I'll be careful.'

The professor sat back, and sighed, 'I expected that. Still, the fact remains, this rapist is dangerous and I'm concerned for your safety.'

'If you're right about Brock, I doubt he even sees me as anything but a teacher. And, if someone told him I was asking questions about the rapes, I doubt he'd see me as a threat. However, if I'm going to attempt to convince Weaver to listen to me, I need some advice.'

'Advice?' Blomberg frowned.

'About cops. I'm afraid I haven't been very effective in communicating with the police officers taking my class. How do you get through their preconceived world view? Because our argument about Brock is really based on his psychological profile, Weaver's response to causation is important.'

'Police officers want to believe their role in stopping crime is significant. They equate talk about social factors influencing criminals with excusing criminal behavior. Further, they see such talk as minimizing their role in protecting the community. '

'So you're saying if I discuss theories of causation, it threatens how officers see their role?' Connors asked. Blomberg nodded.

'They're not the thin blue line protecting the community?' Connors continued.

'Correct. Police are only one of many factors controlling deviant behavior,' Blomberg said.

'How will being sensitive to the police ego help me communicate with Weaver?' Connors asked, a perplexed look on his face.

'In many ways, police officers are like members of a minority group. It's them against the world. They believe only other police officers can relate to the nature of their job. And, they don't think the public understands what they are up against. Further, police officers don't take criticism well and typically respond defensively.'

'So, it's likely Weaver won't listen to me, but you still want me to try?'

The professor nodded, 'You have to give it a shot. Just know that Weaver firmly believes he knows how to conduct an investigation. To him, you're an outsider. That's why I want you to work with Baker on your report. Maybe Weaver will be receptive to Baker's perspective. But, don't bet on it. Still, you need Weaver, or someone in law enforcement, to help you. They have resources you don't have, so it's worth the effort.'

'Okay, get me the appointment. I'll do my best, although given the case facts, it won't be easy. Wouldn't it be best if the police worked closer with the community?'

Blomberg laughed, 'If you want that, you'll have to move to London.'

16

Weaver slammed his fist down on the table. 'God dammit, we need solid physical evidence, not this psychological bullshit.' For a moment no one spoke, the silence hung heavy in the small room.

Allen stole a glance at Connors. She had only just met him and found herself impressed by his youth and his bearing. Weaver's invitation for her to join the meeting was a surprise. 'Some piss-ant professor, a friend of Blomberg, is coming in to share his wisdom about the EAR. At 11:00. I want you there,' Weaver told her earlier that morning.

Now Connors' boldness surprised her.

'Bullshit! Bullshit? Bullshit!?' Connor's tone grew louder and the repetitive outburst created drama in the barren conference room. Outside the glass-viewing windows, the bustle of another day at department headquarters played on.

Inside there appeared to be a face off. Connors stared straight at Weaver and continued, his voice dropping to a normal tone, 'This isn't bullshit . . . this is the essence of modern police work, and you should consider it. I don't see how your department can ignore this information. You've been looking for physical evidence and after twenty-three rapes, twenty-one women and two little girls with their lives ravaged and what have you got? Not a thing!'

'What do you mean, we got nothin'?' Weaver responded, crimson filling his face. 'We've eliminated numerous suspects, including your man Brock. We'll nail this bastard and we don't need a college kid telling us how to do it.' Weaver rose and was on the verge of walking out.

Undeterred, Connors continued, 'You're telling me you eliminated Brock by going to his house on one occasion more than an hour after the rapist reportedly left the crime scene. Brock could have walked home, showered and read the paper by the time your men got to his house.'

Connors stole a glance at Allen. For some reason it pleased him to notice a slight smile on her face.

Allen was taken with Connors' verve. It was unusual for a civilian, albeit one with a degree in Criminal Justice, to march into a meeting with an experienced investigator and argue his case with such passion. She wondered what motivated him.

Weaver sat back down. 'How the hell do you know how we eliminate suspects? Did you talk to Brock? You watch yourself. You're getting close to interfering with an investigation.'

'I have my sources, but there is no way you can call this interfering. I'm here telling you what I know. How is that interfering? And, since you say Brock is not a suspect, there would be no problem if I had talked to him.'

They made a strange trio: Connors, in tailored slacks and sports jacket; Weaver, his large frame spilling over the chair, red faced and angry; Susan Allen, composed in a crisp blazer, slacks and leather boots.

She, unlike Weaver, had scanned the report, with Baker's name and DOJ title prominently displayed throughout the report. She could see a lot of time and effort had gone into it and was intrigued by its focus on Tyrus Brock, the very man she was curious about. Yet Weaver remained adamant in dismissing Brock as a suspect.

Weaver was obviously not interested in the document. It detailed matches from Moran's statements, the Vesta attendance records and profilers' analysis of the rapist. Baker had signed off on the report, including his strong recommendation that the Sheriff's Department consider Brock a 'person of interest' in the case.

Yet, even though Connors had been forewarned about Weaver's attitude, the detective's negative reaction still surprised him. In fact, Connors couldn't believe it. Here was a respected lead detective who would not listen to, or even consider, a special report on a seemingly obvious rape suspect. It didn't make sense. Connors could feel his internal sense of justice escalating.

Weaver returned a cold yet obviously fatigued stare at the interloper. Who was this punk? A kid. A smart-ass college teacher who had shown up in Sacramento and now with a few hours teaching Criminal Justice under his belt he was suddenly some god-damned expert on police investigation.

The lead detective picked up the report again and slowly read its title: *An Assessment of the EAR's Psychological Profile.* It was naïve, this attitude and assessment by a Johnny-come-lately, simply naïve to think such a report could solve a savage series of rapes. He looked up from the report and forced his voice to a normal tone, 'What good does this do me? I've got a madman on the loose and a city about to go ballistic. Did you see the headline in this morning's paper? The city's two dailies are on this every day, and you want me to focus on what makes this freak tick? Hell, who cares about this crap? It don't mean shit. Did Blomberg put you up to this?'

'I've done my own investigating.' Connors answered keeping his voice as calm as possible.

'Well, we've had Brock's name before and he's been checked out. In fact, he's been checked out twice. I can tell you flat out Brock is not our man,' Weaver concluded matter-of-factly. 'Is this all you got?'

It was obvious Weaver thought the meeting a waste of his time. Allen remained quiet, studying both men. She had expected more objectivity from Weaver, more balance and less volatility. She wondered what triggered his reaction but kept her thoughts to herself. Connors had obviously touched a raw nerve, a nerve she, too, had sparked recently.

Connors continued, 'There is more if you would bother to read the report. For instance, your office released information to both Sacramento dailies indicating the rapist might be ex-military or even current military. I questioned some of the people associated with the Vesta program at City College and they told me Brock brags about being in the Army and claims to have served four tours in Vietnam in some type of Special Forces unit.'

Weaver pushed his chair back and stood to leave, 'For that he should get a medal, but again, I assure you we have definitely eliminated him as a suspect.'

Connors decided it was time to push the issue still further. 'I understand you also eliminated him on blood type, but I heard there's confusion as to the actual blood type of the rapist.'

Weaver snapped, 'Where'd you hear that?'

'Again, I have sources,' Connors said coolly, switching his gaze to Allen who was busy writing notes.

'Look kid, if you're trying to play detective, forget it. I was arresting perverts when you were in diapers.' Weaver struggled to control himself. 'Dammit, we've received thousands of tips on who this rapist might be and checking them out takes lots of man hours. We've used more than blood type to eliminate suspects and that certainly includes any creeps who have rape backgrounds.

Brock can't be the rapist, so if you want to play detective, I suggest you check out some of the other cons in that Vesta program. Lord only knows why anyone would put criminals on a college campus anyway.'

Connors pushed further, still with an even tone, 'There are so many leads to check out, are you sure you haven't been focusing on eliminating suspects and neglecting in-depth investigations of convicted sex-offenders such as Brock?'

He pressed on, 'But, since you won't read the report, let me share some of the points: Your department's profilers said the rapist was either not married or recently in a new marriage. *Brock is recently married.* Further, they said the rapist's prior offenses would be indecent exposure. Brock was arrested right here in Sacramento for indecent exposure. *He is a convicted rapist and was paroled just before this series started.* The rapist might have a strong religious background. *Brock is a lay minister.* The rapist is thought to be middle class; *Brock is*

105

middle class. The rapist may have a military background and, as I said, *Brock was in Special Forces.* Further, he fits the physical description.' He took a breath to retrieve some of the air expended in the long counterpoint.

Weaver stood and stomped toward the door. 'Forget it; fuck your report. You're trying to tell me how to conduct an investigation. You come back in here with some solid physical evidence linking Brock and I'll listen to you. Until then enough of this psychological bullshit.' With that he was gone.

Allen and Connors remained seated. Finally, Allen broke the silence. 'You'll have to excuse Bud. He's been under a lot of stress. That and lack of sleep have him on edge.'

Connors sighed, 'My fault. I came in here because I thought he would appreciate the information. I'm afraid I didn't do a very good job.'

'Don't worry. He'll forget it in a few minutes. I have some questions if you don't mind,' Allen said leaning toward him, 'I sense you have more information than you've told us. What else do you have?'

'Yes, I have found out more, but I'm afraid none of it implicates him directly.'

'Indulge me,' she said her voice warm and engaging.

Connors swallowed hard, 'Sure, I'll gladly tell you everything I've found out, but first let me ask you a question. In an investigation like this, where there have been so many rapes and evidence is scarce, isn't the personality of a suspect something the police should be interested in? Shouldn't the methods used to carry out the crimes be compared with personality and behavior characteristics of suspects?'

Allen listened carefully. 'Ideally, such information could prove valuable, but in high publicity cases, there are just too many suspects. We don't have the manpower to do an in-depth investigation on each of their personalities. Plus, personality characteristics are not admissible evidence in court, nor can they be used to support an arrest. That being said, what do you know about Brock's personality?'

'Plenty. He's considered odd and scary by the staff and other cons in the Vesta program. He brags about knowing police officers and the word is he's married to a lesbian . . . which may reflect on his sexuality. Also, one of the staff told me you can see in Brock's eyes that he's a killer. Perhaps the most significant fact is that Brock has failed to check in at the Vesta office every morning following a rape.'

'Interesting, not checking in on days following a rape might mean something. The rest sounds like a lot of speculation. His eyes? That's really a stretch,' Allen chuckled.

Connors couldn't resist a smile, suddenly realizing how much he missed a woman's laugh. He looked at Allen with renewed interest.

She continued, 'As Weaver said, Brock has been eliminated on more than blood type. If it helps any, I've questioned sending detectives to a suspect's house following a reported rape; too much time elapses.' Allen glanced at her watch. It was time to conclude their session, 'Despite Weaver's attitude, I do appreciate your efforts. Thanks for coming down.'

'Wait, can I make one more point about the investigation?'

'Sure.'

'When someone from your department contacted the military to obtain Brock's blood type, they contacted the Air Force at McClellan Field. The Air Force sent back the blood type of Thomas E. Brock, a radio operator for the Air Force, still on active duty. Tyrus Brock was in the army and he was discharged when convicted of rape in San Diego. So, your department has been using the wrong man's blood type to eliminate Brock.'

Allen blushed noticeably. 'I'll certainly check that out. I hope we haven't been that sloppy.' She rose and waited for Connors to leave the room ahead of her. As he passed her, she handed him a business card and said softly, 'Call me if you find anything additional. Weaver has too much on his plate. I might be able to help if it's solid information.'

As Connors left the building, fingering the card in his coat pocket, he wondered if Allen had given him the card to encourage his efforts or just to placate him following Weaver's rude behavior. Before putting the card in his wallet, he turned it over to discover: *398-2552 (home)*.

'Was she asking him to call her at home', he wondered? Connors hoped he would soon have reason to test her interest. He liked having the personal phone number of a beautiful, sharp, female detective, especially a woman who showed appreciation of his investigative efforts.

17

From across the large parking lot, he watched them take her away. She was dead, no doubt about it.

The ambulance was no good for her now. Her death had been quick. Painless? It didn't matter. If she had just honored her marriage contract, but she hadn't and there was no choice. Mission accomplished.

His thoughts grew clearer: 'Now I can move on. No need to worry about her calling my parole officer. I've got a meeting in a couple of days with that parole officer. . . It's best this way. No surprises. Tonight is jazz night,' he said to himself as he casually walked back to his van. He liked jazz. He was not sure why.

###

Although the Emerald Club featured only local groups, they were usually worth the cover charge. He favored the club because of the small crowds and the lack of dancing. Dancing bothered him. Always had. Women shamelessly hanging all over men.

At the bar he ordered a whiskey sour and carried the drink to a corner table. He sipped his drink slowly ignoring the crowd waiting for the liquor and the bass' rhythmic strumming to soothe his mind. She was gone and she no longer posed a concern. Soon, the memories would fade as well.

He sat enjoying his privacy when the scrape of a chair startled him. A man sat down directly across from him, his beer slopping as he banged the glass down on the table. The intruder was a large man with bulging body fat and long, stringy hair. His musty body odor and soiled clothing spoke strongly of a person living on the street. 'I'll be damned if it's not Brock,' he offered his rough hand across the table.

Brock ignored the gesture.

He dropped his hand and sat down hard. 'Been watchin' you since you came in. Took me awhile to be sure. The blonde hair threw me.'

Brock gazed coldly at the man, '*Who* in the hell are you?'

'McGrudy . . . Jeff McGrudy. Basic training. And then Nam . . . we were there, same time. Until they pulled you out. The fair-haired boy got the plum?' he queried.

'Doesn't matter.' Brock said, 'I don't talk about Nam.'

His uninvited guest pressed on, 'While the rest of us crawled through the damned jungle eatin' mud and killin' slopes you were on some kinda special assignment?' He took a long draught of his beer. 'Aw hell, what's it matter for Chrissake? Nobody gives a damn about vets.'

'Not vets like you. Fuckin' doper. A doper gone to fat.'

'Hell man . . . I was only eighteen, scared as hell. We all were,' his voice fell, his head bowed. He avoided eye contact. 'But look at you,' he managed to raise his gaze, 'You look like you done good. Pullin' easy duty musta made a difference.'

For an instant Brock considered just walking away. 'Who needs this', he thought. 'You got no idea what I did in Nam, and I'm sure as hell not going to tell you except to say I killed more gooks in a week than you did in your entire fuckin' tour.' He was emphatic. 'And nobody in my unit smoked dope. If they had, I would've killed them myself.'

The big man guzzled the last of his beer and motioned for the barmaid. 'Whoa there partner, didn't mean to get you so riled. Just wantin' to share a few memories, that's all. Lemme buy you a drink.'

'Look, I didn't ask you to sit at my table. You got problems. We all got problems. My wife was killed today. I'm looking for quiet.'

'Geez . . . killed? Sorry to hear that, you wanna talk about it?' He waited for Brock's reply and when there was none, he offered, 'It ain't easy losing a good woman. My wives both left me.'

'Not the same as dying.'

McGrudy nodded, 'Shit, aint nothin' easy anymore. You're one of them survivors, I can see it on ya.'

Brock was growing irritated with the interruption, the cheap commentary and the Emerald Club. Still he countered, 'Yeah, I'm doing fine.'

McGrudy straightened in his chair and returned to war talk, still hopeful for conversation, 'So they set you up to kill lots of gooks?'

Brock stirred the melting ice in his cocktail with a small red sword designed to hold an olive, 'I went north while you stayed south. That's all.'

'North?'

'Fuck man. I don't want to talk about it.'

Slow on the uptake, McGrudy continued, 'You with any group?'

'Group? What'n the fuck you talking about?' Brock's voice thick with irritation.

'Vets. You know; it helps to get with the guys. Talk about it. Have some laughs, some beers.'

Brock quickly countered, 'Not for me. And, it doesn't look like it's done much for you.'

'I've been worse. Got a part-time job now.' His eyes brightened. 'Gettin' a place of my own at the end of the month. Still think about it a lot. Too much death and dying. Hell, they blew people to pieces. Me holding cover in a bush for days.'

'The killing didn't bother me. Nothing wrong with killing if there are bad people. We were soldiers on a mission to kill. Soldiers kill,' Brock responded.

'What about nightmares? What'd'ya do for 'em? Almost all the guys talk about nightmares,' McGrudy, asked, groping for camaraderie.

'No. I have no nightmares. I found the Lord and He's helped me. Righteous people can kill people. Happened all the time in the Bible,' Brock leaned forward, 'I've been tested by the Lord and I've come out the victor.'

McGrudy sat, silent, his glass now empty.

'Here, buy yourself another,' Brock said, standing and pulling a five dollar bill from his wallet, dropping it on the table in front of the slouching ex-soldier.

As the band warmed up for another set, Brock slipped out the side door into the cool evening, anxious to get home in time for the late news. One story in particular interested him. And, he still had work to do.

18

At 9:00 AM Tyrus Brock was due in her office for their first session and Grant still needed to review Dr. Bevins' latest report. 'Hopefully, there is something new in the clinical report that will give me some direction,' the parole officer thought as she opened Brock's file. She turned first to the therapist's clinical analysis and read:

'I'm sorry you haven't yet interviewed Mr. Brock. I was able to see him again, and now I believe Brock has serious problems with women. After much probing, he has finally started talking about his relationships. Although only 28 years old, his current marriage is his third. He blames the failure of the first two marriages on age and absences – his service years – but I believe there are more underlying causes. Suppressed anger toward his mother stems from her failure to protect him from an abusive step-father (see attached narrative from his journaling). He masks his psychological pain with an air of aloofness. I now believe he needs intensive therapy. We should have a staff meeting in the next few days and discuss petitioning the court to request bi-weekly sessions.'

Grant flipped to Brock's hand written journal entry and began reading:

Dr. Bevins, you asked me to write about my step-father. I guess it's really hard to talk about the old man. But here goes. The most powerful memory, stronger than even those from Vietnam, comes often. Scene by scene my mind plays it out: Paul, all 6'2', 280 pounds of him, is dragging a squealing pig from the pen. With his left hand he holds the pig by the back leg and in his right hand he is wielding a huge knife . . . the silver blade glinting in the sunlight. He drags the pig toward a barrel of boiling water sitting under a large maple tree. Under the barrel red hot coals burn, a block and tackle hang above. He tells me to hold the long end of a rope while he sticks the knife blade into the pig's throat. The pig is suddenly covered in blood and slips from his grasp and begins to rush straight at me. This part is always in slow motion, the pig waving his head and spraying blood, Paul swearing and yelling for me to stop the pig. But, I know I can't. I dodge to my right and the pig strikes me square in the chest. We both fall to the ground in a tangle of arms, legs and blood. I scream louder than the pig and struggle to my feet. I begin running blindly toward the house. Before I take ten steps, the old man is on me. He grabs me by the back of the neck and jerks me to a complete stop, he snarls, 'Goddamn you, no man runs away. Now get back here and do your job.' I'm frightened and covered with blood and I try to struggle free. He slaps me hard across the face. 'Shut up, you blubbering baby. Men don't cry. Quit your whimpering and help me drag this pig back to the barrel.' Not until the pig is dunked in the boiling water and hung does he let me leave. I wash up in the creek behind the house. My left eye is swollen shut. I am dizzy with pain. I yearn to go to my mother. I know what she'll say. Nothing. She is so distant, so detached. I find my bike and ride down the dirt road to the river. I am eight. I hate this memory. I hate them both.

Grant sat pensively, reading and re-reading the entry. Even with her years of work with parolees, she wasn't sure she was ready for Brock. Who was he, really? How would he present to her? She was still contemplating the narrative as Brock arrived.

When he walked into her office, Grant was temporarily taken aback realizing how accustomed she was to lethargic parolees shuffling in, hang-dog and hopeless, quite different from Brock. His fresh, all-American look was genuinely a novelty. He carried himself erect with the gait of an athlete. She stood to greet him and was surprised by his firm, open handshake.

'It's a pleasure to finally meet you,' Brock said, in a confident, pleasant voice. 'Several of the guys in the Vesta program at City College have spoken highly of you.'

'I wasn't aware any of them knew me well enough, but I'll accept the compliment,' she responded, casting a wary eye on the parolee while noting his eager and bright eyes.

He sat down, crossed his legs and smiled, showing a set of very white, even teeth. Grant continued, 'I called you in to find out how you're doing. Having any problems?'

'No, I'm married now to a nice lady. Her name is Janet and we've been married for almost two months. School is going well. Last semester I pulled straight A's. Things couldn't be going better,' he sounded convincing. Slightly stiff, but convincing.

Accustomed to parolees talking a good line, Grant could see what Bevins meant about Brock sounding a little too smooth, too staged. She needed to cut through his façade. 'I see here, you've missed some scheduled meetings with Dr. Bevins. Any reason for the no shows?'

With no hesitation, he responded, 'I called both times. The first one I missed because I had the flu and the second time I had a major exam I needed to study for. But, for the record, I really like Dr. Bevins and believe he is helping me.'

'In what ways do you need help?'

Again, a quick response, with perfect diction, 'Oh, I think in adjusting to civilian life. I was in the army for almost six years and then spent three years in prison. So, it's been awhile since I lived as a civilian.'

'What's been the hardest adjustment?'

'Probably decisions. For years other people made decisions for me. So that's been difficult.'

Grant continued her probe, 'I see you're not working, just going to school. How are you living?'

'My wife has a good job and she wants me to focus entirely on school for now. Once I graduate, I'll get a job.'

'Speaking of wives, I see this is you're third marriage. Aren't you pretty young to have had three marriages?'

Brock smiled at the question and paused. Grant realized the smile bought him time to formulate a suitable response. She also noticed a distinct shift in his eyes. Was it soft to hard, light to dark? Had she triggered him?

'I suppose so. I was married while still in high school. We were just too young. I married my second wife while I was in the military and soon deployed to

Vietnam. When I returned, she was living with another man. I guess you could say I've had bad luck with marriage. You know what they say, third time is a charm.'

Feeling a need to elicit less charm and more content, the parole officer continued, 'I'd like to clarify your relationship to both Dr. Bevins and me. Your psychologist is required to share all clinical reports. This is unlike traditional therapy where everything said in session is confidential.'

'Yes, Dr. Bevins explained that to me.'

'Therefore, you know he has shared with me your journaling. Do you believe you committed your crimes as a result of stress suffered in Vietnam?'

'I suppose that could have been the reason, although I really think it was because I was drinking too much. But now I've found peace through my religion and don't drink.'

'I'm concerned about you missing sessions. If you have to miss another meeting, would you please give me a call, as well as Dr. Bevins?'

'Yes ma'am,' he smiled, 'I don't think I'll be missing anymore sessions, but if I have to, I will call you.'

Grant tried one more time to encourage Brock to open up, 'It seems like you had, shall we say, a difficult childhood. Do you think some of those problems may have caused you to have difficulty relating with women?' Again . . . for a fleeting moment, the parole officer saw something in his eyes, a veil . . . or pain?

'Oh no, it was very sad when my mother died. Now, I'm really close with my sisters and I can't wait to see my nieces and nephews. I have eight of them, but they're all in Colorado. They call me often.'

'Did you have any problems with the law as a teenager?'

'No. I was really into sports.'

'Did you have any difficulty academically in grade school or high school?'

'No. I always got A's and B's.'

'What were your favorite subjects in high school? Brock smiled before responding, 'Ah . . . actually . . . there were several. For the first time he faltered in his answer. 'I . . . liked them all . . . maybe science and history were the best.'

Grant deliberately cut the session short, as it was obvious Brock was not going to reveal much. Inside she felt frustrated over the truncated information offered by this complex parolee. His file seemed incomplete to her. The feeling was uncomfortable. It exacerbated the sense of disconnect she felt with Brock.

Typically, the parolees she counseled displayed emotional hardness, a callous exterior. In contrast, Brock seemed too charming. 'Who was the true Brock', she wondered? And what about those eyes? They were penetrating, that was certain.

Dismissing Brock, she picked up her telephone and dialed her department's central records office. Brock's file was entirely too thin. There was no pre-sentence report, nothing about his family and no reports from his army service. To evaluate him properly she needed more data.

'Records. Gilbert speaking.'

'This is Darlene Grant, a parole officer here in the Sacramento office; I need you to send me the complete file on a Tyrus Brock, B-4183573. He's on my case load and I believe I have an incomplete file.'

'Sure, I can check that right away.'

'How long will it take?'

'If I can get to it today, I should be able send it over by tomorrow.'

'Thanks. I'm on an important deadline for a court hearing,' the parole officer lied, wondering why she felt a need to do so.

Grant made a note of the request in Brock's file, then picked up her dictaphone and began her report on the session:

'Tyrus Brock reported on time as scheduled. He reports everything in his life is going well. He is married, is supported by his new wife, and is a full-time student at City College. He reports a straight A/B average in his high school and college classes. His demeanor and verbal responses contrast with the journal entries submitted in his mandatory therapy sessions. The journal entries indicate some deep-seated emotional problems, which Brock masks well. It will be necessary to contact people in the community to get a better read on Brock. I will attempt to contact his wife, Janet.

Dr. Bevins requests a more intensive therapy schedule. I concur. I will be discussing Brock in our case discussion meeting early next week. My experience with parolees leads me to expect prison time as bearing negatively on already disturbed personalities. Parolees almost always exit prison more hardened and with a greater propensity for

119

violence than when they entered. Is Brock a rare exception or has he evolved a highly developed ability to mask his real feelings? I will submit a follow-up report on Brock within the next ten days. Dated 3-7-76'.

Grant laid the microphone down and paused to reflect. No doubt, Brock was going to be a tough case. Then, almost as an afterthought, the parole agent reached for the telephone and dialed the Sheriff's Department.

'Sacramento County Sheriff's Department, how may I direct your call?'

'I need to speak with someone about the EAR. This is Darlene Grant, I'm a parole officer.'

'I'll put you right through to detective Weaver. He's the lead investigator.'

'Homicide, Weaver,' a voice answered on the third ring.

'Hi, this is Darlene Grant, a parole officer and I'm calling about the East Area Rape case.'

'You and half the city, what do you need?'

'I just talked to one of my parolees. He's on parole for rape and I'm a little concerned about his emotional stability.'

'What's his name?'

'Tyrus Brock, he seems to fit the physical . . . .'

Weaver cut her off, 'Yeah, we've already checked him out. He's not the rapist. He's been eliminated, but I appreciate the call.' The line went dead.

Surprised by the detective's curt attitude, Grant wondered if she should call back. 'I guess they're a little stressed over there,' she surmised and returned to her paperwork.

19

Connors couldn't believe how nervous he felt about making a phone call. Pulling into the parking lot of a supermarket, he parked next to a row of pay phones and began rehearsing what to say. 'God,' he thought, 'I'm acting like a sixteen year old.' He let the phone ring seven times and was about to hang up when she answered.

'Hello.' It was obvious from the tone of her voice she'd been sleeping.

'I'm sorry, did I call too late?' Connors glanced at his watch, 10:10 p.m.

'I suppose it depends on who you are,' Susan Allen answered, the sleepy tone slowly disappearing, 'If you're the Pope, I'll talk, if a mere mortal, call tomorrow.' Allen had come home early, taken a long bath and gone to bed at eight with a new issue of *Cosmopolitan* magazine. She had fallen asleep in the middle of an article entitled: *'Professional Women in the 70's.'*

'I may not be the Pope, but I believe I am a savior, at least as far as the EAR case is concerned,' he answered with what he hoped matched her wit.

'Scott Connors!' Allen exclaimed, her voice warming, 'Now you're haunting my nights. Weaver must swear at you half a dozen times a day. You sure have become an irritant to him.'

'I thought you said he would forget me in a few minutes?'

'Usually he lets nothing bother him, but for some reason you're a sore spot. Enough small talk. What's up?'

'I think we have a big break. Brock's wife, Janet, has left him. She's moved back in with her old partner Kim Henderson.'

'Sounds great for a soap opera, but how does this help catch a rapist?'

Connors chuckled, delighted with her wit. 'Assume for a moment Brock is the rapist. Who better to tell us about his late night, early morning activities than the woman who shared his bed? If she tells us he was sound asleep, snoring loudly, night after night, I'll never mention his name again.'

'Weaver would love that. But, what do you mean tell us? Does this include me?'

Connors felt encouraged by the warmth and humor Allen was projecting. 'I have a meeting with Janet Brock tomorrow night at 7:30 and was hoping you would accompany me and hear for yourself what she has to say about Brock.'

'Hmmm,' Allen said softly.

Connors quickly upped the ante. 'And, to make this offer even more appealing, I'll buy you dinner first and fill you in on what Kate Willis had to say about Mr. Brock.'

'A unique approach I must say. I'll bet not many women, on a first date, get to ask another woman about her sex life with a rapist. In fact, I'm sure I would be the first.'

'Can I take that as a yes?' Connors asked, anticipation evident in his tone.

'How can a woman turn down such an intriguing invitation? Where and when would you like to meet?'

For a long while after concluding his phone conversation with Allen, Connors continued to dwell on her use of the word date. 'It's been a long time since I've been out with a woman as interesting as Susan', he thought. For the first time since coming to Sacramento, he was glad to have something else to think about, something besides a rapist.

###

Allen entered the restaurant looking nothing like a police detective. She wore a tailored cocoa-brown pants suit and a silk camisole, turning heads as she moved through the dining room to where Connors was seated near a window.

He glanced up just as she reached the table and stood to acknowledge her presence. 'You look stunning,' he said as he pulled her chair out.

Allen smiled as she sat down. 'Thank you. But let me be honest, I thought an attractive outfit might work well with the ladies.' They laughed in unison.

Inside, Connors felt an unexpected burst of pride realizing his date was undoubtedly the most attractive woman in the restaurant. They spent the next few minutes ordering wine and studying the menu. Connors decided to bring forth his boarding-school-honed manners and asked, 'Where I come from, when a gentleman takes a lady to dinner, he places her order. May I do that for you?'

Allen's smile indicated she felt very comfortable with such a formal, if old-fashioned, dating ritual. 'That would be very nice. Exactly where do you come from?' the detective asked, realizing Scott Connors was not like the California men she'd dated. His unique style, politeness for politeness' sake, was a refreshing break from the macho male personas she so often encountered.

123

'Colorado mostly, but I spent my high school years in a Wisconsin boarding school and came back West for college,' Scott responded. 'How about you?'

'I'm a California girl, born and raised. My mother now lives in the Mendocino area, near the coast. I originally came to Sacramento to get my masters. Then I was hired on at the Sheriff's Department . . . ,' she paused, 'I'm giving you a bio.' Again they laughed.

A waiter appeared with a small carafe of wine.

'Well, with those brief background checks behind us, I'll propose a toast: To two intelligent sleuths in their pursuit of a high-profile criminal.' He clinked glasses with Allen. Their eyes met and both allowed the connection to linger beyond the moment.

Connors felt a wave of emotion course through his chest. Whatever it was, it felt good. For several minutes they sipped their wine and watched the sky change from bright to dusty rose, reflecting off the Sacramento River.

'Boy, it feels good to relax, I needed this. The entire city is on pins and needles over this case,' Allen sighed.

'I know,' Connors responded. 'And, I hate to break the mood, but there are some things we should go over before the interview.'

Taking his lead, Allen started the discussion with a question. 'You talked with a Kate Willis. Is she the same Kate Willis who has been bugging Weaver about Brock?

'One and the same. She told me she'd given up on Weaver and talked with you just a few days ago.'

'She did call. Did you get the feeling she really

124

had something on Brock? Weaver thinks it's just a personal vendetta,' Allen commented.

'Her information is pretty consistent with what I've found from other sources; no hard evidence linking him to the case, but she had some compelling things to say about Brock, things which could lead one to conclude he is the rapist.'

'And those are?'

'Kate has the same physical features as the victims of the rapist. She is white, tall and slender. Like all of the rape victims, her hair is long and dark. From the time she first met Brock, he appeared to fixate on her. She finds him constantly staring at her whenever they are in the same group. Several times she's even caught him following her in his white van. And, there are the phone calls . . . . '

'That's what she was telling me,' Allen broke in, 'some guy calling her late at night saying he was on the East Area Rapist task force. I told her it sounded like a random crank call to me.'

'Did she mention she recognized the voice as Brock?' Connors asked.

'No. When I told her it probably was nothing, she hung up.'

Connors nodded, 'Yeah, she said she is very disappointed with the whole Sheriff's Department. Apparently, she has been calling Weaver since late January telling him Brock was the EAR.'

'I'm confused. How does Brock's wife fit in with this?' Allen frowned.

'Kate is the manager of their softball team. She's known Janet for three years and is very open about being gay. She also said Janet is gay and that none of their friends could believe it when Janet announced she was getting married.'

'That's a key point. If she's gay, why did she marry a guy like Brock?'

'Kate said it was because Janet wanted children and didn't want to raise them without a father. She met Brock when he was in Folsom prison. She was on a Christian mission. Apparently, she thought he was a wonderful guy and married him within a few months after he was paroled. That's when Kate first met him. After that, Brock was always hanging around softball practice, which made all of Janet's teammates nervous. Kate said everyone knew Janet was not happy with the marriage, right from the beginning.'

'Did she give any specific reasons for Janet's unhappiness?' Allen asked.

'No, she suggested I talk with Janet herself and that's why she set up the meeting tonight. In fact, we'll be meeting Janet at Kate's house.'

'This'll be very interesting. Obviously you should do most of the talking . . . unless their intimate life comes up. Guess it should be me to ask those questions.'

'Sounds like a plan,' Connors said, impressed that Susan was such a quick study.

'By the way, you were right about Brock's blood type. We did have it wrong. I can't believe Weaver sent a request to the Air Force. We now have a request in to the Army. Thanks for giving me the information.'

Connors couldn't help smiling.

The comfortable, light mood vanished when they arrived at Willis' house at exactly 7:30 p.m. Connors rang the doorbell and was shocked when Kate opened the door. Her eyes were swollen and tears streamed down her cheeks. She startled them with an abrupt announcement, 'Janet's dead,' she half cried, half whispered.

Stunned, they followed the sobbing woman into her living room. Connors recognized Nancy Fischer, Kate's partner, but the other six women, also in tears, were strangers. No one spoke while Connors brought two chairs from the dining room, and he and Allen sat silently waiting for someone to speak.

Finally, Kate composed herself, 'I'm sorry I couldn't call you and tell you not to come. We just got back from the hospital. Janet died this afternoon. Kim is still in the hospital.'

'What happened? Feel free to talk openly. This is Susan Allen, a detective with the Sheriff's Department. She's working on the East Area Rape case and wanted to speak with Janet. Can you tell us what happened?' Connors directed his question to Kate.

'We're all in shock,' it was Nancy who answered. 'We only know it was a motorcycle accident. Apparently they ran into a wall at the Safeway on Folsom. Janet died at the scene. The doctor said Kim sustained multiple bruises, but would be okay. We weren't able to speak with her. That's all we know.'

Connors realized nothing could be gained with Janet's friends in such obvious grief. 'What hospital is Kim in?' he asked.

'Sutter on 29th Street,' Kate responded.

'Do you know who was driving?' Allen spoke softly, directing the question to the entire group.

127

'Janet was driving, but no one at the hospital knew anything else about the accident,' Nancy answered.

Expressing their condolences, Allen and Connors excused themselves. As they left, Allen gave Kate one of her cards, 'You call me with anything at any time. I want to help.'

Once in the car Connors spoke first, 'God . . . this is incredible. Dead. She's actually dead. I'm sorry I brought you in on that. This is shocking.'

'No need to apologize. What I would suggest is you drop me off at my car and then go to the hospital and see if you can talk with Kim. Under the circumstances they may be lenient about visiting hours. Meanwhile, I'll call city PD and find out who's handling the investigation of the motorcycle accident. They need to find out where Brock was this afternoon.'

'You think Brock might have caused the accident?' Connors asked. This had been his initial thought, and it encouraged him to find Allen thinking along the same line.

'I have no idea, only intuition at this point. Brock may have killed her to keep her from talking. He may have realized he was losing his control over her.'

'Okay, I'll go over to Sutter and talk with Kim. Hopefully, she'll be able to tell us what happened,' Connors said. 'Sure you don't want to go with me?'

'No, it's better if I stay behind the scene at this point. Just drop me off at my car, but keep me informed of what you find out.'

Connors pulled in and parked next to Allen's car. As she started to open her door, he stopped her,

'Please, wait just a minute,' he reached over and rested his hand on her arm. 'There is something I need to tell you about Brock and you need to hear it before you get more involved.'

'You don't think I know enough now?'

'It's just that he is more dangerous than you may think. Brock served four tours of duty in the army assigned to Special Forces doing what was called deep reconnaissance. A few days ago, I talked with a retired Marine colonel. Among other things, he said Special Forces purposely select men who are loners. They're given intense training and sent on missions that could cause psychological damage to the enemy, whatever that means. I think Brock was one of those men. If this is true, he is very dangerous.' Connors studied Allen's response to the information carefully; he felt it imperative she understand the seriousness of the situation.

Allen sat for a moment, the passenger door half ajar, then turned to face him, 'Scott, I appreciate your sharing this with me, but it does nothing to change my mind about working with you. Actually, I insisted on working this case well before you came on the scene because I felt there was something wrong with the investigation. I have been questioning Weaver about Brock for months. All over the city women are being terrorized and brutalized. If Brock is the rapist, he must be stopped. I see your involvement as an important aide in the investigation.'

Connors entered the emergency room and went straight to the registration window. 'I'm here to see a Kim Henderson. She was brought in earlier this afternoon following a motorcycle accident.'

'Are you a relative?' asked the admitting clerk, a small woman with thick glasses.

'No, just a close friend.'

'Have a seat. I'll call the charge nurse.'

Connors had been seated for only minutes when a large woman, dressed in nurse whites, came rushing into the waiting area. She addressed the room, 'I'm looking for the man who said he is a friend of Kim Henderson.'

'I'm Scott Connors,' he stood to greet her, 'and actually I am a friend of a friend, but I was hoping I could talk with her for a few minutes.'

'We would like to talk with her, too. Unfortunately, she left the hospital without checking out,' the nurse reported, wearing a confused, disturbed look.

'You mean she isn't here? But I heard she was injured.'

'Kept in for observation, and, yes, she was badly bruised and needed to be x-rayed. For some reason she made the decision to leave without telling anyone.' The nurse shook her head in disbelief.

Connors walked to his car perplexed by the evening's events.

20

Connors' lecture was disjointed and he felt out of sync with his students while his mind continued to fixate on the news of Janet's death and the events of the night before. It didn't help his concentration to see Brock come into the classroom, a few minutes late and set down like he had not a care in the world. How does a man attend class so soon after his wife dies?

He tried not to look at Brock but could not push the thought of the bizarre accident from his mind. Is Brock connected to the accident? Over and over, questions played in his mind. Despite his best effort, he was too distracted to lecture effectively; and, as a result, he dismissed class after twenty minutes, citing an unexpected department meeting.

As Brock left the room, Connors observed his student talking with another man, and when Brock said something, causing them both to laugh, the professor was appalled. Even if Brock wasn't the rapist, how could he display humor so soon after his wife's sudden death? He was indeed one complicated man.

The young professor hurried to the faculty lounge and placed a call to Kate Willis, determined to track down Kim Henderson.

Kate answered on the first ring, 'I was hoping it was you. I just finished talking with Kim. She left the hospital because of Tyrus. She thinks he's responsible for the accident. She didn't want him to come to the hospital looking for her.'

'Did she tell you where she's staying?'

'She's at a friend's apartment.'

'Will she talk with me?'

'I told her about you and how you are working with detective Allen. She said she'd talk, but you need to see her soon. She's in a lot of pain. I'm picking her up at one to take her to my doctor.

'Give me the address and I'm on my way.'

'Make sure no one is following you,' Kate said.

The thought gave Connors a chill.

The apartment building was one of many look-alike three story buildings, side by side, along Fulton Ave. Fortunately, Kate's directions were precise and he found the correct apartment easily. When Connors knocked, Kim took a few minutes getting to the door and then opened it only after checking through the peep hole.

Connors entered and spoke first, 'I'm sorry to ask you to talk so soon after Janet's death, but what you know may be important.'

Kim nodded her agreement and directed him to sit at the kitchen table, explaining, 'It feels better to sit in a hard chair. My head is throbbing.'

Connors couldn't help but wince when he saw how swollen and purple the left side of her face was, and he purposely found himself choosing a chair to her right, the side with an open eye. He started to speak when Kim interrupted.

'Kate said I can trust you, but promise me you won't give this address to anyone else.' She paused momentarily. 'I swear he wanted to kill us both.' She spoke slowly, through puffy lips.

'I assure you I will tell no one where you're staying,' Connors replied.

He felt unsure of his questioning. Was he pushing too hard, too soon for details? "Could your arm be broken?" he continued anyway.

'I can't tell for sure. All I know is that it hurts like hell. I've been keeping ice on it, and Kate's coming to take me to see her doctor.'

'I promise I'll keep this brief. You said he wanted to kill . . . are you referring to Brock?'

'Yes . . . he is horrible, evil . . . why . . . oh why . . . did Janet ever get mixed up with him?'

Connors could see tears welling. 'I know you're tired and probably in a lot of discomfort, but can you remember what happened?'

'I've been . . . had . . . been teaching Janet how to handle my motorcycle. She learned fast and was doing a great job. She was driving and I was on the back. We stopped at Safeway to pick up a few groceries. When we came out and got back on, Janet kick started the bike and for some reason the throttle stuck.' Kim paused, struggling to hold back tears. 'Before . . . before she could do anything we hit the wall. The next thing I remember I was in the hospital.' She lowered her head and reached for a Kleenex to dab her open eye.

'As you came out of the store did you see anything unusual?

'No, nothing strange, but we were talking and not really paying attention.'

'Have you ever seen Brock around the bike?'

133

'No, but the bike had never done that before. Something was different. And, we had caught Brock following us on a couple of prior occasions.'

'Did you see him following you before you stopped for groceries?'

'No, at least I hadn't and Janet would have said something if she had.'

'What kind of bike was it?'

'A new Harley. Only two months old. Never had a problem.' Kim answered in a fading voice, her weariness evident.

'That's enough for now. After the doctor patches you up, I would like to talk again. Get some rest and thanks for taking the time to meet with me. I'll be in touch soon and if you think of anything else, please give me a call, night or day.'

He left his name and telephone number on the table and walked to the door. Kim followed closely. Connors heard the firm click of a deadbolt.

Connors found Mike's Motorcycle Shop listed in the yellow pages. If he were to make any sense from the details of the accident, he would need to talk with someone who knew bikes, especially Harleys. He parked in front of the shop, entered a small office, and waited behind a dirty, paper-strewn counter. Several minutes elapsed before a burly, bearded man came in from the shop, wiping greasy hands on his pants.

'Need some help young man?' he asked in a squeaky voice, the antithesis of his stature. Looking past Connors toward the street he asked, 'Watcha ridin'?'

Connors laughed, 'Actually a Ford Mustang, but I came in for some information. A friend of mine was killed when she kick-started her bike. For some reason it roared ahead; and before she could stop, the bike crashed into a wall. I was hoping you could tell me how that could happen.'

'God damn that's a hard way to ride. What kinda bike? Bet it was a Harley.'

'How did you know that?' Connors asked, surprised.

'A Harley and an old one at that. Harley's had that trouble because they had no throttle spring. Government last year made 'em add one. Before '75 if you left the throttle on, 'stead of turnin' it to off when you killed the engine, bike might jump on ya.'

'No, this bike was only two months old.'

'Hmmm,' the mechanic scratched his beard. 'Would'a had a throttle spring. Shouldn't been a problem. You say the friend was a woman. If somethin' went wrong with the spring . . . you say she kick started her?'

'Yeah, that's what the passenger said.'

'A woman would'a had a tough time ropin' in a Harley if the throttle was stuck open.'

'Once I locate the bike, would you be willing to take a look at it?' Connors asked, convinced he'd uncovered a key piece of information.

'Sure . . . I could check to see if the throttle was working okay. Just gimme a call and let me know where I can find it.'

Connors immediately called the Sacramento Police Department and asked to speak to the officer investigating the fatal motorcycle accident. After several transfers he was given the name of Officer M. R. Melton. The report, he was told, would not be available until Monday. However, he could talk to Melton if he called at 4:00 p.m. during shift change.

At exactly 3:58 p.m. Connors called and after waiting on hold, officer Melton came on the line, 'Melton here.' His voice sounded flat.

'Officer, thanks for taking my call. My name is Scott Connors. I'm calling about the woman killed yesterday on the Harley at the Safeway on Folsom. I understand you were the investigating officer. I wonder if I could meet with you to discuss the accident.'

'Not much to discuss. Couple of broads on a bike, met a hard fate, that's all. The Brock woman was just learning to drive and made one helluva mistake. She hit the wall like a torpedo. Accident report will be ready in a few days.'

'I need information now. This woman, the deceased, was only recently separated from her husband, and he was taking the separation hard. The husband has a history of violence. It's my understanding the throttle can be manually jammed or the throttle spring removed on a Harley, so when the bike is kick started it takes off like a rocket.'

'Well, it certainly did that. Look, we check out the mechanics in every fatal accident, but let me tell you this bike is a mess. No way to check the throttle now, too much damage. It's a wonder the other broad isn't dead as well. You saying the guy killed his wife? That's a stretch.'

'So, you don't think her husband could've been involved. Does this mean your report will just write it off as driver error?' Connors asked.

'Nothin' else to say. Hey the bike, what's left of it, is impounded over in our corps yard, 12th and D.'

'Okay if I go take a look at it?'

'Sure. It'll be easy to find, only bike there that could fit into a bushel basket,' he chuckled.

The corporation yard encompassed several acres, including a storage site for wrecked vehicles. An eight-foot cyclone fence surrounded the yard. When Connors arrived, he could see mechanics working in three long sheds, doors open to the front. No one acknowledged his entry to the property. 'I'm looking for a wrecked Harley,' he called out.

'Motorcycles 'round behind the shop. You lookin' for the one came in yesterday?' A young man said, pulling out from under a car's hood.

'Yeah, actually I am.'

'She's a doozy. Not much left of that one. Looked at it myself this morning. Shame to do that to a brand new bike. You from the insurance company?'

'Yeah,' Connors appreciated the convenience of an easy fib. He walked to the back area where he found several damaged bikes leaning against the fence, each wearing a red ID tag. Spotting the Harley was easy.

The entire front end was crushed into a mass of chrome, metal and fiberglass. Because the bike parts were tangled so dramatically, it was several moments before Connors realized both handlebars were missing. Every part of the bike was covered in dirt,

137

grease and dried blood except the stumps of the handlebars. Both featured square, clean cuts.

Despite a thorough search, he could find no evidence of either handlebar. Connors stood, briefly, stunned in disbelief. 'Damn, look at this . . . someone has cut the handlebars off, right at the base,' he muttered out loud, running his index finger over the smooth cuts.

Quickly, he returned to the shop. 'Excuse me, but what kind of security does this area have at night?'

The mechanic looked at Connors quizzically, 'We throw a padlock on the main gate, mostly to keep the winos out, and anything of value is put in the sheds. The only thing left out are the wrecks. Why do you ask?'

Connors stood for a moment, shook his head and replied, 'No reason.' However, in his mind, the impact of his discovery was growing in significance by the minute. He needed to call Allen.

'Sorry, Detective Allen is in the field and unavailable, may I take a message,' the dispatcher droned. It was the third time Connors had tried to reach her and he was beginning to fret.

At 7:15 p.m. the phone rang. It was Allen, 'Hi . . . got a message you called.'

'Actually, I called three times. You must've had a busy day,' Connors responded.

'Yeah, Weaver had us working on neighborhood checks. How 'bout you? What's happening?'

'Quite a bit. Is this a good time for you to talk?'

'It is. I'm home now, holding a hot cup of tea, ready for a meaningful phone conversation,' her voice grew lighter, even playful.

Connors' intensity contrasted with her tone. 'I talked with Kim. She's pretty banged up and told me she thinks Brock tried to kill them. The motorcycle was new and apparently the throttle stuck. Very unusual.'

'I found out the name of the investigating officer at city PD, his name is Melton, you might call him tomorrow and see what he says.' Allen interjected.

'I'm way ahead of you. Already called him. But, he's not going to be any help; he's writing it off as driver error. I saw the bike and both handlebars are missing. They were cut off and the cuts are fresh. This means there's no way we can check for a faulty throttle.'

'Let me guess, the bikes in the corporation yard and was left there without security?'

Connors detected frustration in her voice. 'Right, but think about it. Who else would climb into the yard and cut two handlebars off a wrecked motorcycle?'

'True, only Brock has a motive, but remember there is such a thing as chain of evidence. Without security, if we try to connect Brock with the missing handlebars, we're left with a gaping hole any defense lawyer could walk through. It would never stand up in court or even serve as a basis for a warrant. I'll agree more should be done, and I'll call one of my friends at city PD to see if they will take another look at the bike. But, I wouldn't hold out much hope.'

'We may not be able to link Brock to the accident, but I'm willing to bet there will be a change in the rapes. A major change.'

'What kind of change?' Allen asked.

'Either the rapes will stop completely, at least for a time, or they will become more violent. It's only logical if Brock is the rapist. And, if I'm right, and there is an increase in the level of violence, wouldn't you have to concede Brock has to be the EAR?'

'I'm not totally there yet. The blood type problem confuses the issue, but I am getting closer every day. Let's hope you're wrong about the violence level increasing. The rapes are bad enough now.' Allen paused, her tone serious. The two communicated in silence for several moments, a silence of collective thinking.

It was Connors who spoke first, half statement, half thought, '*Res ipsa loquitar.*'

'Scott Connors!' Allen sounded amazed, 'You speak Latin. And maybe you're right: *the thing does speak for itself.*' Continuing she asked, 'Where'd you learn Latin?'

'Four miserable years in a military boarding school. What about you?' His interest suddenly diverted from a serial rapist to Allen's academic history.

'I can top that. Try twelve years with Catholic nuns.' Suddenly, the mood was personal. Allen continued, 'I want to thank you for dinner last night. Very pleasant, a calm before the storm.'

'Nice way of putting it.'

'You know Scott, I've been thinking and I have an idea which might help. What if I give you a call around

140

seven tomorrow night and I'll buy the dinner? We can meet at the Hudson House. I want to talk to you about my idea.'

Connors quickly agreed. The invitation from Allen seemed friendly and it pleased his weary spirit. A phone conversation with Susan, he concluded, was a nice way to end the day.

21

Here's where I'll leave my real mark,' he sneered, glancing around the room to survey the carnage.

'Fuckin, bitch, shoulda been alone,' he reflected back to the events of the past few minutes.

This mission had been planned carefully, very carefully. She was a banker, jogger, Sunday school teacher and on his list for a long time. He had often stopped and listened while she read to her class.

Tonight his image of her was shattered. 'What a hypocrite, teaching Sunday school and she takes a man into her bed'. Finding the man shocked him, and then when he tied the man's hands, the idiot had foolishly tried to fight.

He cursed himself for firing three shots, and now the man lay dead, his blood spilling out in a gathering pool. Three shots probably awakened neighbors. 'My own fault, it's been too long since combat. Next time I'll use a knife,' he muttered behind the mask.

Her name was Kathy and she lay frozen on the bed, gripping the sheet as if it were a shield. He grabbed the cover, ripping it from her hands, revealing the full length of her naked body. 'Turn over bitch,' he snarled, now making no attempt to disguise his voice.

She did not move.

'Turn over,' he barked again, roughly yanking her right arm, and in one motion, flipping her onto her stomach. Laying the flashlight down, he jerked her left arm behind her back and carefully knotted her hands together. His mind was torn between this mission and the need to flee. 'Dammit, three shots are too many', he thought. 'What a waste and all because this prick had to play hero. Well, he's no hero now, just a fuckin' dead man.' Angrily, he rolled her back over.

She stared at him, her eyes filled with shock and fear. *'God what a screw up,'* he mumbled to himself, 'All this planning for nothing.

Still holding the revolver in his right hand, he rolled her off the end of the bed; she fell clumsily, landing on her face, right leg draping over the dead body of her lover. Stepping carefully to avoid blood, he moved to stand over her.

Bending slightly, he shifted the revolver from his right hand to his left, placed the barrel against the back of her head and pulled the trigger. Her head bounced from the shock and then she shuddered and lay still. Still careful to avoid the new trickling blood, he stepped back to evaluate the scene. There was no time to recover bullets.

With that thought, he picked up his backpack, shoved the knife, gun and flashlight inside, and moved toward the slider, stepping into the night. His thoughts turned to the unused vial of blood, 'No sense wasting it, maybe two, three days at the most.' Instantly, his mind anticipated a new reality: 'What the hell, from now on I might as well kill them all.'

Weaver sat at his desk, his head pounding. Massaging both temples brought some relief; the detective had already thrown down four aspirin and was considering more when he thought of his sister. She had called yesterday to wish him happy birthday, and they talked about his headaches. 'Bud, you've got to get yourself to a doctor and get something done about your blood pressure,' she admonished. 'You need to take care of your health.'

'Still the big sister', Weaver thought. 'Unless you know a doctor who can catch this rapist, ain't nothin' can be done about my head,' he told her.

This morning, a new case file lay unopened in front of him. He loathed the thought of reading it as he knew it contained details of the dreaded crime he'd been expecting for weeks: Homicide. A double murder committed by the EAR.

Something that had seemed so simple in the beginning was now out of control. 'It should never have reached this point . . . what was the old man thinking,' Weaver thought. Muttering to himself, 'Sure as hell will make my life easier when this mess is all over.'

Slowly, he opened the file folder. 'No choice. Got to read this,' he continued to mumble. He skipped over the face sheet, aware of the basics after a telephone call from the crime scene. Flipping directly to the preliminary lab report, he forced himself to focus.

As Weaver read, he made notes on a yellow legal pad concerning the double homicide committed March 17, 1976, between the hours of 0300 and 0330.

- *11743 Hollister Ave., Rancho Cordova: owner –Kathy Reimer, WF-29, Banker*
- *2nd victim – Jay Westly,WM-37, medical doctor*
- *entry – rear slider   exit – bedroom slider*
- *Westly shot three times at close range*
- *Reimer – executed by single shot to back of head – shooter left handed*

144

- *Bullets – Super Vel: .357 Magnum, 110 grain soft point*
- *Bullets fired from: Smith & Wesson, any model – or a Ruger*
- *No cartridge cases – eliminates automatic – must be a revolver*
- *Twine samples at the scene – all 3 strand nylon cord – 1/16 inch diam.*
- *IDENTICAL TO NYLON CORD FOUND AT OTHER EAR CRIME SCENES – also new shoestrings – 2 pair – same brand as EAR has used prior*
- *Victim – female type O blood, male type B blood No foreign blood found.*

As he finished, Weaver leaned back in his chair. 'Damn', he thought, 'It looks as if there finally was a guy with the guts to fight this bastard and what does he get but dead.'

He continued to read until he felt a tightness creeping into his chest. Weaver stood and shook both arms trying to will the feeling away. 'Fuckin' angina,' he muttered. When the tightness persisted, he decided to take a walk. Three times around the parking lot and back to the break room seemed to release most of the tension. The detective brought another cup of coffee back to his desk.

Allen's arrival startled him. 'Find anything?' she asked.

'Yeah, take a look,' he answered, shoving the note pad across the desk. 'Everything matches with our rapist. Nylon cord checked out to be the same, new shoe strings, location, entry, description of female victim, everything the same. He's left-handed, but we already figured that. No strange blood this time and

145

no mention of semen. Also, no indication of genital trauma. The bastard left in a hurry after firing four times. Smart, 'cause neighbors heard the shots. This is one crafty son-of-a-bitch.'

Allen nodded, thinking back to Connors' prediction just two days ago. A silence followed as the two detectives considered the impact of the homicides. She studied her boss' face, noting the dark skin under his eyes, which spoke volumes about the stress of the past several months. She felt a sense of pity, 'Bud, you look terrible. You need some time off. Get some rest. I can handle the neighborhood check. Go home and get some sleep.'

'No way. Don't you start in on me; my sister's on my ass all the time. I don't need two women giving me hell.'

'Not too defensive,' Allen tried to infuse her statement with humor, 'How long has it been since you've had a physical?'

'Three . . . maybe four years, but I'm okay. Damn doctors are all the same. Pills. Pills. Pills. The bastards probably own the damn drug store.'

'So, are you taking the pills?'

'Hell no. I don't need pills. My blood pressure would be okay if we'd get a break and catch this fuckin' rapist or if Phillips would quit callin' press conferences.'

'Alright, but why don't you stay in the station today and leave early? Get a good night's sleep and, Bud . . . ,' she hesitated, 'lay off the booze. I'm worried about you.'

Weaver nodded without looking up. He wasn't used to anyone worrying about him, but he sensed

Allen was sincere. 'She'll make someone a good wife someday', he thought. He rustled through his desk drawer, found the flask and threw it in his briefcase. 'Here, you drive,' he directed, tossing Allen the keys, 'Probably be best. I'm coming with you.'

She shrugged and headed for the parking lot. 'Let's go recheck with the neighbors. Maybe somebody saw or heard something. And I've got a line on a couple of delivery people who may have been in the area early morning.'

22

He woke up covered in sweat. The dreams had been so vivid he had saturated his sheets. He forced his sleep-deprived brain to order his feet to the floor and sat up on the edge of the bed. Reaching to his left, he turned off the alarm. 'No need for that,' he muttered, 'when the Lord calls, he doesn't use an alarm.' A distant train sounded its horn. He knew the crossing at 19th and W. He'd heard it before - many times.

The clock read 3:00 a.m. Standing, rubbing his eyes and stretching, he threw the quilt to the floor and pulled off the sheets. He wadded them up and proceeded toward his laundry room. Dirty sheets were something he could not tolerate.

He reached for a shirt, but then thought against it. 'Best to submit myself unto my Lord naked,' he admonished himself.

He lifted his old black Bible from a dresser drawer, the one his grandfather had used as a circuit preacher, and headed back to his bedroom and the closet. His neatly lined shoes had to be moved. But, he didn't mind. This drill was routine for him. An empty closet floor allowed him to prostrate himself.

Each time, when called in the middle of the night like this, he felt the cleansing begin almost immediately. It filled him from his solar plexus to his heart to his head and, finally, to his tongue. The process began quickly and would continue until he felt the release.

And, always there was a release, a coveted, cleansed feeling. 'Though his sins were as scarlet, they would be made white as snow, thus saith the Lord,' he mumbled over and over.

'When thou prayest, enter into thy closet.' And, so he did, turning off the light, pursuing his God with passion. At first the words came slowly, buried in the tears and sobs of a man-child aching from a deep, distant, dark time. Then, the tone and cadence began to lift:

'Aya mi resto win selahe wenday . . .
Win selahe wenday . . . wenday . . . wenday
Mi corrindo . . . win selahe . . . aya . . . aya . . . aya'

He spoke in a tongue unknown to him. And he spoke alone without translation.

He did not care. The compulsion to pray in this strange language was deep. Something inside drove him long into the early morning. At times he would stop, grab a flashlight, frustrated by the interruption and begin frantically paging through his Bible. The Old Testament lured him like a moth to a candle. Especially the verses of vengeance.

'Vengeance is mine, thus saith the Lord.' He agreed and begged. 'I am wretched . . . a worm . . . oh God, help me.' Crouched alone in the closet, the man-child cried and beseeched his unseen God. The relentless cries led him back:

'Aya mi resto win selahe wenday . . .
Win selahe wenday . . . .wenday . . . wenday
Mi corrindo . . . win selahe . . . . aya . . . aya . . . aya'

And so it continued. He recalled a verse he craved in John: 'I will not leave you comfortless'. He begged for comfort. He begged and he cried and he

149

begged. Then the chill he felt began to annoy him. He reached for a shirt, and quickly thought against it. Malachi 3:3: 'He shall purify the sons of Levi.' He wanted so desperately to know the purity, to be purified. He believed passionately that his willingness to be alone, naked, cold and prostrate could speed the purification. Such discipline he craved.

Slowly, the release came. He knew he was cleansed. Sleep or no sleep, he felt whole again.

23

Charlene Mathews' telephone call surprised Connors. He'd tried for days to reach her and had given up. However, she sounded friendly, explaining that she'd been away on a family matter and upon returning had been faced with a desk full of requests. But, yes, she would be more than happy to see him. 'This morning would be fine.'

Less than an hour later, he walked into the River City Women's Center with an open mind, eager for information.

Mathews was one of those people who engendered herself to others. She was warm and friendly, a large woman who seemed always to be smiling. 'The work I do,' she told Connors, 'you have to keep smiling to stay sane.'

The two sat in her office, a comfortable, musty smelling suite in an old medical office building. 'We're funded by grants from both the feds and state in addition to support from local businesses and charities. But every year we struggle to stay open and provide all the needed services,' she sighed.

'So, this is more than a rape crisis clinic?' Connors asked.

'Absolutely. We're a full service agency. Actually, spousal abuse victims take a lot of our time, but we also deal with pregnant minors, women's health issues, runaway teenage girls, incest, birth control, and a variety of other services important to women. And, of course, we provide counseling for women who are victims of rape. You name it, we handle it.'

This was Connors' entry point. 'As I explained, I am researching sexual deviancy and hoping to gain insight from your experiences, as well as get your views on incest and teenage pregnancy. However, right now I am focusing on forcible rape, more specifically stranger rape.'

'You mean, even more specifically, the Sacramento rapist?'

'Exactly.'

'Well, I'm probably the wrong person to talk to about why men rape. I see the victims and it's hard for me to be objective about rapists. Also, I see the problem in the broader sense of how we, as a society, raise our boys,' Mathews said, for the first time sitting forward in her chair, her face void of warmth. 'Violence and masculinity seem to go hand in hand in this country.'

'You see rape as a reflection of our society's culture of violence?' Connors asked.

'That's right. Rape is more about control and anger toward women than it is about sex. It's about violence. Boys are raised to be tough, show little emotion, and not talk about feelings. Their games are about winning, competition, putting others down. The national sport has become football, a violent, savage game.'

She sat back, her voice rising with each word, 'Then we have sex, a basic instinctual need and drive, mix it with how boys are conditioned and the result often is domestic violence against women and, in too many cases, rape and murder.'

'Tell me about the impact of rape on women,' Connors asked, realizing he needed to bring her back
152

to the subject of stranger rape.

Mathews paused, 'It varies, but many rape victims have recurring nightmares that can occur anytime, night or day. They often suffer physically with chills, heart palpitations and even panic attacks. They typically develop low self-esteem, feel emotionally detached, and withdraw from friends and family. It's not uncommon for them to have serious depression. Most of the women I've counseled develop eating disorders, headaches and sleep problems.

'So the damage touches every part of their lives.'

Mathews nodded, 'And other family members as well, especially husbands. Every part and usually forever.'

Connors nodded.

'It's very difficult for women to deal effectively with the post trauma associated with violent rape. The symptoms usually appear within several weeks, but some victims have delayed symptoms, months, or even years later.'

'Can you tell me if you've counseled any of the EAR victims?' Connors asked.

Mathews hesitated, as if studying Connors to assess his intent and sincerity. 'Actually I have. One of the first was last year; several more in recent months. It's important to start therapy as soon as possible, and that has been difficult if the woman has been injured. We often must coordinate with the hospital and, unfortunately, some women refuse to talk about the attack, even to a counselor.'

'What happens in those cases?'

'They try to tough it out, sometimes with tragic results. One victim, Beth Heatherton, committed

153

suicide just two weeks after being attacked. We had tried repeatedly to get her into counseling, but she refused. Just withdrew. Quit her job, wouldn't leave her house. Nothing we, friends or family could do. Finally she overdosed and died.'

'That's horrible, Connors shook his head in disgust. 'Can you share anything you learned in the counseling that might be helpful in an investigation?'

'My impression is that this particular rapist is very complex. Now it is true many rapists have serious sex problems, but the control and anger this man expresses exceeds anything I've ever encountered.' Mathews leaned back in her chair, 'I'm not a police officer or a psychiatrist, but I think there must be some significance in why he only chooses victims in one area of the city and often with a man present. You would think that would make him easier to catch.'

'Why do you think he stays in just one area?' Connors asked.

'My guess is it is not just women he hates. First, what other rapist has deliberately chosen victims where he knows men will be present? Second, he stays in one area because he wants to humiliate the police, demonstrating his power to the whole city. He shows his control. It's as if he uses women as a means of attacking society. This means he must have reasons for not only hating women, but hating society as well. Let me tell you . . . this man is terrifying.'

The words of Charlene Mathews lingered, their after-taste a reminder of the increasingly appalling crimes. The suicide of one victim stirred up the

154

memories of his own family, also haunted by a violent death.

He remembered the difficult struggles of his sister because of the death of her daughter, his beloved niece: Annie. How his sister's once happy marriage had ended in a bitter divorce. There was also the anguish the crime caused his parents and the resulting damage to his nephews and the angst he himself endured because of Annie's kidnap, rape and death. His continual guilt left him with the ever-present question: 'Could I have saved her?'

24

Connors rose as soon as Susan entered the small dining room of The Hudson House. He adjusted her chair and she sat down across from him.

She spoke first, 'Sorry to cancel dinner last night. We worked on those homicides until well after midnight. And you certainly were right about the rapist becoming more violent. The man fought and the rapist killed. Executing the woman makes no sense. Unbelievable.'

Sweeping the peanut shells onto a wood floor already thick with broken shells, Scott responded, 'This is one time I feel terrible about being right.'

They sat in brief silence as the bus boy poured fresh water and brought two menus. 'I like your choice for dinner,' Scott offered, hoping to lighten the mood.

Allen smiled, 'Yeah, this is a favorite of mine, and probably the place I frequent the most. But what are your thoughts on the killings?'

'Anyone with a brain should be able to see that the rapist is coming apart. Did Weaver show any interest in taking another look at Brock?'

'I brought it up, but he was dismissive. Said the shooter was left-handed and Brock is right-handed, instant elimination.'

'Is that how he does all his investigations, focusing on elimination?'

'Seems to be a pattern in this case, but he has a reputation as an excellent investigator, so I'm truly at a loss.'

'But you do agree, Brock must be the rapist and now the killer?'

'Let's just say I believe the odds of him being the rapist have increased dramatically. And, I'm definitely not swayed by the left-handed versus right-handed theory. Scott, you're right, everything seems to point to Brock, but the blood, I can't figure out the foreign blood.'

'I know. So many blood types. It's a real puzzle, but there must be an answer. You're sure the lab isn't making mistakes?'

'Blood typing is pretty basic. Three times I've sent samples to the state lab and received identical results.'

'You said something the last time we were together about having a suggestion for me?'

Before Allen could answer a large pizza arrived. Taking two slices and placing them on her plate, she answered, 'You're going to need some help. If you're right and Brock killed his wife and now these two people, investigating him is not a one-man job.'

'I would agree. What do you suggest? With no money to pay anyone, and your department not willing, I'm a little short on options.'

'You better take some of this pizza, I can't eat the whole thing,' Allen directed, placing a slice on Connors' plate, aware he hadn't shown any interest in eating. 'Actually, I have someone in mind, despite some reservations. Money shouldn't be a problem. Remember the reward is up to fifty thousand.'

'First the reservations and then the name,' Connors insisted, taking a sip of his beer.

'The person I have in mind was fired by our department seven or eight years ago. To put it politely, he's a little rough around the edges. He was a ten-year veteran, with a great arrest record. Unfortunately, he logged more personnel complaints than the entire detective division. They kept him on because of his ability to make major arrests until he finally crossed the line.'

'What line was that?' Connors asked.

'Supposedly, he pistol whipped a guy he thought was a doper. I guess he thought he had someone who knew a major dealer and really worked him over before the poor guy could prove his identity.'

'And the department couldn't cover for him?'

'No, this doper turned out to be the son of a local County Sheriff working undercover. The injuries put him on permanent medical disability. Best Sheriff Brandt could do was avoid having Graham prosecuted.'

'What does he do now?'

'He works as a private investigator in San Francisco and still has a reputation for violence. His customers, attorneys of questionable ethics, love him because he gets results. My hesitation about him is not just the violence, but that he often operates outside the law.'

Connors frowned, feigning confusion, 'So, you're wondering about using this PI to help stop a violent rapist turned killer, knowing he could be a big help, while at the same time considering not using him because he's a little heavy handed. What's wrong with this picture?'

Allen grinned sheepishly, 'I see your point. I'm not making sense. His name is Frank Graham and he's good at what he does. Could be the best on the West Coast. And I hear he pulls in five, six times what he made with our department. He'd like the reward money.'

'I'm not doing this for the reward. He can have that. How soon can you set up a meeting with him?' Connors asked.

'I'll call him tonight. Are you sure you want to go in that direction?'

'Look, you're right, we need someone. I'll admit I need help. Brock is good and very tough. I think it's obvious your department can't catch him. Sorry if I offend, but he has to be stopped.'

'Okay. I agree.' Allen continued, 'There's still another meeting we need. Can you arrange something with Kim Henderson? I know she's in bad shape, but I need to hear in detail what Janet told her about their married life and how often Brock was gone at three a.m.'

'Sure, should be no problem. When I get it scheduled, you want me to pick you up at your place?'

'No, with this homicide investigation, my days are impossible to predict. Call me at the office and just leave an address. Try to set it up for the evening. And don't leave your name.'

'Can I take this as a full commitment on your part? Now you're willing to help me in an active way?'

'With limitations. I believe were on the right track, but understand I can't give you any inside information about the investigation,' Allen said.

'I understand. We can keep this above board,' he

159

smiled reassuringly. 'Don't forget my intern work at DOJ gives me access to information. Let's put this aside for now, change the theme and take a walk. We need some night air.'

'I'd like that,' Susan responded.

'We've spent so much time talking about Brock and Weaver and now the murders. What I would really like to know about is Susan Allen. Who is she? What does she enjoy besides police work?'

Susan laughed. 'I'm afraid there's not much to know.'

They left the restaurant and walked into the cool evening. As Allen started to put on her coat, Connors took it from her, stepped behind her and held the jacket wide for her arms. 'Such a gentleman. Very refreshing,' Susan commented, turning to face him.

Scott took her hand as they walked toward the river. 'How did you wind up as a policewoman?' The soft glow of streetlights reflected off the slow moving river. A horse drawn carriage clip-clopped nearby.

'My dad was a police officer in Los Angeles. I was nine when he was killed.' Allen surprised herself with such immediate openness on a topic she rarely discussed.

'I'm sorry . . . was it while he was on duty?' Connors sensed the delicate nature of his inquiry.

'Yes. A high-speed chase. Another officer lost control of his car and hit my dad's car. Dad was killed instantly. Both my brother and I grew up worshipping his memory. There were pictures of him all over the house. My brother is a California Highway Patrol officer and . . .'

'You are a deputy sheriff,' Connors finished her sentence.

'I guess I really never considered anything else.'

'Isn't it hard being a woman working in a traditionally male field?'

'At first it was. I had to learn how to put up with a lot of crap. And, of course, it ruined my marriage.'

'Why do you say 'of course' so matter-of-factly?'

'Working shifts, especially graveyard, the long hours and all the stress. The job comes home with you, not the best recipe for romance. A high percentage of the deputies in our department have been divorced, so I'm in the majority. Not much comfort.' she laughed, a nervous laugh, intended to mask her pain.

'What kind of work did your husband do?'

'Attorney, a tax attorney. He hated the thought of me being with other men all the time, one of those traditional guy types.'

'I haven't heard you mention children.'

'Fortunately, I don't have any. Divorce is so hard on kids. We were only married a year and a half.'

'And, you still like this work, knowing it ruined your marriage?'

'Actually, I appreciate it now more than ever, especially since there is so much testosterone in the field. Society needs some female energy, especially from police officers,' Allen spoke with conviction. She turned to assess Scott's reaction.

'You make a valid point,' he responded, placing his hand on the small of her back to direct her across the street toward her parked car. They said good night just as a light rain began to fall.

###

The young professor was at his best the next morning in class. Despite the stress of the rape investigation, thoughts of Susan put him in extremely good humor. She was, perhaps, the most stimulating woman he'd ever met. And, she hadn't hesitated when he took her hand. Her ready laugh and easy conversation brought him a level of comfort he needed.

He would have remained in this semi-state of reverie, routinely going about his lecture, had it not been for an intense debate breaking out in the classroom. He had posed the question: *'Given that every man has a mother, why do men abuse women?'*

He was surprised when Tyrus Brock responded immediately. That Brock would speak up so directly in class was unusual and offering commentary about women even more surprising. 'It sounds to me like your assumption is that every woman is warm and loving to their children. While it's true women give birth, how about the women who have no business being mothers? Mothers who actually destroy their children.'

Brock's remarks gave the class a momentary pause, but remained unanswered as the discussion returned to point, the question of why men abuse. The atmosphere in the class crackled with intensity during a mostly male-dominated discussion. Connors found it odd that Brock never offered a single counterpoint. Rather, he sat with a wry smile, seemingly enjoying the fray.

Soon the class hour ended and Connors walked out of the building, far away from students and into the warm, afternoon sunshine. He was anxious to be on time for an appointment at the Women's Crisis Center. The director had called earlier in the day with a provocative offer, 'I have something you may be able to use in your investigation.'

Charlene Mathews was eager to begin. Connors had no more than entered her office and settled into a chair when she asked, 'What's this I hear about Sheriff Brandt not liking you and being upset with you.'

Connors was shocked. 'Where did you hear that? I've never met the man.'

'Oh, I have my sources. I understand he's even talked to the DA about having you arrested for interfering in the EAR investigation.'

'Seriously?' Connors questioned, 'This is news to me. I can assure you I have not interfered with the investigation. I even met with the lead detective on the case, Weaver is his name. True, we did exchange words, but since I provided him with information about the case, information I have uncovered, there is no interference. I have uncovered a suspect and all I was trying to do was encourage Weaver to investigate him.'

Mathews seemed satisfied and continued with a more reassuring tone, 'Blomberg swears by you and since I don't think much of Brandt myself, I'll work with you. But, please keep my name out of any discussions with the Sheriff's Department. My position is very, very political and I can't afford to have the Sheriff upset with me. It could cost me a lot in terms of financial help from local business leaders.'

163

'No problem. I can understand your position,' Connors reassured. 'Was there another reason you wanted to talk to me?'

'Yes. After meeting with you, I reviewed my notes on the rape victims I've counseled and one thing jumps out at me. Several of the women said the rapist whimpers after he climaxes. He changes from a snarling, threatening attacker to a whimpering intruder. Many of the women said this unexpected whimpering would sometimes turn into open crying. And, it left them more confused than ever. How could such a savage attacker cry in their presence?'

'You have this from more than one victim?'

'Yes. Many of the victims report some version of the whimpering. I'm used to hearing about strange sexual behavior on the part of rapists, but this is a first.'

'What do you think this tells us?'

'It tells me that he is one very disturbed individual. This double homicide didn't surprise me one bit. I just pray he will be arrested soon.'

Connors left Mathews' office with two questions: 'Why would a rapist cry and, more importantly, how many more victims would have to endure this sick behavior before the terror campaign ceased?

25

Kim Henderson led Allen and Connors into her living room. An uncomfortable silence loomed until Susan introduced herself and explained they needed more background information on Brock. 'Can you tell us why you left the hospital without checking out?'

'I was scared, really scared,' the bruised woman replied.

'Scared of what?'

'Of Tyrus . . . the monster!' Kim sparked quickly. 'I knew the minute I gained consciousness after the crash that he'd done something to the bike.'

'What do you think he did?' Allen asked.

'I don't know, but it had to have been him. The bike was brand new; we'd never had any problems with it.'

Before Allen could continue to question, Connors interjected, 'But, how do you know . . . and forgive me for asking . . . that it wasn't driver error?'

'Two reasons and they both point to Tyrus. Janet had started the bike many times. He razzed her about learning to ride. He called her a dyke. He was like that . . . biting and sarcastic.'

'Is there anything else that made you think Brock wanted to kill Janet?' Allen continued. Although direct, she had a presence that seemed to make Kim feel at ease. The detective could tell that, while Kim was sharing sensitive, personal details, the information was flowing freely. Kim trusted her. This was exactly as Connors had hoped and he decided to take a back seat and let the women talk.

'Well . . . he has always resented me. Janet and I lived together before she married Brock, and he knew we were still intimate. Even after they were married, Janet would spend a lot of time in my apartment. He was furious when she moved back in with me. He had been by my place several times trying to talk Janet into coming back to him,' she paused. 'Tyrus has this odd way sometimes. Janet called it a cold anger.'

'Cold anger?' Allen asked.

'Yeah . . . it's a strange, chilling way of showing anger. Most guys start yelling and swearing. Not Tyrus. He would get really quiet and almost spit words out in a low voice. It's hard to describe, but you would find it strange if you were to experience it. You could feel the anger, despite his calm exterior.'

'How did Janet respond when he became angry?'

'She'd ask him to leave.'

'Would he?'

'Yeah, except the last time. I think it was last Thursday. He wouldn't leave, so she said she would call his parole officer.

'Did he leave after that threat?' the detective asked.

'Yes, but not right away. He sat for a moment staring at her, us, with an icy look. When he left he made a point of closing the door really slowly.'

'Did she actually call the parole officer?'

'No.'

'Going back to when Janet was still living with Brock, you mentioned Janet would sometimes spend the night with you in your apartment. Exactly what days of the week would that happen? Can you recall?' Allen asked, jotting notes in a small spiral notebook.

166

'Sure, it was normally after softball practice. We practiced every Tuesday and Thursday evenings. On those nights she would stay until at least midnight. And often would spend the night.'

'Did she say how Brock would react when she got home either real late or the next morning?'

'She said when she left real late it was no problem because he usually wasn't home anyway. He never seemed to mind that Janet and I were still lovers, but he was really mad about her actually moving out and ending the marriage. It was hard to tell they had a marriage. What he seemed to want was the husband-wife façade.'

'Did Janet tell you why she was leaving Brock?' Allen pressed further.

'She'd been thinking about it for some time. Initially, she really wanted the marriage to work, but it was a mistake from the beginning. Tyrus was gone a lot at night, said he was playing pool, but bars close at two a.m. He often didn't get home until five or six in the morning.'

'Did she talk about their sex life?'

'Sure, we were a committed couple until Janet got the idea she wanted to have kids.'

'I hate to ask such personal questions,' Allen said, aware of Kim's pain. 'But we think there's a possibility Brock may be the East Area Rapist, and it would be helpful if we knew how he related sexually with Janet.'

For a moment Kim sat silent, studying her guests, 'Actually, Janet and I both thought he might be, but she said he couldn't perform. He had little interest in sex. At first she really tried, but he kept

167

avoiding her and when he did try he couldn't . . . you know . . . get hard. The few times they did have sex, after he climaxed he would curl up in a fetal position and whimper. We figured he was just too odd. We didn't think he would make much of a rapist.'

'Actually many rapists are sexually impotent. But, this sounds bizarre. Rape is more about rage against women than sex. Did she describe this whimpering that he did?' Allen queried.

"It was almost like he was crying," Kim said.

'Cry?' Connors surprised both women with his abrupt re-entry into their conversation. 'Did you say he would cry after intercourse?'

'Well . . . well yes,' Kim said, 'Janet said it happened several times.'

Allen studied Connors with a perplexed look.

'I'll explain later. Go on with the questions,' he said.

Allen turned back to Kim, 'Did she elaborate on what she meant by crying?'

'She said it was really weird. I think she said it was kind of a combination of whimpering and crying, almost like a child.'

'God, that's bizarre,' Allen couldn't help her reaction, 'Anything else odd?'

'Actually, there is. I heard him talk about the rapes from the articles in the papers, usually joking about how stupid the cops are. Janet said he even cut news clippings, supposedly for a class he's taking at City College.'

Allen looked up from her note taking to glance at Connors.

168

'One time he showed us how to take off a locked, sliding patio door from the outside.' Kim added.

'You're kidding, what was behind that? Allen asked.'

'He's a know-it-all, always has answers for everything. One day a bunch of us were talking about getting locks for our doors and he said it would do no good. That's when he showed us.'

'Did Brock have a job?'

'No, he just went to school. He did get some money from the GI bill, but he was always bugging Janet for cash. Even after she moved out, she had to give him money.'

'Had to?'

'She was afraid of him and gave him money to pacify him, get him off her back.'

'Did he ever physically abuse her?'

'You mean hit her?' Allen nodded.

'No, but she was always afraid he would.'

'Did she ever say anything about Brock having a gun or knife?'

Kim paused, 'Only once when they were first married. She said they went on a picnic up in the mountains, and he told her he was going to teach her how to shoot a pistol. She was afraid of guns and wouldn't even try. He shot up almost a box of shells. Janet said he was really good. He could hit a tin can almost every time – with either hand.'

'Did he keep the gun at home?' Allen asked.

'She said she never saw it again. When she asked him about it, he told her he had returned it to a friend.'

'Did she tell you the name of the friend?'

169

'I don't think so. If she did, I don't remember.' Kim answered.

'Do you know the names of *any* of his friends?' Allen asked.

'No. In fact I never once saw him with any guys. He was always alone or with Janet. I don't think he had any friends, except maybe at his church.'

'Can you think of anything else about Brock that might connect him to either your motorcycle accident or the rapes?'

'You said something earlier,' she looked at Allen, 'about rapists being angry. Tyrus hates women. He once said his mother was a poor excuse for a woman.'

'Did he stay in touch with his mother?'

'I believe she's dead. Janet wasn't sure.'

'What about his dad?'

'I think he only had a step-dad. Janet said he never talked about family.'

Allen and Connors walked slowly to their cars. 'Boy that was some interview,' Allen said, breaking the silence. 'Why the big reaction when she said Brock cries after sex?'

'I was shocked. Yesterday I interviewed the director of the Women's Crisis Center, Charlene Mathews. She's talked with a number of women who are victims of the EAR. She said some of the women she interviewed reported the rapist cried after the assaults.'

Allen shook her head and said nothing and Connors wondered if she was simply overwhelmed with the details of the case.

'The connections are shocking. Where do we take this from here?' the detective glanced at her watch, "I think I've had enough for one afternoon.'

'Got time for a drink?' Connors asked, eager to change their focus and hoping she, too, had her fill of criminal investigation for one afternoon.

'Thought you would never ask,' Allen smiled the warm smile Connors was growing to love.'

'Let's meet at the Back Door Lounge in Old Sac. I hear my students talking about their Happy Hour,' Connors suggested.

'Great choice,' Allen said as she headed across the street.'

Connors stood for a moment transfixed, watching the tall, graceful figure walk toward her car.

After settling at a table, the two sat in silence for several minutes, sipping beer. Connors wanting to retreat from a hectic day, while Allen's silence was harder to read.

'What are you thinking? Connors asked.'

'I'm still trying to put it together logically. Nothing Kim said eliminated him as a suspect. Much of what she said certainly sounds like he must be the rapist. However, you understand nothing Janet told Kim is evidence that could be used in court. It's all hearsay.'

'I noticed you didn't ask her about Brock's religion?'

'We can get that from the church where he sometimes preaches. I didn't want to push her. She's pretty banged up and still obviously distraught over Janet's death. We can talk to her again in a few days.'

171

'So you don't think I'm crazy thinking Brock is the rapist?'

'No, I don't think you're crazy. Have you contacted Graham yet?'

'Yes. Meeting him tomorrow afternoon at two. On the Wharf in San Francisco.'

'Be careful with him. He can be a loose cannon. As far as I know you can trust him, but try to stress that we want him to stay within the law.'

'It doesn't sound like ethics is his strong suit.'

'True, but do what you can to keep him in line.' Allen urged; then, suddenly, 'I have an appointment to see Sheriff Brandt tomorrow morning. I'm going to discuss Brock with him.'

'Does Weaver know about the meeting?' Connors asked, surprised by Susan's announcement.

'No, it's something I feel I have to do. It's not clear to me why Weaver shows no interest in Brock. I plan to tread lightly, but I need to know if it's Weaver's inflexibility, or if it runs deeper.'

Scott decided to change the subject, 'I should be back from San Francisco by seven at the latest. Can we meet for dinner somewhere and compare notes?'

'I've got a better idea. After I meet with Brandt, I'm taking the rest of the day off, I need a break and I have to get my hair cut. How about I make some spaghetti, toss a salad and we eat dinner at my place?'

It was an invitation that Scott eagerly accepted. 'I am totally in the mood for home cooking.' He smiled and offered a little wink, a gesture Susan had seen only once before and one she liked.

'See you at seven.' Susan confirmed, aware of the comfort level growing between the two of them;

172

and already her mind was piecing together a grocery list for dinner.

26

The pensive detective sat alone in the break room with a cup of black tea when Sergeant Howell of Internal Affairs entered. Howell, a grizzled cop, seven years past retirement age, plopped down on the chair next to Allen. 'Understand you're about to brace the old man about Brock.'

The combination of his position in internal affairs and his mention of Brock abruptly brought Allen out of her daydream. 'How in the world do you know that?' she blurted.

'Been lookin' to catch you alone for some time now. You got a future with the department. Never thought I would say this to a woman, but you got class and how you row your boat is making me change my mind about female cops. But, this is not a smart move.'

'Wait a minute. How do you know I plan on talking to Brandt?'

'Honey, there ain't no secrets around here.'

'I guess not,' she wondered how much irritation her voice displayed. 'What's wrong with my talking to Brandt. He's always bragging to the public about his open-door policy and I have a serious problem on my hands. I would think he would want to hear about something which might blow up and get him hammered by the press.'

'This situation with Brock won't make the papers. Look, I'm only trying to help you. Reminds me of how naïve I was in the beginning. I learned only after it was too late. Hate to see you make the same mistake.'

'What are you talking about? I'm only trying to stop a series of violent crimes. Isn't that my job?' she demanded.

Howell paused, took a sip of his coffee and refusing eye contact said, 'You gotta understand there's lots of things you don't know. I can't deal in specifics. I can only tell you you're way over your head. Brandt has lots on his plate. Elections are coming up in November. Elections are all about emotions. Voters are dammed fickle. Plus county brass has to worry about civil suits. Wrong move might cost the county plenty. You stirring the pot could cause him a lot of trouble . . . .'

'Am I hearing what I think I'm hearing?' Allen interjected, her tone incredulous.

'Calm down, you're a smart dame . . . just trying to give you a word to the wise. You're looking at only this one case. Brandt, he's gotta see the big picture. Me, I broke in under that old stiff-necked Watkins. Made the mistake of getting frustrated about a gambling operation and went to the papers. I'm lucky even to be wearing these stripes. Gave up long time ago thinking I could get past sergeant. Don't see why you should go the same route.'

'I don't like the sound of this. I was hired to be an officer and people expect me to protect them. What am I missing here?'

'You can only help people if you're working. Can't help them much if you're not working or on permanent assignment to warrants.' He paused to read her reaction. 'Now understand, this is a conversation that didn't take place. You go to Brandt and raise hell, you'll get a jacket you can't shake.
175

Brock will be taken care of . . . Brandt's been on that for some time. He'll do it his way. May not be your way.' With that he rose and left.

Allen sat stunned, telling herself she needed to refocus, redirect her thoughts and intentions. 'Who was this wizened old cop who could so brazenly butt into her affairs? Just because he works in internal affairs, that's supposed to scare me? Maybe I should be, but I can't let myself be intimidated.' With that she dismissed his intrusion and within a few minutes she felt ready. She stood, placed her coffee mug in the break room sink, and walked confidently to her appointment with the sheriff.

Sheriff Brandt greeted Allen with a loud, booming voice, 'C'mon in my little gal. Grab a chair. Hear you're doin' good work, even trying to keep old Bud off the booze.' Brandt was a large man, 55 years old, his huge girth camouflaged by his carefully tailored suit. 'Get you anything to drink?'

'No I'm fine,' Allen responded as she settled into a large leather chair directly across the wide desk from Brandt. The chair was so large Allen immediately got the feeling of being very small. She felt like Alice before the Queen. Brandt's office appeared tailor made with a wall of photos showing him hobnobbing with celebrities. Dominating one corner of the room was a large silver-adorned saddle draped over a steel sawhorse. On his credenza sat the requisite family portraits. Allen noted her superior appeared to have only daughters.

Not waiting for her to continue, Brandt said with a smile, 'Hope you're not here to tell me you're pregnant and want me to come up with a maternity-leave policy.' He laughed, enjoying his own humor.

'No, I'm not pregnant,' Allen responded dryly. 'I'm worried about a case I'm working and thought you could provide some counsel.'

'You talk to Weaver about this before coming to see me?'

'Not exactly, although I have discussed the problem with him several times, with no success.'

'You talk with Captain Phillips about this?'

'About coming to see you?'

'That's my question,' Brandt said in a firm voice.

'No, I didn't clear this visit with the Captain.'

'Well, then the first advice I'll give you is go through the chain of command.'

Allen rose to leave, 'I stand corrected. I'll go . . . .'

'Sit down girl.' Brandt shifted back to a friendly tone, 'You're here. Might as well get it off your chest. Next time remember to do it right.' Brandt waved her back down into the chair. 'Now what's this problem that's stuck in your craw?'

Allen wasn't sure how to proceed. The words of Sergeant Howell still rang in her ear, and it was obvious Brandt was taking control of the meeting. She knew she needed to choose her words carefully. *'How do I raise this issue without proving Howell right,'* she wondered? 'I've been assigned to work with Weaver on the EAR series. I'm afraid we may have overlooked a suspect.'

'Wouldn't be the first time. You've been a detective long enough to know investigation is more an art than a science. Bud's been a little overloaded, but my money says he'll nail the bastard soon.'

'Well, that's part of the problem, so many leads, not enough time, but we've had a number of calls on one particular ex-con. Every time I mention this suspect's name, Weaver says he's been eliminated. The problem is I can't find any rational reason for the elimination. I think we need to set up a surveillance.'

'Slow down young lady. Don't you worry your pretty little head. I'm sure Bud has everything under control. Isn't this the series with one rapist but many blood types? Bound to be confusing. You just work with Bud on this one. You'll learn a lot.'

He paused momentarily, then continued, 'Now I have a meeting coming up with the mayor of Galt so just go back and keep up the good work. More and more, voters like to see women in leadership positions. I've got my eye on you, so just keep your nose clean and who knows where you might be in five years.'

Allen left Brandt's office incensed. Had she just been warned to keep quiet and then offered a bribe of future promotions if she did as she was told?

Brandt was a good politician, but was he a good cop? Allen was shaken with the realization. 'Something is very wrong here,' she thought. Her mind brimmed with questions: Was her activity on this rape investigation common knowledge with the brass? Why would Brock be getting special dispensations? How could the welfare of women be so secondary? Why were they afraid of focusing on Brock? How did Brock figure in an election? And what had Howell meant with his comment about civil liability? So many questions; so few answers.

'Damn them,' she thought. 'I'm tired of being the token female, tired of not being heard, not respected, yet expected to be the good little woman and follow orders. If they won't go after Brock, I will,' she decided.

Allen glanced around at the empty squad room, thankful no one was there to see that she was close to tears. 'If Brandt knows Brock is the rapist and is deliberately, for whatever reasons, not arresting him, only trying to force him out of the area, then he is merely giving the women of the county an illusion of safety,' the thoughts disgusted and ultimately saddened her.

Her mind shifted to her afternoon plans and the upcoming evening with Scott. 'Thank God, I have someone to share this with,' Allen glanced at her watch: 10:43 a.m. 'Time to get on with the day - away from this place.'

27

Frank Graham sat in a small Italian bistro, overlooking the bay, enjoying an unusually sunny afternoon in San Francisco. He held a bottle of Heineken and puffed on a cigar.

Connors spotted him immediately, recognizing his large stature and shaved head, exactly as described by Allen. Approaching the table, Connors extended his hand, but quickly pulled it back when Graham showed no interest in the formality. Instead, Graham leaned forward and pushed aside two empty beer bottles and a slender box of Dino cigars.

'My office. Grab a chair,' he said, motioning to his left. Graham continued in a blustery voice, 'The name's Frank. Susan probably told you all about me, mostly the ugly stuff I'm sure,' he laughed a throaty laugh. Giving Connors no chance to respond he continued, 'Hear you got a line on a guy with a pricey head.'

'Pricey head?' Connors frowned, momentarily unsure of the connotation.

'Reward.' Graham clarified.

'Oh, yeah, yeah,' Connors blushed, embarrassed to have missed the cue.

'Well, how much?' Graham asked fixating on the reward.

'Right now it's at fifty thousand, but it seems to go up every week.'

'Then maybe we should just sit and wait until it reaches a hundred thousand,' Graham offered with another throaty laugh, leaning back in his chair.

Connors wasn't sure how to interpret the man and he struggled not to form a negative first impression, after all, Susan had recommended Graham highly. 'Fifty thousand is a lot, even with the split. And, the longer we wait, the more people who are hurt, maybe even killed.'

'Split? What kind of a split and with who for Chrissake?' Graham reacted, obviously irritated.

'We got the tip from an ex-con who knows the suspect. Initially, he was promised half the reward.'

'You tellin' me some dickhead gets twenty five g's just for givin' a name?' Graham demanded.

'No, I'm saying, if . . . when we collect, the reward has to be split. The reward was at twenty thousand when he gave the name up, so his share would be ten thousand,' Connors was growing uncomfortable with all the money talk. He and Allen were thinking about victims and Graham could only think about money.

'Ok I'll settle for forty. Understand, I'm a businessman. Gotta think about the cash.'

'Don't worry; the reward will be more than fair. Can we move on to the rape series and our suspect?'

'I guess that means there is no up-front money?'

'Sorry, I'm still a graduate student.'

'So, I do this job on the come? What if your guy ain't the rapist? Then I'm out in the cold with nothing,' Graham said.

'I guess it's the chance you take, but I really believe we've got the right man. Let me fill you in and then you make a decision. If it doesn't sound worth the risk, you're only out a couple hours.'

'Well, Allen said you were onto something. She's a good broad and seems to think you need help. Hell,

181

even the Bay papers are starting to follow Sacramento's folly.' He motioned to a waiter, 'Another round over here. I got a guy dying of thirst. You like Heineken or you one of those wine drinkers?'

'No, beer will be fine.'

For the next few minutes Connors reviewed the rape series, the double homicide as well as the information developed to date on Brock. Graham sipped his beer and listened, although Connors found his finger tapping annoying. Connors wondered if Allen's recommendation was really the best, he had concerns about Graham's impatience and air of condescension.

When Connors finished, Graham responded with surprising accord, 'Sounds like you might be right. This Brock guy is a real odd one. Loose wiring, that's for sure.'

'There is one complication.'

'Always is. Shoot it to me straight,' Graham instructed.

'There's confusion about the rapist's blood type. They've found foreign blood at the crime scenes, but when the lab runs the blood type it comes back different, again and again. Looking at the lab reports, you'd think there are four or maybe five rapists. But, the M.O. is so distinctive, there can only be one.'

Graham sat silent for several moments, downing a long draught, before declaring, 'You gotta problem with your lab.'

Connors waited, knowing Graham had still more to say.

Suddenly, Graham sat upright, 'The bastard plays games. That's it! This fucker isn't bleeding at every

182

rape, he's leaving a signature. God, Weaver really is as dumb as I thought. Only question is where is the rapist getting the fuckin' blood? Could there be more bodies?'

'But, it's always a different blood type. They've found A, B, and O, secretors and non- secretors. And, there's no pattern.'

'Like I said, lots of bodies. Okay, okay, forget the goddamned blood for now. I learned long ago, instinct is often better than science. Anyway, I'll go with your guy having his wires crossed and being the rapist.'

'Does that mean you'll take the case?' Connors asked.

'I try to limit pro bono cases to one every fifteen years. Your lucky number just came up,' Graham said, draining the last of his beer and smiling broadly. 'Order whatever you want. The ribs are great. I run a tab here.' He signaled for a waiter, shifted in his chair, then continued, 'I guess that's why old Weaver hasn't jumped all over Brock. Something like a few bad lab reports would confuse the hell out of Bud.'

'He seems to focus on eliminating suspects. Allen thinks Brandt may be giving Weaver orders.'

'Brandt is a political animal and he may be sitting on something rotten in Denmark. Probably why Weaver's still there and I'm gone.'

Connors smiled and then turned serious, 'Speaking of Brandt, Allen is talking to him about the case today. Maybe she'll gain some insight.'

Graham frowned, 'Weaver know she's talking to the old man?'

'I don't think so, at least not as of last night.'

183

'Either way, Weaver's not gonna be happy. He's a bull-headed bastard, one of Brandt's favorites. Might be trouble for Allen.'

'How so?'

'Career. She could fuck up her career. She pisses off Brandt or steps on one of his deals, she'll get a jacket. May wind up being an empty holster for the next twenty years.'

'Empty holster?'

'Assigned to records or some other shitty job. It's what every department does with malcontents, incompetents or people who don't follow orders.'

'Let's hope not. Getting back to the business at hand, what do you need to get started?'

'Leave this asshole's rap sheet and mug shot with me. Then write down his full name, address, DOJ, FBI, and social security number. Oh yeah, and his phone number. Might want to call and hear his voice. Give me a couple days to wrap things up here and then I'll head up to Sac town. I'll want to tail him everywhere for a couple of days and then focus on the hours after midnight.'

'Remember, he prowls houses and selects his victims prior to the night of the rape.'

'I get the picture. Lemme guess, he prowls after the broads go to work. You did say all his victims had jobs?'

'Yeah, according to the police reports. At first they thought there might be a religious angle, but only the first four or five women were church goers. There doesn't appear to be anything else the victims share in common, except of course their physical appearance.'

'Skinny, white meat, with long dark hair, right?'

Connors shook his head, amazed at Graham's colorful language, 'Yes, all white women and none of them over thirty five. But, he doesn't pass up young girls if they happen to be available.'

'That part really fries me. It'll be a pleasure to grab this guy. I got no use for kid fuckers. I'd love to pop him.'

'Be careful, this rapist is good at what he does. He's ruthless. His first homicide was because a guy tried to fight. Then he executed the woman in cold blood. Keep in mind, Brock is an ex-Special Forces soldier.'

'This Special Forces shit don't impress me much. Soldier boys real tough when surrounded by lots of support and following orders. When I'm on his ass, it ain't gonna be like no dumb chink.'

'You're not concerned about Brock having special skills?'

'No. I've dealt with some really bad bastards. I'm still in one piece. Far as following him, hell, I can shadow coyotes without 'em ever knowing. No, if you're right about Brock, I'll be banking that reward money within the week,' he answered with an assumptive close.

'Do what you have to, but remember we talked about staying within the law.'

'Don't worry; I want to make sure I collect the reward. But, no one will shed tears if I drag him in with his guts hanging out. Now, how about those ribs?'

'Thanks for the offer, but I'll have to pass on the food. I've got a dinner date back in Sacramento.'

28

The drive out of the city, over the Bay Bridge, took Connors longer than expected, and he thought about pulling over and locating a pay phone. He decided against it, confident Susan would understand if he showed up a little late. The night before, Susan had drawn a map to her place on the back of a napkin. He recognized a hint of her perfume when he retrieved the map from his pocket. Her scent was beginning to grow on him more and more.

'An invitation for dinner,' he mused. Connors had called Susan at home several times in recent days, always about the EAR, but had never seen her apartment. He thought now about the fleeting images he'd entertained during those phone conversations. 'After tonight I'll have a whole new picture; I think I'm going to like seeing her domestic side.' Thankfully, the traffic began to move swiftly. Instead of turning on the radio, Connors decided he'd use the drive time to review the past two hours spent with Graham, hoping to quell his unease with the PI's bravado.

At 7:15 p.m. Connors pulled up to the Curtis Park address, fashionably late he thought. He could hear music playing as he approached Susan's door, the Carpenters, their unmistakable harmony in *Close to You*.

She answered the door after one crisp knock, wearing a colorful batik kaftan, her hair pulled back in a single braid. Connors smiled and held out a bottle of *Chianti*. Susan laughed, her warm, welcoming smile, the one that so instantly put Connors at ease. 'How nice! After today I need this,' Susan said, leading him into the living room. The room was large, comfortable and filled with hanging plants, floor pillows, and a beautiful macrame wall hanging.

Connors went immediately to the wall hanging. 'This is incredible. Did you do this?' he asked.

'My therapy. It's amazing how tying little knots can remove the knots in my mind and my shoulders at the end of the day,' she chuckled. 'Tell me, how did it go with Frank?

'He'll take the case. You were right about him. But, he's like no one I've ever met. Very egotistical and cocky.'

'Cocky, but very good. I guess when you're six feet four, two hundred twenty, you can afford to be arrogant. It also means he's a risk taker.'

'And likes money. He made it clear he expects at least forty thousand of the reward, but enough about that. What happened in your meeting with Brandt? Graham seemed to think it was dangerous for your career.'

'It was one strange meeting.' She poured two glasses of the wine and handed one to Connors. 'And, yes, it could easily damage my career.' As they settled on the couch, Allen hesitated, suddenly aware she felt vulnerable. This was a new experience for her. Ever since her divorce, she had programmed herself to be guarded around men. Earlier in the day, thoughts of Connors had left her feeling energized; now she felt unsure. Did she want to open up to Scott and expose more about her personal life? His welcome smile told her she did and so she continued, 'Before I even met with Brandt, Sergeant Howell came into the break room and warned me not to talk to Brandt.'

'Who's Howell?'

'A sergeant from internal affairs. He said I shouldn't talk about Brock.'

'He knew about Brock?'

'Yeah. Internal Affairs has a reputation of knowing about a lot of things. In fact, when I think about it, he seemed to know exactly what Brandt would tell me.'

'But, you went ahead with the meeting?'

'Scott, I can't let myself be intimidated.' She studied Connors' reaction, took another sip of wine and paused before continuing, 'Brandt was obviously ready for me. He took control immediately and never gave me a chance to even mention Brock's name and why he should be a prime suspect. Then he wrapped it up with a veiled threat. In a nutshell, he said if I would back off, I would have a chance at a promotion.'

Connors shook his head, a combination of disbelief and disgust. 'Meaning that if you didn't, you could forget about ever advancing?'

'Exactly. Brandt is capable of anything and I have no protection. Being the ultimate politician, he chose his words carefully. He'll never be accused of either a threat or a bribe.'

Connors nodded, 'It's strange, this business about Weaver ignoring Brock as a suspect. Graham picked up on that angle and questioned why Weaver wasn't putting Brock under surveillance.'

'I can't answer that either, but I definitely got the feeling today the hands off policy regarding Brock starts higher than Weaver,'

Scott nodded, sensing she had more to say.

Susan continued, 'It just hit me . . . Brandt never even asked who my suspect was. Isn't that bizarre?'

'I'll say . . . he obviously intended to move you through his office quickly and cause you to stop questioning Weaver.'

The couple sat in silence, watching a fire grow in the fireplace, letting the conversation settle until Connors broke the silence, 'Graham needs two days to clear his calendar. Said he'll be in Sacramento later this week. Do you think you could meet with us and help give him some direction?'

'I'll be real busy during the day with these homicides, but an evening should work. Let me know when and where.' Susan was back to efficiency and planning. 'I don't think Graham will take any direction. But, it'll be good to see him again.'

Connors took a deep breath, 'Enough shop talk. It's been a long day, and whatever is cooking in your kitchen is about to drive me crazy. It smells wonderful, and I'm suddenly famished.'

'Likewise, but one last thing on the case, I'm not going to let Brandt or Weaver tell me what to do. My career is not worth losing my personal integrity, I've decided to help your investigation as much as I can.' With that, Susan stood and walked towards the kitchen, 'Come help me make the salad. I certainly can't let my ace investigator in this case go hungry.'

As she anticipated, Connors raved about her sauce. 'What's in these meatballs? They're very, very good,' he asked as he helped himself to another serving.

'Well . . . I don't give my culinary secrets out to just anyone, but if you'll promise not to alert Julia Child, I'll tell you: veal, pork and beef. All three mixed together in equal amounts with fennel seed, salt, pepper, garlic, one egg and a half cup bread crumbs.'

Connors laughed, obviously pleased with his hostess' ready response. 'Time for a toast, to a darned good cop who happens to be a terrific cook,' he clinked her glass.

'And macramé artist,' she winked, adding a personal boast.

'And macramé artist,' Connors smiled, his charm matching hers.

As Susan watched him eat, she felt amazed at the ease with which a woman could hold sway over a man -simply through his stomach. They lingered at the table. With a fresh pot of decaf and seemingly unlimited conversation, the evening easily became late night. It was Allen who signaled a conclusion. 'Scott, I've got a staff meeting tomorrow at seven thirty, I'm afraid I have to get some sleep.'

Connors couldn't resist a little jibe, 'That early? About the time I decide whether or not to sleep for another half hour or get up and read the paper. I guess we can't all have a professor's schedule.'

'Yeah, but at least I don't have to correct papers,' she stood and began to gather their dinner plates.

'Here, let me help,' Scott rose. Instead of reaching for the dishes, he walked toward Susan, his hands finding her shoulders. 'Didn't I hear you say earlier your shoulders were tense?' he began to massage gently.

'That feels heavenly,' Susan sighed a deep, satisfied breath and leaned back into his grip.

Slowly, he turned her to face him. Two strong arms now wrapped around her waist, his boyish, pleased smile gazing into her eyes. 'Susan you are the most beautiful woman I have ever held.'

She thought of protesting, but instantly dismissed the notion. Why should she deny herself this moment she'd considered many times since meeting Scott Connors? Instead, she smiled and felt a gentle butterfly flutter somewhere in her stomach.

At first they lay together in front of the flickering fire, draped over the floor pillows, letting the embers warm them. Then Scott assumed another lead, 'Let me make love to you tonight,' his eyes fairly pleaded. There was no answer, no decision to be made; Susan instinctively reached for his belt buckle, taking their passion to a new dimension.

For Scott, Susan's embrace was open and yielding, her readiness spiced with an innocence he hadn't expected. She sensed him studying her, her thoughts and emotions. 'Scott, I'm not like a lot of women. Too much Catholic teaching to make me facile or predictable, but right now I can't even explain how you make me feel.' They paused for a moment to gaze into each other's eyes, to relish each other's naked bodies and delicious warmth.

He placed his left arm under her waist and his right under her head, 'Come to me.' And she did. Together they swayed in the motion of lovemaking, with Scott thrilled by his ability to bring Susan to pleasure several times over. He glanced down at her, still in his embrace. She had tears in her eyes. 'You're crying?' he asked, 'Have I hurt you?'

She smiled and shook her head, 'No, no . . . you've just taken me someplace I've never been before.'

With that he stroked her forehead, buried his lips in hers and then lifted himself higher to find his own vista.

The clock on Susan's mantle struck three, as the couple rested side-by-side. Scott reached up to grab a few logs and gently set them in the fireplace. Susan was quiet, observing, watching his strong arms deftly handle the task. He laid back down and drew up the thick afghan that had fallen by their sides. For several minutes they talked, of nothing really, more engaged in the re-growth of the fire embers than conversation. Then Scott spoke, 'I realize it's late, but you've made me a very hungry man, again,' he laughed.

'Not a problem . . . let me grab a couple of robes and I'll whip up some eggs and toast.'

'Any possibility of stirring up some more of those meatballs?' he asked, with feigned contriteness.

'Meatballs for a meatball,' she teased as she walked to the bedroom closet.

Scott lay back and considered his reply for a moment. He repeated after her, 'Meatballs for a meatball . . . I must say, you're the first person to ever label me with such an endearing term, especially given the past hour.'

'I warned you . . . I'm not your typical woman,' she responded from the kitchen.

'That you are not,' he agreed, settling into the terry robe she tossed him. He walked towards the kitchen. 'But, I like what those Catholic nuns did for you.'

She tossed him a spatula and offered a command, 'Stir the eggs.'

29

Connors arrived on campus at 9:15 the next morning, almost an hour later than usual. He met Blomberg in the hallway outside his office. 'I need to catch you up on my investigation. Do you have time for coffee?'

'Actually, I was just thinking of calling you. Let's go to the faculty lounge,' the professor responded.

They found an empty table in the far corner and as soon as they were seated, Connors began to bring his academic mentor up to date. It was a rapid fire verbal report detailing, among other things, meetings with Allen and the difficulty she was having getting Weaver to recognize Brock as a suspect, her recent meeting with Sheriff Brandt, the pending involvement of Frank Graham and the missing handlebars from the motorcycle.

Instead of focusing on any of the key points, Blomberg surprised Connors, with a personal question, 'Do I get the impression there might be a relationship developing here?'

Connors blushed and stammered, 'She's a very special lady . . . I'm . . . I'm trying to keep this on a professional level. But she is a big help and willing to take risks,' he stopped to collect himself. 'Frankly, I'm concerned her involvement could hurt her career. Which leads me to questions. Why is Weaver refusing to even consider Brock a suspect and why did Brandt make a veiled threat to Allen?'

His mentor sat, quiet and thoughtful, carefully weighing Connors' words. A vast valley lay between the light, humored reaction to Connors' romantic

194

interests and the more serious talk about Sheriff Brandt.

'Have I said something wrong?' Connors sensed the professor's unease.

'No, not at all. On the contrary, I think you've discovered a serious problem, one I'm sorry to say isn't all that surprising.'

'What do you mean?' Connors asked.

'I should have used the name of a third party weeks ago when I turned Brock in as a suspect.'

'Why would you need to do that?' Connors asked.

'I'm only guessing. We may never know for sure. But, Brandt may have been concerned I would get credit if Brock turned out to be the rapist. He could be worried that I might use the information against him in the next election. He knows I have formed a committee to find someone to run against him.' Blomberg continued. 'As these rapes continue they could impact the next election.'

'You think he's worried about being re-elected?'

'All politicians worry about elections. And rape is a big thing for women voters.'

'This is hard to swallow.' Connors said, 'You're saying political considerations have impeded this investigation?'

'Maybe. I hope there is another explanation. But, didn't you say Howell brought up the election to Allen?'

'Yes, and she also told me Howell said Brandt is taking care of Brock. What could that mean?'

'Brandt must be putting pressure on parole to either violate Brock or force him to move.'

'Would his parole officer do that?' Connors asked perplexed.

'Probably not, since most of them have no use for Brandt. Unfortunately, again, we may never know.'

'I think I should talk again to Brock's parole officer,' Connors said, surprised by his professor's analysis. Both men sat quietly. 'It's strange. All my courses in criminal justice and, yet, what I've learned here in just a few weeks was never discussed in any of them.'

'Welcome to the real world. It's certainly one of the problems of academia. How can we prepare students for the realities they will actually face on the job?'

'Yeah, I guess you're right. I don't ever remember a professor talking about police corruption.'

'Yet there is a long history of corruption, not only with police, but in the courts as well. Corruption will occur anywhere there are people. And, I'm not talking about just money. That's bad enough, but abuse of power is epidemic.'

'Even if it leads to exposing women to rape and murder?' he asked.

'Unfortunately, sometimes even that,' Blomberg replied.

'One more question.' Connors began, shaking his head in disgust, 'Why does an ex-soldier go into the homes naked? Somehow that doesn't sound like a soldier to me.'

'No, but it does sound like a smart criminal. Have you ever heard of the Locard principle?'

Connors shook his head and the professor continued, 'It means this rapist has been exposed to
196

some aspects of criminal investigations. The principle is named after an old French guy who came up with the theory that a criminal entering a crime scene will bring something with him and leave with something from the crime scene. By taking off his clothes this rapist minimizes that possibility.'

'No wonder the police are having trouble catching him,' Connors said.

'I'd even bet he showers before he leaves the rape scenes. The police obviously haven't made that connection,' Blomberg suggested.

Connors glanced at his watch. His class would begin in less than ten minutes. 'You've given me a lot to think about. I'm certainly seeing the criminal justice system in a different light now,' the young protégé said.

'Let's get together at the end of the week. I want to keep tabs on your investigation and especially on Graham's progress. He's one of the best.'

30

How come you wanted to meet off duty, away from the station? I can't afford another wife, so it can't be that.' Weaver offered with a shy smile.

'No, it's not that Bud. Nothing against you, but I'll never marry a cop. I just want to get some straight answers. It's easier to talk off duty,' Allen responded.

The pair sat face-to-face over a table in a quiet bar in Old Town Sacramento. Soft-rock music played in the background.

Allen had called him at home to suggest the meeting and Weaver agreed readily. It was Allen who deliberately showed up almost an hour late, knowing full well Weaver would be on his second or third drink. For a moment, she felt a combination of guilt for staging his vulnerability and pathos. He appeared so alone, so tired.

Weaver nodded, as if to say he was expecting serious dialogue, 'I understand, we've been so busy, no time to really talk. You got somethin' on your mind?' He downed the rest of his drink and waved to the waitress, 'Another round here.'

'I need some straight answers.'

'Straight answers to what?' The detective avoided her eye contact.

Allen reached across the table with her left hand and placed it over Weaver's right wrist. 'Bud, I like you. I don't want you to get hurt, but something is wrong, really wrong with our investigation. And, I don't get it. This is a rape and now a homicide investigation. Why are you screwing it up?'

Weaver stared at the table, still refusing to make eye contact. When the waitress returned with another glass of scotch, no ice, he sipped slowly. Allen sat patiently.

Finally, he began, 'I'm fifty seven. Been payin' child support on four kids now for seems like forever. Two of 'em in college. My second wife keeps threatening to come after my pension. My car is ten years old. I'm close to retiring' . . . to what? A trailer parked in some dumpy lot in Rio Linda? Life seems simple to you, a good lookin' broad and young. You'll be able to grab some rich guy and bank some money. Me . . . I got nobody and nothing.' He took a long swallow.

'But, Bud . . . a rape case. Why a rape case?'

'Rape? It's got nothin' to do with it. I'm not sayin' no more.' He looked away. Allen could see tears welling in his eyes.

She sat for a moment. What could be said now? The reality: She worked with a broken man, a man broken by bad decisions and poor choices. Inside she felt her anger rising.

Obviously, money was involved. Weaver had sold his oath and his soul for the almighty dollar. Now it was clear. Sheriff Brandt was dirty. The thought sickened her while, strangely, steeling her resolve. From now on, she would have to press for the answers herself, seeking an outcome she knew women all over the city desperately needed.

'You want a beer or anything?' Weaver asked, half hoping she would stay.

'Sorry, Bud, I have to get going. Thanks for meeting me. Get some rest. I'll see you tomorrow.'

199

When she reached the door she stopped, turned and watched Weaver still sitting, staring toward the bar, an empty glass before him.

Allen didn't stop to call. She parked a block from Connors' address and satisfying herself no one was watching, went quickly to his apartment building and knocked on his door. On her third knock, Connors answered, surprised, 'Susan, what's going on?' And then, 'Come in.'

She walked directly into Scott's embrace. 'Just hold me. Don't say anything. Just hold me.' They stood for several minutes until Susan stepped back, refreshed by their connection.

'Let's sit down,' Connors said as he led her into his living room.

'Scott, don't comment. Please, just listen. I had a talk with Weaver. I couldn't stand it anymore. Everything you've found out about Brock points to him being the rapist, and now a murderer. Yet, Weaver refuses to do anything to stop him. I let him get drunk and then I challenged him. Asked him straight out why he was ignoring the evidence.'

'And he admitted it?' Connors asked in disbelief.

'Not directly. But he might as well have. He implied there was money involved, said he was old and broke. That's his reason. But, where can there be money in protecting a rapist? You've got to help me, I'm confused and don't know what to do. It's Brandt, I know it's him. That's why Howell warned me. I can't believe it. I've worked hard for years, put up with all their bullshit and now I find out they're corrupt.'

200

Susan was near breathless, her pent up frustration and anger erupting.

Connors pulled Susan close to him again, 'Slow down, slow down. There's got to be some answers. We'll figure it out. Baker will help us. DOJ has an investigative division and Graham will be a big help. Let me start water for tea. I'll get you some Kleenex.'

Allen wiped her eyes. 'I'm sorry. I'll pull it together. This has been haunting me for weeks, so at least now I know. It's just so unbelievable.'

'But, we can't lose our focus,' Connors responded, handing Susan the tissue. When the water neared boiling, Connors poured two cups and dropped in the tea bags. 'How about some lemon?' he asked.

'Sure.' Her calm returning.

Connors continued as he brought the tea to the table, 'Let's approach this rationally, analytically. What could be the connection between Brandt and Brock? You're right . . . it must involve money. Brock was a soldier and then he spent three years in Folsom prison. So, he couldn't be the source of money. What does Brock have that keeps Brandt from having him arrested?'

'Brock doesn't have anything to offer except a demented nature and a propensity for killing,' Susan answered matter-of-factly.

Connors' eyes widened, 'That's it!'

'What?'

'Killing. You just hit on it. Killing is the only thing Brock has of any value to anyone. It's what he's trained to do. Think for a minute. Has there been any big case, really big, after July sixth of last year, after

Brock was paroled? One that involved murder?' Connors asked, his intensity rising.

Susan relaxed, sipping her tea, thinking, then suddenly, 'Yes!' She sat up, 'There was and it actually involves two homicides.'

'Two homicides?'

'Yes, two.' Setting her cup on the table, she continued, 'We call it the Demitrus case, after one of the goons arrested. A major drug bust came down from Tri-County narcotics. Heroin, lots of it, forty some kilos. Sergeant Sawyer, one of our best, got a tip from a snitch. Based on that information, a judge issued a search warrant. The narcs walked in on three guys and found the heroin in plain sight. It looked like an airtight case. All three were mafia types. Despite high bail, they posted that same night. And, immediately Tony DiGriggo, a known mafia mouthpiece, appeared from San Francisco to represent them.'

'When did this happen?'

'October, I'm sure, first week or so. Then on Christmas Eve Sergeant Sawyer was shot to death in his bed. One week later the body of his snitch turned up floating in the American River.'

'What happened to the case?'

'Charges dismissed. Although the search warrant was valid on its face, the judge used their deaths as an excuse to dismiss. So, the judge must also be involved,' Allen replied. 'All three thugs walked. It was really tough. I know Kimberly, Sawyer's widow, and their two teenage kids.' Now Allen was on her feet, pacing.

'You might just have made the connection. If Brandt is caught up in the dope trade and had Brock hired to do the killing, he doesn't dare have him arrested. Too big a chance he would talk. I'll have Baker at DOJ pull the reports. We might be able to establish a connection through the M.O. I'll call you tomorrow as soon as we finish.'

'Can you trust Baker?'

'We have to. Blomberg swears by him,' Connors assured her. 'But do you think Weaver will tell Brandt that you're onto them?'

'That I don't know. Weaver was pretty drunk. He didn't tell me anything directly, just indicated he was desperate for money. He might be too embarrassed to tell Brandt he was drunk and talked. I'll try to smooth things over in the morning.'

'Speaking of the morning, isn't it time we called it a night?' Connors remarked as he reached for her, caressing the nape of her neck.

'So . . . I'm more than a one night stand?' Susan tilted her head, smiled and waited for an answer.

Scott studied her for a moment. 'How could you even ask such a question? You are much, much more.'

Connors sat with Baker at his desk, several opened crime reports scattered in front of them.

'Hard to compare these homicides with the rapes. A paid killing is a long way from a rape, but we can check for similarities or find differences which would eliminate Brock,' Baker offered.

'Where do we start?' Connors asked.

'Start with the weapon. Sawyer was killed with a .357, which is the same caliber used in the rape series.

203

But it's a common caliber,' Baker began, turning the report pages slowly. *'Johnson, the snitch, undetermined cause of death, too much deterioration from river water. Both killings look like mob hits although typically, according to our organized crime experts, their hit-men use small caliber weapons.'*

'But, if they hired someone outside the mob, he would use his own gun,' Connors noted.

'Could be.' Baker flipped back through several pages. 'Look here! It says the entry was made by removing a sliding glass door in the Sawyer killing. Didn't one of your sources say Brock bragged about his ability to take off sliders?' the analyst asked.

'God, that's right,' Connors replied. 'Kim Henderson. She was with Brock's wife when he demonstrated how to remove a patio door from the outside. But, Sawyer's wife wasn't raped. Whoever killed her husband just killed him. Wouldn't Brock have raped her?'

'Not necessarily. If it was Brock and he did it for money, he wouldn't have taken the risk. He left the deputy's wife and two kids alone,' Baker explained. 'The killer wanted in and out fast.' The summation made perfect sense.

'So, there's a possibility it could have been Brock?'

'A strong possibility,' Baker emphasized.

'What's our next step?' Connors asked.

'I'll ask our organized crime section to research Brock's finances in the days following Sawyer's killing. Any significant infusion of cash into a bank account could implicate Brock in the killing.'

'They can get that kind of information?'

'They have their ways. We probably won't be able to use the information in court. But the banks will provide details if they think it's needed for an organized crime investigation.'

'So much for privacy laws.'

'Favors. Happens all the time,' the analyst explained matter-of-factly. 'I'll get right on this. Also, I'll contact a captain I know at Folsom and check on Brock's associations with any mafia types during his prison time.'

'How soon can you find out? I'm meeting with a private investigator later today. This is information he should have,' Connors urged.

'I'll do my best. We'll see if we can match ballistics. The reports indicate bullets were recovered from the Sawyer killing and the two EAR killings. I'll put a rush on it.'

Sacramento's afternoon rush hour traffic seemed heavier than usual as Connors merged onto the highway 50 to meet Graham at The Hilltop Diner in Rancho Cordova. Graham was already working on a platter of seafood when Connors sat down. 'I ordered you a beer. Grab a plate and have some crab,' Graham said, licking his butter-coated fingers.

'Thanks, but I have to make a phone call first,' Connors excused himself and headed for a pay phone. Fortunately, Baker was still at his desk and answered on the first ring, full of information.

'Looks like you might be right about Brock. He deposited nine thousand eight hundred dollars in *First Savings and Loan* on January third,' Baker said.

'That was quick. You sure they got the right account?'

'These guys are good. They can get almost any information as long as it's not intended to be used in court.'

'Any luck on the mafia connection at Folsom?'

'All I could find out is that there were three or four guys with organized crime jackets serving time while Brock was in. No info on any relationship. Anyone suspected of having organized crime connection is kept separate from the general inmate population, with the exception of chapel when the entire prison population is allowed to mix.'

'Damn,' Connors exclaimed, 'If Brock was recruited as a hit man, they did it in church.'

'It's entirely possible. You can share with your PI about the deposit, but don't mention how you got the info. And, don't say the name of the bank.'

'Any match on the bullets?' Connors asked.

'Not yet. That'll take a few days.'

'Okay. I'm thinking more and more everyone needs to tread carefully. We might need to back up our PI. If you can think of anyone, let me know.'

'I'm afraid there are not many people who will volunteer to stalk the likes of Brock,' Baker said.

Connors returned to the table to quickly bring Graham up to date on Baker's information regarding the Sawyer murder and its connection to Brock.

At the mention of Sawyer, Graham lost all interest in eating. 'No shit, Sawyer was a friend of mine and a damn good cop. You're tellin' me it was Brock . . . he killed Sawyer and his snitch?' Graham said, staring hard at Connors.

'Nothing we can prove at this point. But, it's likely he made an organized crime connection while in Folsom. After the two killings, Brock deposited more than nine thousand dollars. Where does a convict get that kind of money right after being paroled? Another consideration . . . there may be a match on the bullets in the Sawyer case, as well as the recent killings by the rapist.'

'I know Sawyer's wife, Kim, went to high school with her. Hell, they invited me to their kids' first communions,' Graham sat back in his chair and immediately begun to reflect on the news.

Connors could see the details hitting Graham hard and he waited for the private investigator to speak. Shortly, both the old Graham and his fiery spirit were back. 'If this bastard is the one that offed Sawyer, I'll cut his balls off before I drop him at jail.'

'Easy, easy,' Connors cautioned. 'You must understand how dangerous Brock is. I want to be with you before you make contact with him. You'll need a backup.'

'I don't need no help,' Graham said, his jaw tight. 'I want this guy all to myself.'

Connors knew there was no use arguing the point, but he couldn't shake a sense of foreboding.

31

The seasoned investigator parked down the street from Brock's house. He waited until dark before approaching Brock's white van in the driveway. A light rain was falling and he held an umbrella which gave him ideal cover. He paused directly behind the van, stooped and quickly fastened a magnetized transmitter to the inside of the rear frame.

The act was completed in a seconds. Back in his car, he felt himself relaxing enough to lean back and cat nap, his confidence buoyed by the silent trap he'd just set. Should Brock move the van, the transmitter beep would instantly alert the PI that Brock was on the move. When 3:00 a.m. passed with no action, he waited an hour and then drove back to his motel, took off his shirt and shoes and lay down. He awoke at 7:30 a.m. without an alarm.

By 8:00 a.m. he was back, parking within two blocks of Brock's house. At 9:30 the transmitter alarm sounded. As soon as he determined the van was headed in the direction of City College, Graham dropped back and drove slowly, following the signal to the City College campus. He found Brock's van parked on the east side of Hughes Stadium.

The PI quickly cheated the door on the driver's side, and made a complete search of the vehicle. It was clean. This didn't surprise him. He figured Brock was too smart to carry anything linking him with the rapes.

Back in his own car, Graham cursed, remembering something he had forgotten to get from Connors. 'Should have Brock's class schedule,' he thought. He drove around to Land Park, a quiet city park just west of the campus. The park was already filling with joggers and day walkers as Graham parked and continued on foot to the campus quad. He found a bench just outside the Criminal Justice building and sat drinking a cup of coffee, watching students as they walked by.

At 12:15, he saw Connors come out of the building and begin walking toward the faculty parking lot. Graham moved past a group of students and quickly caught up to him, 'Good morning professor. Beautiful day isn't it?'

Connors turned, obviously startled. 'Good to see you,' he spoke in a hushed voice, 'Brock is coming right behind me. Meet me over by the tennis courts.' He broke stride with Graham and continued walking.

After a few minutes the two reconnected on a bench facing the tennis courts. 'So your suspect made it to class this morning. He must not be grieving his newly departed wife, or at least he's not letting it stop him from getting an education,' Graham said with a short laugh.

'Yeah, he actually hasn't missed a single class,' Connors responded. He paused. 'Allen mentioned she would like to see you. Maybe later this evening?'

'Suppose she's got to say her piece, give her input, but I've got this fucker bugged and he can't go anywhere without me knowing. If you guys really think we need to talk, how 'bout we meet over dinner, your nickel? And, bring me a copy of Brock's class schedule.'

'No problem. Any suggestions for dinner?' Connors asked.

'How about the Landers Supper Club . . . say eight?' Graham suggested.

'Eight sounds good. Susan often works into the evening, so this should be okay for her.'

'Susan . . . eh,' Graham smiled. 'She's Susan now. Must mean things are getting thick. Lucky you. She's a damn fine lady.'

Connors nodded as Graham turned to leave. Here was the second person in less than a week who had detected something between Allen and himself. He wondered if he was 'letting his feelings see daylight' as his grandmother used to say when she detected an emotion playing prominently on his mind.

Graham spent the rest of the day tracking Brock. By 4:00 p.m., the suspect was at his house. Graham took advantage to return to his motel and slept until 7:00 p.m. Following a quick shower, the detective arrived at the supper club, just as Allen was getting out of her car. She greeted him with a warm handshake and a smile.

'You're lookin' good, too good for a cop,' Graham said with a mischievous grin. 'That smile says the lady has a lover. It's in your eyes.'

'Frank, you never change, nosy and irritatingly personal,' Allen smiled.

For the next two hours Connors enjoyed listening to the two old friends exchange stories about their time with the department. Twice during the conversation Allen tried to stress how dangerous Brock was. Both times Graham dismissed her concerns with a joke.

The $60 dinner and drink bill put a strain on Connors' monthly budget and a fresh sense of apprehension in his mind. Was Graham too much bravado and too little caution? In a few days, they would have an answer. After Graham left, Connors walked Allen to her car. 'Thanks for trying to warn Graham, but it didn't appear to have any impact.'

'No, but it was worth a try. Frank's a big boy and it could be he's right. Maybe Brock is really no match for him. It's his call. Thanks for picking up the dinner tab.' She smiled and leaned forward to offer a kiss.

Connors pulled her close. He couldn't remember any woman's scent and eagerness to kiss ever thrilling him as much as Susan Allen.

'Meet me back at my place. Let's start a fire and cork some wine,' Susan said as Scott opened her car door.

'How did you know I was thirsty?' he smiled.

32

Graham was back within sight of Brock's house at 11:45 p.m. With no action by 3:30 a.m., the PI returned again to his motel. He attempted to rest, but found sleep elusive and by 8:30 a.m. he was repositioned once more. For the next couple of hours he watched patiently until the van began to move.

Brock exited his driveway, drove north on 65th Street, and entered Highway 50 headed west. Graham followed in his light blue BMW, quickly determining that three quarters of a mile was sufficient distance to keep the receiver signal strong. When Highway 50 became I-80, Graham realized Brock was heading for the Bay area. 'I'll be damned, he's taking me home,' he said aloud.

Tailing the van was a little more difficult as they approached Richmond. With many exits, Graham needed to jockey up close to keep the van in sight. At University Ave., the second Berkeley exit, Brock turned off the freeway and headed east into downtown Berkeley. Graham drew up close and then dropped back again as he saw Brock turning right onto Fifth Street. The PI drove one block beyond, turned right and parked. He sat, listening to the beep of the transmitter. Within minutes the tone steadied and Graham knew Brock had stopped the van.

'He's at Aquatic Park,' the PI surmised, wondering what the reason could be. As Graham drove into the park, he spotted the van near the men's rest room. 'The bastard's a fuckin' queer,' Graham exclaimed out loud, knowing the reputation of this particular location. Parking as far from away as possible, Graham maintained his vigilance.

Brock was obviously in the rest room, but what was taking so long? Encounters in the Aquatic Park bathrooms were known to be brief. Four men entered and exited the bathroom and still no Brock. Graham could wait no more. Pulling on an old hunting cap and eyeglasses with neutered lenses, items of disguise he always kept in his car, he entered the restroom.

No Brock. Puzzled, he ventured outside and began walking along the east bank of the lake and saw two men sitting on the ground. They were no more than 30 yards from him and he quickly moved behind a tree, surrounded by bushes on his left to avoid detection.

One of the men was definitely Brock. He appeared to be talking with an unkempt drifter. 'What-in-the-hell is he doing talkin' to a bum?' Graham whispered to himself. He watched as Brock stood, shoved something into his coat pocket and turned to walk back toward his van. The bum remained immobile, still on the ground, head bent.

'Goddamn!' Graham muttered. 'What's this all about?' He continued to watch as Brock walked across the park through the parking lot to his van and drove away.

By the time the PI reached the bum he found him lying on the ground asleep. 'Gotta wake this bastard up,' Graham thought as he circled the man looking for clues. For a moment, he stood looking down at the old man before kicking him sharply in the shoulder.

The man grunted and opened his eyes, reeking of cheap wine.

213

'Wake up you old geezer,' Graham barked.

'Please, I'll leave,' the bum pleaded.

'Just sit the hell up. I got questions for you,' Graham ordered, dropping down on his knees. He grabbed the man's shoulder and jerked him to a sitting position. 'You talk, understand?'

'Ain't got no money,' the man blubbered.

'Not after money,' Graham barked. 'What business you got talkin' to that young fella?'

'What . . . what young fella?'

Graham held him by his jacket collar and slapped his cheek, sharply. The bum whimpered and Graham asked again, 'What did he want? Saw you talkin' just minutes ago. Tell me or I'll drown your sorry ass.'

'Wasn't nothin',' he muttered as a grimy twenty dollar bill fell from his hand.

'What'd he want?' Graham persisted, shoving the bill into the man's pocket.

'Blood,' the man said. 'He wanted blood.'

'What the fuck . . . ?' Graham was incredulous, 'Did you give him blood?'

'Yeah . . . he took some. I . . . need a drink. Gimme a drink.' He clutched at the paper bag lying on the ground beside him.

Graham grabbed the bag, pulled the wine bottle out, unscrewed the cap and held it up to the man's lips. The sour smelling alcohol poured into his slimy mouth and down his matted beard.

'There, now tell me, how'd he take blood?'

'Needle . . . here, see,' the old man said, trembling, as he stretched out his dirty left arm, revealing a trickle of dried blood.

214

'Damn, the fucker used a syringe. Pretty damned clever,' Graham said.

'Whadya say?'

'Nothin' old man. Now you gotta give *me* some blood,' with that Graham took the man's arm and squeezed hard, reactivating the puncture. A bright red thread squirted up and then down his arm. Graham paid no attention to the whimpering captive and pulled a handkerchief from his pocket to sponge up a silver-dollar sized sample.

He carefully folded the handkerchief in on itself and returned it to his pocket. 'Go back to sleep,' Graham ordered, as he walked away.

33

Connors was just finishing a TV dinner watching the evening news when the phone rang. 'Hey kid, Graham here. Better get those folks with the reward money on the line. I'll be collecting come daylight.'

'What in the world are you talking about? You haven't been in Sacramento but three days.'

'Don't take this man long. There'll be a rape tonight, and I'm going to be waiting for the bastard when he takes his sorry dick out the door.'

'What makes you so sure?'

'I got the riddle solved. Followed your guy Brock to Berkeley. He goes to Aquatic Park, finds a wino, uses a syringe and draws blood from the guy's arm. Damn near brilliant. Yes sir, no run-of-the-mill rapist, this one. He'll be hitting tonight, wanting to use this fresh liquid as soon as possible.'

'What?' Connors demanded. 'You're saying he uses another man's blood to contaminate the crime scene? Well, it does make sense and sure complicates any investigation.'

'You heard me right. I'm coming by your place to drop off the golden sample. Get it to Allen ASAP.' His instructions were crisp and full of confidence. 'I'll bet the full reward money it matches the samples found at the scene of the next rape.'

'Hold on . . . hold on. It sounds like you're planning to let the rape happen before you grab Brock. We can't do it that way. We can't knowingly let a woman be raped. Let's get some help and stop him as he's going in.'

'No, no, no way. Get too many people involved and I don't get my forty grand. No, I'll nail him myself. Nice and clean,' Graham was firm.

'But, what about the woman? You can't allow a woman to be raped. Did you forget he just killed two people? What makes you think he won't kill tonight?'

'He killed because the guy fought. Chances are nobody'll get hurt. Don't play Pollyanna with me, kid. Sometimes sacrifices have to be made if we're gonna get a good case against Brock. In the long run it'll save other women,' Graham replied.

Unconvinced, Connors countered, 'Frank, we have to rethink this . . . . '

Connors stood staring at the receiver, realizing that Graham had ended the conversation without fully considering the dangers imagined by Connors.

Connors placed a call to Allen, but there was no answer at her house. He called the Sheriff's Department and asked the dispatcher to have Allen call him, leaving their agreed upon code name of Brian Foster. The name signaled to Allen he was at home and needed her to get in touch as soon as possible.

Within five minutes she called back, 'What you got?'

Connors could tell from her tone that she was probably with Weaver and unable to talk.

'Can't give you all the details, but Graham has found out the reason for the many blood types and believes there'll be a rape tonight. I'll fill you in later. Graham's on his way here. He plans to follow Brock, allow a rape to take place, and then take Brock into custody. We can't let that happen!'

'Okay, thanks for the update,' she ended the call abruptly.

Connors sat nervously, waiting for Allen to reconnect.

Ten minutes later, the phone rang and Allen blurted, 'Graham can't do that. He can't let a woman be raped and possibly killed. What's he thinking?'

'He's got thousands of reasons in his head and they all look like dollar signs. I'll try to talk sense to him when he gets here. Call me when you're free, so we can figure something out.'

'I'll be finished around ten and come by your place then.'

Connors sat alone, a heavy sense of concern. Unfortunately, he knew there would be no other way with Graham. 'What in the hell have I gotten myself into?' he asked himself, staring out the window at the city lights. His thoughts swiftly retreated to another early spring evening years before. The memory of his young niece, Annie, still brought so much pain, especially as he thought of the months of devastation his family endured after her brutal murder. The thought of another family experiencing such a loss was staggering.

He sat quietly for several minutes before he realized what Allen had said. 'She's coming here tonight,' he jumped up and began tidying his apartment. Two armloads of newspapers to the trash and a quick rinse of the dishes spruced up the small space. He changed into a fresh shirt, took a minute to gargle and turned on the TV to national news.

Five minutes into the program, a new reality hit. There was no one but himself to protect the next victim. There were no choices. He needed to talk with his mentor. Suddenly, he wasn't going to be just checking around the edges; he was headed directly into the fray. He reached for his phone. Blomberg answered on the third ring.

'Are you sure Graham intends to let the woman be raped. That's crazy,' Blomberg said.

Connors replied, 'He seems set on it.'

'Why do you feel you have to get involved? This isn't what I had in mind when I asked you to investigate Brock. Do you realize you'll be directly between two very violent men? Men who have killed and are capable of killing?' the professor asked, his voice heavy with concern.

Connors hesitated, 'Sir, can I share something with you, something that's been eating at me for years.'

'You know you can.'

'I'm . . . afraid I wasn't completely candid with you when I told you about my niece being raped and murdered.'

'I sensed something more . . . ,' Blomberg responded.

Connors felt himself swallowing hard, 'I've . . . I've never told anyone this.'

'Maybe it's time?'

'It was partly my fault,' Connors said softly.

'Your fault?'

'I was supposed to be watching her. It was spring break and I was babysitting while my sister and her husband were away for the day. I was fourteen.' The

219

words were now coming in a rush. 'Two friends came over and we were in the back yard playing basketball. Annie was with us, but she went inside and then apparently decided to play in the front yard. That's where she was snatched. It was my fault. I should have made sure . . . .'

'Hold it,' Blomberg interjected. 'You can't carry the guilt. Little girls have a right to play in their front yard. The only one at fault was the pedophile who kidnapped and killed her.'

Connors sat slumped in his chair. 'That's what the family said, but I knew in my heart she would be alive if I had been more attentive. You asked, should I get directly involved? I need to. Maybe, just maybe, I can save a life . . . and maybe I just need to do this for myself.'

'And erase some guilt?'

'Perhaps.'

'Is that why your engagement failed?'

'Actually, it was my second failed engagement. I haven't been able to trust myself in a committed relationship where someone I love counts on me.'

'I understand. Now it makes sense,' Blomberg paused, weighing the information from Connors. 'I don't necessarily agree, but I see where you're coming from. But, you can't go into this unarmed. I don't suppose you have a weapon?'

'No.'

'Do you even know how to shoot a pistol?'

'Yes, my dad taught me at a young age.'

'I'm on my way over. I'll drop off my service revolver. It's a .38 special, four inch, Smith & Wesson.

It's old but it served me well for twenty years. Are you familiar with a Smith?'

'Yeah, my dad's favorite revolver.'

'This turn of events worries me. However, I can't let you go into this unarmed. Just be very, very careful,' the senior professor sighed as he hung up the phone.

34

Connors had only a few minutes to get a feel for the revolver before a knock on the door interrupted.

It was Graham. The PI knocked once, opened the door and tossed a baggie containing a blood-soaked handkerchief at Connors who had just shoved the revolver under a pillow on the couch. 'Put that in your refrig with your un-edibles, kid.'

Surprised, Connors barely caught the small bag before it hit the floor. In the past two hours he had fielded three intense phone conversations, met briefly with his senior professor, received a gun, and now another visit from the burly, brusque Frank Graham.

'How in the world did you get this?' he exclaimed, holding the bag up against a light to study its contents.

'Don't ask. You really don't want to know, but it's the real thing. I'll give you a complete, signed statement verifying the time, date and place of collection sometime tomorrow. Only thing, would be wise if you put a lock on the old refrig, chain of evidence and all that bullshit.'

Connors carefully placed the bag into the crisper section of his refrigerator. 'I'll have to figure a way to secure the evidence. Can you take time for coffee? We need to talk strategy.'

'Cup of coffee would really hit the spot. Been a long day and will probably be an even longer night,' Graham responded, his voice filled with anticipation. Then his tone changed to dead serious. He chose his words carefully, 'There's only one strategy. I bring this bastard in myself. There's no doubt this Brock is good, and if we get a bunch of uniforms around, he'll flare like a gut shot tiger. You try to arrest him before he enters and you may wind up with a not guilty verdict from twelve stupid jerks. No, the only way is my way.'

'Exactly what is your way?' Connors asked as he poured the coffee and directed Graham toward a large leather chair.

'As I said, it's the only way,' Graham repeated, taking a swallow. 'I follow him to the house, he goes in a back door or window and I wait several minutes. Remember, if he follows his usual pattern, he goes in naked as a jaybird. I disable his van and pick up his clothes. Then I enter the same route he takes. Everything breaks right, by that time old Brock is doing his thing with the lady, I break up the tryst. He tries to duke it out or whatever, but I got a light in his eyes and I got the drop on him. If he's smart he'll give up. If not he'll be dead. And, either way I get the money all to myself and the world has one less rapist.'

'That easy?' Connors sounded doubtful.

'Even if he runs, he'll be naked. And it should be pretty easy to spot a naked man running around a neighborhood.'

'Sounds good in theory but there are many things that could go wrong. It seems to me you're putting an innocent woman into a very dangerous position. Also, isn't there a problem of legality? You're no longer a police officer.'

'Boy kid, you really are green. Take this to your class. A citizen can make an arrest for a felony committed in his presence same as a policeman. Since this here felony is going to be committed in my presence, I can legally arrest the bastard.'

'Okay, you got me on that point, but isn't there a good chance he'll park his van and then disappear? How are you going to be sure which house he actually enters?'

'Could happen I suppose, but he still has to come back to his van and I'll nail him there.'

'What about the woman? What if she's already been raped and possibly killed?'

Graham studied the young professor, 'Yeah, it's a risk we run.'

'We? I think it's more like a risk the woman runs and I don't think we have the right to make that decision for her,' Connors argued, shocked by Graham's callousness.

'Look, I told you coming in I had to do it my way. This is my way. You want Brock busted, I can do it. How many more people will die if I don't stop him? This city keeps counting on old Weaver and that's trouble. Keep riding that horse and a whole bunch of women will be raped.'

He stopped and stood to leave. 'Thanks for the coffee. I got work to do. Be sitting on Brock's house all night. Call ya later.'

Allen called at 9:55 p.m. and was sitting in Connors' living room by 10:25. She'd kissed him warmly when she first entered, then stepped back. 'No more of that tonight. We've got work to do.'

Connors nodded. More and more he realized how much seeing Allen infused him with energy. 'You're right of course, but you have a way of distracting men, especially this man.'

'Forget about distractions and think about the task ahead.' She walked toward his dining table.

Allen's ready sense of directive leadership and her crisp professionalism were characteristics Connors respected, and he responded like a courteous student, 'Yes ma'am.'

She countered with a brief smile and sat down, 'Graham's strategy is exactly why I had reservations about getting him involved. He operated the same way when he was with the department. Somehow he always seemed to pull it off, until the pistol-whipping incident.' The detective leaned back in the chair, closed her eyes and sighed deeply. 'But, the life of a woman is at stake. What do we do?'

'Tell Weaver or go it alone?' Connors half suggested.

'No, I'm afraid the whole thing might blow up in our face if we call in Weaver. I hate to admit it, but remember my department won't even consider Brock. Sheriff Brandt gave me a clear message that Weaver is following orders.'

'What if you explained to him how Brock is able to contaminate crime scenes with other man's blood. Would that sway him?' Connors asked.

'Just how did Graham figure that out? And will it hold up in court?' Allen asked.

'I don't know all the details. Graham just said Brock collects blood from bums. He brought me a bloody handkerchief.'

'A bloody handkerchief? It's too bizarre. Weaver would never buy it. Where's the handkerchief now?'

'My refrigerator. I'll give it to you when you leave. Graham's sure it will match blood found on the next rape victim. He's probably right.'

'Or, homicide victim,' Allen interjected. 'The blood on the handkerchief is of no value unless there is a new rape and your sample matches the blood type found on the victim. Even then, we may have a serious problem with chain of evidence.'

'So Graham is right, we do need a new victim. God this is complex. I just can't get past the risk for whoever is next,' Connors responded.

'Yeah, I'm with you on that. The best scenario is to stop Brock before he rapes and ideally catch him with the blood in his possession. Again, as far as Weaver is concerned, he's not well physically and burned out emotionally and definitely compromised. He's of little value, and I no longer trust him,' she summarized.

Connors replied, 'The only thing I can think to do is for me to track Graham. Once he follows Brock into a house, I go to a phone and call your dispatch. How long will it take to get deputies to the scene?'

'That's not what concerns me. The time it takes you to find a phone could be a problem.'

'Is there any way to alert patrol deputies in the area beforehand?' he asked.

'Too risky. Maybe I should pick up a two-way radio from the station and go with you and . . .'

'No Susan, I can't let you do that. This is something I have to do myself. However, the radio would be a great idea. Can you check one out?' Connors' tone was firm.

Allen studied Connors and decided against arguing the point. 'Since we don't know for sure Brock will hit tonight and you sound so definite, I'll pass, but you be careful. And, yes I will get the two way and meet you somewhere on Folsom Boulevard.'

'Good plan.'

'Wait, you don't even have a gun. You can't go unarmed.' Allen sounded concerned.

'But I do. Blomberg loaned me a revolver.'

'Okay then, and since you'll have the two way to communicate, I'll alert the graveyard sergeant. In fact, I'll also memo Lieutenant Jenson. He's the officer in charge tonight for graveyard. Might help some,' Allen sounded fatigued.

The two sat in silence for a few moments as Connors' small cuckoo clock sounded eleven times.

He was about to change the subject and tell Susan a light story about the clock when Allen blurted, 'Wait . . . do you know how to use a gun?'

'Learned as a boy,' Scott smiled. 'I've never shared much of my past with you, but I was raised in the country and my father was a hunting fanatic. He started teaching me how to shoot handguns, rifles and shotguns when I was ten years old. It's been several years since I fired a revolver, but at one time I was considered an excellent shot. Not bragging, but I could hit a running rabbit at twenty yards with a handgun. We even loaded our own ammunition.'

Allen sat forward in her chair. 'Wow, this is a side of Scott Connors I hadn't imagined. You come across as a bit of a city slicker, always dressing so well, those impeccable manners. But, you were raised on a farm?' She shook her head, both amused and surprised.

'Not exactly a farm. It was a Colorado cattle ranch. My dad made his living raising blue ribbon bulls. As a result, I can saddle up, work the range and shoot pistols and rifles. As to how I dress, I guess I have to cite my mother. She was an interior designer from Chicago until she married my dad. Always insisted I be properly socialized, boarding school and all that goes with it.'

'Aren't you the versatile one? Riding horses won't help us on this, but since you can shoot, I'm feeling a little better.'

'Don't worry I'm not the hero type. I'll radio if there's any trouble,' Connors assured her, 'I'm thinking, most of his rapes have been in Rancho. Brock must drive to the east area down Folsom Blvd. I'll find a place along there and watch. I should be able to spot Graham's car.'

'Good idea. I would suggest the parking lot of Lloyd's furniture at 75th and Folsom. It's a big lot, and if you park next to the key-making shack, no one will notice you. I will meet you there at eleven forty five and give you the radio.'

'Thanks. 'Now, I'll get that bloody handkerchief and walk you to your car.'

As they approached her car, Susan turned to face him and reached for his hands, lifting them up and resting them over her heart. 'Be careful. Promise me you'll be very careful Scott. I'd never forgive myself if you were hurt.'

Then, with one quick kiss, she was gone.

228

35

Thirty minutes past midnight Connors parked with a clear view of the intersection at 75th and Folsom. Blomberg's gun, the two-way, and a full thermos of coffee lay next to him on the front seat.

Traffic was light, with a small flurry of cars around 2:00 a.m., but no sign of Graham's BMW or Brock's white Ford van. Fighting sleep, he used the time to review his days in Sacramento. Blomberg, Moran, Baker, Weaver, Graham, Brock, and most of all, Susan ticked through his mind.

'So much has changed,' he said aloud. He wondered about his plans at the end of the semester. Last December, when he and Laurie had called off their engagement, it had been with the understanding that during Scott's guest teaching in Sacramento, the two would re-think their relationship. They planned to meet again in June and perhaps try again.

Tonight Connors realized he could never be happy with Laurie. Despite two years of what had felt like a growing and fulfilling relationship, the couple had experienced too much vitriol together. And Susan? More and more he found himself thinking of her, craving her infectious laugh, wanting to be with her, anywhere, for any reason.

The young professor was still contemplating his life as the early morning sky began to fill with light and color. He glanced at his watch and was surprised to read 5:40 a.m. Got to call Susan,' he thought. Instead of using the radio, Connors found a phone booth adjacent to the parking lot and was surprised to find her line busy. On his second attempt, she answered on the first ring. "Susan, there's been nothing here. No sign of Graham.'

'Can't talk, dispatch just called to report a woman and her daughter murdered in Rancho. Sounds like it could be the EAR. You didn't see Graham's car or Brock's van?'

'Neither. Graham said last night he was going to sit on Brock's house. He's probably still there. I'll see if I can find him. Call me when you get a chance.'

'Scott, do you realize what a disaster this would have been if Graham had been following Brock. Because, if it was Brock, Graham would have allowed the murders to happen. Not a pretty picture.'

'Right, but maybe we're wrong about Brock,' Connor sighed.

'Double damn,' Connors mumbled to himself, as he drove towards Brock's house. Sure enough, he found Graham, sitting in his blue BMW, three blocks from the suspect's house. Connors touched his horn and waved for Graham to follow. He drove to an empty school parking lot and talked between cars. 'What's up kid?' Graham asked.

'A woman and her daughter were murdered last night. Allen says it sounds like the EAR. How could you not see Brock leaving in his van?'

'No way! I had a visual, plus the van's bugged,' the PI emphatically justified his tactics. 'If Brock pulled those homicides, he didn't drive the van.'

Connors shook his head in disbelief. 'I need to go. I have a class to teach this morning. Can you meet me at noon in Blomberg's office at City College? We're missing something in Brock's agenda or were wrong about Brock. Maybe the professor can help us figure it out.'

Scott paused, then continued, 'Weaver claimed he eliminated Brock by finding the van cold on the morning of a rape. That and the blood type mystery makes Weaver's position understandable.'

'No, I still think it's Brock. And, I'm not sure Blomberg will be any more help than Weaver; but if you wanna talk, I'll be there. This Brock is even smarter than we thought,' the PI concluded.

###

As Weaver and Allen pulled up in front of a small bungalow on Cedar Ave., they found three patrol cars parked shoulder-to-shoulder in front of the house, blocking the street. They watched as a group of children walked by, around the yellow crime-scene tape, heading to the corner bus stop.

Allen glanced at the time: 7:25 a.m. She couldn't help but think how innocent these kids looked. 'I wonder if the girl victim was normally part of that group.'

Weaver's thoughts were elsewhere. 'Will you look at that, Allen? It's the God dammed EAR again. There's an empty lot just south of the house.' Then, as an afterthought, he continued, 'The bastard comes and goes like a phantom.'

'Don't jump to conclusions. Let's talk to Garcia. He was the first deputy on the scene,' Allen admonished. 'Remember objectivity.'

'This bastard is turning objectivity on its fuckin' head,' Weaver growled. 'Where's Garcia,' he said loudly as they approached the front door. Garcia, a 30-year-old deputy, stepped out to meet them only to be greeted by Weaver's blast of frustration, 'I hope the hell you've kept everybody out and away from the bodies.'

Garcia nodded, 'Relax Bud, in case you haven't noticed, I'm getting lots of experience protecting crime scenes lately. Volk is on the patio making sure no one goes into the back yard or comes close to the side fence where we think the killer entered the yard. Collins is just inside the front door positioned to prevent any reporters or brass from getting anywhere near the actual crime scenes. There is a young girl's body in the back bedroom and a woman's body in the master bedroom. Any questions?'

Allen stepped in, ahead of Weaver. 'Good work. Just give us a quick overview and then get on the neighborhood check.' Allen liked Garcia and knew Weaver wouldn't contribute anything helpful as he treated uniforms like pieces of furniture, so she continued. 'We've been impressed with your reports. They've been accurate and complete. So what've we got?'

'You the first officer on the scene?' Weaver interrupted, still irritated.

'Yes, at exactly 6:17 a.m. Volk and Collins arrived at 6:21. I'm the only one who has viewed the bodies. Volk found the dog.'

'Dog?' Allen asked.

'Yeah, there's a dead German Shepherd in the back yard. Apparently, it was the dog's yelps that alerted the neighbor, Arnold Melton, a captain at Mather Air Force base. Says he first heard noise when he stepped out to get his paper. He looked over the fence and saw the dog bleeding badly.'

'How'd he enter the house?' Weaver asked.

'No one answered the front door, so he kicked it in and found the woman's body.'

Weaver's impatience was growing. 'Allen, you take his statement. I'm going to get a look at what we got.'

Allen turned to Garcia, 'Give me an overview.'

'Entry was through an unlocked rear window. Evidence of a struggle near the fence in the back yard between the intruder and the dog. Woman's body on the bed in master bedroom. Lots of blood.'

Allen instructed, 'Make sure the coroner checks the dog's teeth for fibers or blood. Keep talking while we check out the side yard.'

The deputy continued. 'Melton's wife made the call. He was waiting at the front door when I arrived. He said he saw a bloody footprint and ran home to alert his wife. Story seems pretty straight. I talked briefly with the wife, and Melton's had no blood on him.'

Allen kneeled to examine the ground next to the fence and said, 'See these footprints? We'll have the lab guys make some casts. What kind of shoes did Melton have on?'

'Tennis shoes. I didn't pay attention to the kind,' Garcia replied.

'Get them from him and check his closet for any other tennis shoes. If he's not involved, he'll have no reason not to cooperate. While you're in the house, check the sinks for traces of blood. Get a statement from both Melton and his wife. Keep them separated so we can make sure their stories jibe.'

233

Allen was glad to have this facet of the investigation all to herself without Weaver's annoying interruptions. She continued, 'For the neighborhood check, get Collins and Volk to help you. Tell them to move fast before people have time to leave for work. We need statements as soon as possible. Let me know if any of the neighbors knew the victims or Melton well. We'll have some other detectives down here soon, but anything your guys get quickly will be a big help.'

Garcia hurried off to retrieve the other officers while Allen returned to the front yard, where she noticed a small garden sign in the front shrubbery:

WELCOME.
There's No Place like Home.

36

Allen and Weaver sat in Captain Phillips' office. Phillips leaned toward them, tension oozing from his voice, 'What in the hell is going on? Twenty seven rapes and now four homicides and you're telling me you don't have anything. How the hell can this be?'

Weaver squirmed. 'Nothin' but God damned dead ends,' he offered.

'Not good enough. Not by a long shot. The media is killing us.'

'We got more now with the homicides than we had with the rapes. We know he's using either a Smith or a Ruger, three fifty seven magnum and we got more on the bullets he's using,' Weaver continued, hoping any details might calm Phillips.

'Great! That narrows the field significantly somewhere between two, three million of those models in circulation.' The Captain used cynicism deftly. 'The bottom line is you've still got nothing.' Phillips stood, walked to the window and muttered, 'Shit.'

Neither Allen nor Weaver had ever seen the captain so upset. 'Hell, we've got NBC, ABC and more calling us every day. This case is making us look like keystone cops. I go to neighborhood meetings and the citizens are hot.'

It was Allen who decided to bring the tone down. 'Look, it doesn't do us any good to accuse and argue. We have a serious problem. This guy may be . . . must be, crazy. Crazy with a plan. He's yet to show us any flaws and we've not found his weakness. We need to come up with a strategy that works.'

Phillips nodded, 'You certainly are right about that. I just left a meeting with Brandt and the old man is about to explode. He loves the media, but not when the story reflects badly on him. Need I remind you that he is the boss? We have to do better.'

'Let's review it then,' Weaver jumped in, glancing at Allen. 'What's different about this last case?' He could feel his chest tightening.

Allen took up the challenge. 'In the previous double homicide the killer used a revolver and shot the victims. In this case he killed both the mother and her daughter with a knife. There's no indication the victims fought. Obviously, the killer intended to kill them, since there's no evidence they resisted in any way. He's escalated from rape to homicide.'

She focused on Phillips before continuing. 'Also, while there have been reports he was torturing his victims, this case marks the first time he has taken it to such an extreme degree. Without even waiting for the medical reports, I can tell you he sliced these women up before killing them. And why did he stab the teenage girl so many times? This progression of violence tells me the killer is doing exactly what the profilers said. He is starting to come unraveled.'

'I agree,' Phillips said, lighting a cigar, leaning back in his chair, directing the exhaled smoke across the desk directly into Weaver's face. 'He's bound to make a mistake soon. Maybe that's our answer. Just tread water and wait for a break.'

Maintaining her poise, Allen shot Phillips a hard glance, 'I disagree with that approach. Basically, that's what we've been doing with no success. Why don't we try putting all the deputies and whatever officers the city will loan us in unmarked cars? We've tried flooding the area with marked cars and they're just too easy to spot.'

'Oh no,' Phillips quickly replied, 'We can't do that. With no obvious patrol cars in the area, the public will feel we're not giving them protection. Every old lady in Rancho will be calling with complaints. The letter writers will go crazy.'

'With all due respect Captain, you're wrong,' Allen paused to give her words impact. Weaver shifted, obviously uncomfortable.

Phillips carefully placed his cigar in his ashtray and leaned forward, 'Excuse me?'

'It's time we stopped worrying about the media and public relations and started putting the priority on protecting the women of this community,' Allen said. 'We might have a chance with unmarked cars. People are just going to have to realize that if they can see patrol cars, so can the rapist. Because all the crimes have taken place between three a.m. and six a.m., the unmarked cars would be needed for four, possibly six hours. Not too many of your old ladies up at that time.'

'But we've never done anything like that before, and it would mean lots of liability. The old man would never go for it,' Phillips shook his head. 'Let's wait for the crime lab reports. Maybe there will be something there. Meet here tomorrow at four p.m. and we'll all go over the lab results.'

Neither Allen nor Weaver spoke as they left Phillips' office. Weaver had begun to feel stronger angina and was thinking only of finding some aspirin, while Allen nursed her anger over Phillips' thick-headed theories.

She couldn't believe the self-serving rationale preached by the captain. Further, she couldn't be sure of his motives. Whether it was stupidity or dereliction of duty, the women of the city were obviously of secondary importance to him.

They had almost reached the squad room when Weaver heard someone call his name. It was Sergeant Howell. 'I need to talk to you,' he said to Weaver.

Allen nodded and walked on, giving the appearance of not paying attention, but she wondered what Howell wanted with Weaver that he didn't want her to hear?

Howell motioned Weaver into his small, internal affairs office and promptly shut the door. 'Bud, this has gone far enough. We want the guy taken out now. We no longer give a shit how it looks.'

'Not gonna be easy,' the weary detective responded.

'Just get it done. The old man will cover you on the investigation. Time is of the essence. Got it? But, I warn you, Brandt's getting ready to bring Stringer in.' Howell's tone was firm and flat.

'Never shoulda got to this point,' Weaver declared as he turned to leave.

37

Connors was relieved and surprised when Graham walked into Blomberg's office at 12:08, his prediction of Graham being a no show proven wrong.

The professor remembered Graham from a class several years ago and greeted him warmly, 'Good to see you Frank. Hear you're knocking 'em dead in San Francisco.'

'Managing to survive. You look pretty fit yourself. You don't seem to change much. What's your secret?' Graham's question sounded genuine.

'A good wife,' the professor responded, glancing at Connors.

After several more minutes of small talk, Connors redirected the conversation to the purpose of the meeting, 'I just explained to the professor that you have solved the mystery of multiple blood types left at the rape scenes. I gave your sample to Allen last night and if there's a match, is this enough to justify an arrest of Brock?'

Blomberg answered, 'Arrest maybe, but a conviction, I don't think so. What's your read, Frank?'

'Knowing how picky the courts are, if nothin' else showed up at Brock's house, I'll put my money on the bastard walkin' back into daylight,' Graham answered. 'Brock keeps nothin' around his house. And I've searched his van and it was clean. So it would be next to impossible to get a conviction. I gotta find out how he's getting to and from the crime scenes. He's definitely not using his Ford van. That's for damn sure.'

'Dare I ask how you know he keeps nothing at his house?' Connors asked, studying Graham closely.

'Trust me. His house is clean. Only thing strange is the number of candles and crosses. The house looks like a damned shrine. He's lucky it hasn't burned down. Strange thing . . . the bastard has twenty-two pairs of tennis shoes and army boots, all lined up neatly in his closet. There are three different sizes. Even the five new pair are different sizes.'

'Has anyone thought to run a DMV check to see if he has any other car registered in his name or in his wife's name?' Blomberg interjected.

'Damn,' Graham slapped his leg, 'Talk about overlooking the obvious.'

'Any reference to Brock owning another car besides the van in any of the police reports?' Blomberg asked, turning to Connors.

'None that I recall. His wife had her own car and he probably has access to that now, but whether he could have used it for the rapes, I just don't know.'

'Let me give a call to one of my students who works in the records department at city P.D. He can run Brock's name and check right now,' the professor said, reaching for the phone.

Connors and Graham talked for a few minutes until Blomberg interrupted, holding his hand over the telephone mouth piece, 'Bingo. A 1968 VW sedan is registered to a Janet Brock on 61st St.' The professor finished on the phone before continuing, 'Gentlemen, my guess is our Mr. Brock keeps the VW parked somewhere near his home. A second car allows him access to the crime scenes without using the van everyone thinks is his only car.

'You would be exactly right professor, I take back every bad thing I ever said about you teachers,' Graham said, shaking his head and turning to Connors, 'Kid, you awake enough? Let's go comb the area around his house and find this second vehicle. We find it, and the next time this son-of-a-bitch drives out at one or two in the morning, I'll be on his ass.'

Connors followed Graham's BMW to a service station on Folsom Blvd. where they pulled out a city map to study. They divided the area around Brock's house into grids, Graham taking the northern half and Connors the south. An hour later, Connors met Graham at a parking lot on Folsom near 58th street. He could tell from Graham's body language, as he got out of his car, that the search had been futile.

'Find anything?' Graham demanded.

'Nothing.' Connors replied.

Graham shook his head, 'Bastard has to keep it somewhere. He's got no time to walk more than a mile.'

'Could he use a bicycle?' Connors asked.

'Yeah, that's a possibility. The bike would have to be in his back yard or somewhere close. I'll check out the area on foot tonight, but right now I gotta go, I'm getting a beep. Brock's on the move. Call you later.'

Connors spent the early and late evening catching up on course paperwork. He prided himself on bringing current issues to class along with the standard curriculum, and he felt his students should write, and write often, about criminal justice issues. His teaching standards were high for both himself and his students and recently he'd felt himself slipping behind and feeling frustrated. 'I need a secretary', he thought as he shuffled through a stack of short essays about the death penalty.

The past several days had brought increased stress to the young professor; and, he realized the most desirable thing he could wish for was a solid night of uninterrupted sleep. Such hopes were destroyed by the telephone. 'Who could be calling at this hour?' he sighed, reaching his left hand back over his shoulder to the kitchen wall phone, 'Hello.'

'Glad to hear you're up kid, Graham here, got some paper and a pen handy? You, need these addresses.'

'Addresses?'

'Look, just take these down. I'll explain what you gotta do.'

'All right, I'm ready. Go ahead,' Connors directed, turning over an envelope for open writing space.

'11375 Carter Drive, 23765 Salishan Court, and 67786 Baker Place, all out east of town. These are three houses Brock prowled today. We need to know which one is the crib of the broad most likely to tickle his fancy.'

'You mean you followed him and watched him go into these houses? Didn't he see you?' The disbelief in Connors' voice obvious.

'Look kid, I'm good. I was on him tighter than a tick on a dog. He hasn't a clue.'

242

'I'm sorry, but this is getting dangerous. You've got to promise me you'll get help before you actually confront Brock. This is. . . . '

'Stop worryin'. Things are under control. Also, I found the bike. He hides it in an empty lot, barely two blocks from his house. Got it chained behind an old Dempsey dumpster. I'll find his VW. Just give me another day or so. First thing tomorrow morning, you gotta knock on doors and give me your read on which of those houses will be his number one target. Do it early, before these women go to work.'

'Ok, we'll do it your way,' Connors sighed, unsure of his assignment and not totally convinced Graham had the situation under control.

Connors set his alarm for five a.m., but found it difficult to sleep. A chilling dread was creeping into his spirit. Too much was happening too fast and he felt overwhelmed, even to the point of wishing he were back in Phoenix. Sacramento wasn't the sleepy little river town he'd been told to expect.

The city, with its unsolved rape series and now killings, was fast becoming a scary place to live. The young teacher realized he was right in the middle of the action and wondered how his involvement had escalated to this level. Graham might think things were under control, Connors was not at all sure.

He waited until 5:15 a.m. and then called Susan. She answered on the tenth ring with a sleepy, 'Hello.'

'Susan, sorry to call so early.'

'Scott, what time is it? For heaven's sake, its dark outside. What's going on?'

'I couldn't sleep. Graham called last night. He followed Brock yesterday afternoon and watched him

243

prowl three houses. I'm heading to Rancho now, I've got to contact three potential victims before they go to work. They won't know me. I need to have them call you, and wanted to make sure you would be at the department when they call.'

Allen was now wide-awake, 'Okay. Use my business cards I gave you and ask them to call between seven and eight. I'll make sure I'm at work by seven. I've got lots to do in the field, but I won't leave the office until after eight.'

'Graham feels Brock will hit tonight. I have to warn these women.'

'Absolutely. I heard from the lab late yesterday. It's only a preliminary report, but it indicates all the blood found on the latest two victims is their own. That could change when we get the actual report. But, it looks like Brock didn't use his syringe full of blood. Which means he has to hit again soon or the blood will be too old to use effectively.' She paused, 'This blood Brock's collected has me stymied. If Brock means to use it, why not on this last attack?'

'I don't get it either. Is he even smarter than we imagined?' Connors questioned. 'Graham, on the other hand, may be more difficult to reign in than you predicted.'

'What do you suggest?' Susan asked.

'We've got to establish a plan. He's got to let us help. He can't confront Brock alone.'

'I agree, but Graham is Graham. When you talk to him today, ask him to be at your place tonight between eight and nine. I'll meet you there and maybe the two of us can talk some sense into him.'

'Got it.'

244

The morning light was just beginning to fill the horizon when they ended the call. Connors had a difficult time focusing on the task at hand. Thoughts of Susan snug in bed threatened to dominate his mind. 'Stay on task,' he admonished himself aloud. 'This may be your chance to save a woman's life.' The admonishment was exactly what he needed to spur himself out the door.

38

The house at 11375 Carter Drive was not difficult to find. Connors arrived at 6:30 a.m. and waited for signs of life inside the house. Within five minutes both an upstairs and a downstairs light flicked on. 'Good, they're up.' He decided to wait a few minutes before knocking. Just as he approached the front door, it opened and a tall man, wearing a robe, stepped out in search of the morning paper.

Connors spoke first, 'Good morning, sir. Sorry to bother you so early. My name is Scott Connors, and I'm working on the East Area Rape investigation, Detective Allen, with the Sheriff's Department, can verify.'

Connors extended his hand with Susan's business card. 'We have reason to believe a rape suspect prowled your house yesterday,' Connors spoke rapidly, perhaps too quickly he thought.

The man cast a wary look on Connors. 'What? Is this some sort of a prank? Prowled . . . what are you talking about?'

'Sir, this is unusual, I know. But, I'm telling you a rape suspect was seen yesterday entering your house when both you and your wife were away. This is very serious.'

'What the hell do you want me to do? Who are you?'

Connors instantly felt awkward and unsure of his approach. Although time was of the essence, he himself couldn't imagine a stranger approaching his door so early in the morning like this. He pressed on, 'I just need your wife to call Detective Allen at the Sheriff's Department. It's important that your wife talks with her between 7 and 8 this morning.'

'This better be on the up and up. How come you're not in uniform?'

'I'm a volunteer and I'm just here to warn you. There are several other women who also are in danger. You need to understand the urgency. Allen will be at the department by seven, waiting for your wife's call. I can't stress how serious this is. She must call Allen before eight a.m.'

'Okay, but this is hard to believe.'

Connors thanked him, turned and walked to his car. The man was still standing in the doorway as Connors drove away.

His reception on Salishan Court went better. A young lady, dressed professionally, was approaching her car when Connors pulled up in front of the house. The woman seemed very trusting. She assured Connors she would call Allen. Connors noted her short red hair. 'Would Brock be attracted to red hair?' he wondered as he drove toward the next address on his list.

Baker Place was more difficult to find, a tiny court off a small street, and it was almost 7:15 a.m. when Connors found the brick house with an empty lot on the east side of the residence. A tall, young woman with short ash brown hair answered the door. She was clearly disturbed by the knowledge that someone had prowled her house, especially a rape suspect. 'Oh, my God. This is horrible. I'm getting out of here and going to my parents' house after work.

247

What's happening to this city? Why can't the police catch this man? I can't believe this,' a tone of panic peppered her voice.

Connors spoke quickly, reassuringly, 'Please, try not to worry. You'll be safe with your parents, but you must call Detective Allen as soon as possible.'

Connors felt somewhat relieved after talking with two of the women and the husband of the third. However, he was disappointed he had not been able to actually see the woman on Carter drive. Did she match the profile? Neither of the other women fit the description of Brock's victims.

He needed to call Susan at the Sheriff's Department and have her find out if the woman on Carter Drive was a match for Brock. If the woman was slender with long dark hair, she would be his next victim.

The past hour, an hour spent warning unsuspecting women they may be in the path of a killer, left Connors more determined than ever to press on. Brock had to be stopped.

39

Parole officer Darlene Grant flipped through a thick file sent over from the Department of Corrections. The interview with Tyrus Brock was still fresh in her mind and the inconsistencies between his statements and what she was finding in the file were glaring.

He'd said he did well in high school and had no criminal record during his juvenile years, exactly the opposite of what the file revealed. Brock's high school transcript was filled with D's, F's and suspensions.

Further, the file noted his juvenile record was sealed. It was obvious that if there had been no incidents, there would be no need to seal the record.

Surprisingly, she found that the Oregon Department of Social Services had filed to have Brock removed from his home. 'Home deemed unfit,' the report stated. Checking the date against his date of birth, she could see he was eleven years old at the time. She wondered why no explanatory records indicated either a foster home or group home placement. She was left with many questions: Why did they find it unfit? His step-father? His mother? Both? 'Unfit could mean many things,' she muttered.

Grant placed a call to her supervisor, Connie Miller. Within twenty minutes she was sitting in Miller's office. 'You wanted to see me about this parolee?' Miller asked, thumbing through Brock's parole file.

'Yes, I'm extremely concerned. His psychologist, Dr. Bevins, has him journaling and Brock has written some rather disturbing essays about his military experiences, as well as childhood experiences, most notably, an early molestation. Yet, when I talked with Brock, he came across like there had been no problems in his life until he drank too much and forced a woman sexually. He also told me he had done well in high school. I finally received his complete file and he's lying on many counts.'

Grant paused, then continued, 'Interestingly, I was just handed this envelope before I came here. Apparently, Brock dropped this off at the front desk.' She held up a large envelope and took out a lined yellow sheet of paper.

Recognizing Brock's small, cramped writing, she said, 'It's a message from him.'

'Read it,' Miller said, leaning forward in her chair.

Grant began:

'Dear Ms. Grant. Dr. Bevins wants me to write about Nam. I tried, but just can't do it. I followed orders and tried to survive. But I did things I can't tell others. We all did. And when I got back to the States, I got nothing but a few cheap medals and criticism. Even though people sent us there and we did the best we could, they hate us. I had problems when I came back home, and what did they do? Within just a few weeks they sent me to prison. Despite spending time in prison, I'm still a soldier and, no, I don't want to talk about things that happened in Nam. I survived and I'm still surviving, best I can. Always will. No way, folks like you would ever understand me anyway. None of you with your soft and easy life could ever understand. Nor will you forgive much less honor me and other soldiers. Every fellow soldier I fought with was from a poor family

250

and all you rich folks just used us and don't really give a dam about us. Well, my God forgives me and cleanses my soul. So, you folks need to let me be. Tell the doctor I don't need him. I have my God. I hate this country. Soldiers are used to fight your wars and then you neglect them. VA is a joke. You think of me as a dumb kid from the Oregon hills, but I've read Hemingway's A Farewell to Arms. He's right. 'The world breaks every one, and afterward many are strong at the broken places.' That's me. I will show them. You and your precious country will have to learn. If you keep making us into killers there will be a price to pay. T. Brock.'

Miller, an intense woman with a large commanding presence, sat upright in her chair. 'Wow! That's a little strange. Odd you should want to discuss him. I've received several calls regarding Brock from the Sheriff's Department. The first call came in January wanting me to either violate Brock's parole or relocate him away from Sacramento. It was unusual because they offered nothing to support their request. I didn't alert you because it sounded like it was just that blow-hard Sheriff Brandt flashing his badge around. I saw no reason to bias you toward Brock.'

'Did Brandt himself call?'

'Not at first. It was someone named Howell,' she said, flipping through a phone log.

'They called more than once?' Grant asked.

'Actually, four or five times. The last time it was the Sheriff himself. He bullshitted for at least ten minutes, but was never able to give me anything concrete. I told him we were looking closely at Brock. I could sense he was very frustrated, but he seemed angry and just hung up. The whole episode was most unusual.'

Grant shook her head, 'That's strange, I called the Sheriff's Department and tried to tell them I was suspicious of Brock in relation to this violent rape series. I said Brock fits the general description of the rapist and started to say why, but a Detective Weaver interrupted and said Brock had been eliminated, then abruptly hung up.'

'Well, in none of their calls did they claim he was actually in violation. They just gave me the impression they didn't like him. Tell you what, why don't you give Sam, Sam McKinley, a psychiatrist out at Folsom prison, a call. See what he has to say about Brock. Have you talked to Brock's wife?'

'I've tried to, but so far I haven't caught anyone at home. She must work odd shifts. I've called all times of the day and evenings.'

'Depending on what McKinley tells you, let's set up a meeting with Brock and confront him with the contradictions you've found. Bring Dr. Bevins in. Let me know when the meeting is and I'll sit in with you. And, Darlene, give this some priority. Let's find out what's going on here. I don't like the sound of this.'

Grant had no sooner returned to her desk when her inter-com interrupted her thoughts,

'Darlene, there is a Scott Connors here to see you,' her secretary's voice informed her.

Grant replied, 'Sorry, I don't have the time right . . .,' she broke off in mid-sentence, as a dark haired young man walked into her office.

'Hi, I'm Scott Connors, a teacher at City College and I really need to talk with you,' he said.

252

Grant remained seated, 'Generally I appreciate a call for an appointment,' she said dryly, accepting the handshake. Despite his assumptive approach, she couldn't help but note his pleasant manners.

'I realize that. Forgive my abruptness, but I have some pressing questions about one of your parolees.'

'Well, you're here, might as well grab a chair and tell me about it,' Grant said motioning toward a chair. 'Just put those files on the floor.'

'Thanks. My concern is about Tyrus Brock. I'm on a temporary guest-teaching job at the city college and Brock is enrolled in my class. I learned he is a suspect in the local rape case and I've done some checking into his background. I'm beginning to believe he might be the rapist. Is there any information you can share with me about Brock which might have a bearing on my investigation?'

The timing was too coincidental to believe. For the past hour she had been focusing on Brock. His file still lay open on her desk. Now she was talking to a total stranger who also was suspicious of him. Grant tried not to show she was taken aback. 'I'm afraid my work with Mr. Brock is confidential. I can't discuss my parolees with anyone who happens to walk through the door. Do you have any agency credentials?'

'Actually, in addition to teaching, I work as an intern with DOJ.'

'Unpaid?'

'Unfortunately.'

'Then I can only receive information, not give it. If you want information on this man, perhaps you should contact the Sheriff's Department. But why, may I ask, are you interested in Mr. Brock?'

Connors shook his head, obviously disappointed, needing her help but unsure how to convince her. 'I was given his name as a possible suspect and I've talked to people who know him. There are a number of people who believe he may be the rapist and *now* a murderer.'

Grant shook her head, signaling she was still not inclined to cooperate.

Connors continued, 'What if my boss, Jeff Baker, an analyst with the DOJ, called? Could you forward any information on Brock to him?'

She sat for a moment, considering. Her intuition told her this visitor was possibly onto something valuable, yet she was powerless to offer him any privileged information. 'If it's any consolation to you, I, too, have questions about Mr. Brock. Questions but no answers. Have your boss call me Monday. I'm leaving this afternoon for a conference,' she'd stood and escorted Connors to the door.

'Let's hope Monday isn't too late,' Connors said as he left her office.

40

'Take some notes for our meeting with Phillips . . . okay?' Weaver motioned for Allen to sit down in the chair next to his desk. 'The lab report on the Davis homicides just arrived. We gotta make some sense of it.' He flipped hastily through the pages, not bothering to look up.

'Sure,' Allen replied dryly, sitting down and taking the notepad Weaver handed her. 'It's a pleasure to take the role of personal secretary. What would you do without my note-taking skills? Write your own, perhaps?'

'I'm more than frustrated. Cut me some slack, Allen. I feel like hell,' Weaver growled. He began to read the lab report: 'Entry via unlocked side window.' He paused and then offered, 'Here's something new. The screen was found on the ground. He's never done that before.'

Allen nodded, writing her version of shorthand notes. She glanced at her boss. His eyes were puffy and she could tell he hadn't shaved recently. 'Poor man,' she thought, 'old before his time.' More and more she vacillated between feeling irritated with her superior's directives, compassion for his personal dissipation, and upset by the knowledge he was compromised.

'Damn, it is our guy. Says here, nylon cord found at the scene matches nylon cord found at numerous EAR crime scenes. Also, more fuckin' shoestrings. Why can't we find out where'n the' hell he's buying all those shoestrings?' Weaver leaned back and slammed his fist on the desk.

'Calm down Bud. We've got a notice out to every shoe store north of Fresno. But he may have bought them anywhere,' she advised.

'Damn!' Weaver responded to something in the report, his mind moving beyond shoestrings.

Allen continued, 'This is our case alright. What about the blood found on the telephone? Any mention of that?'

Weaver flipped through the pages, 'Yeah, here it is. Blood from victim, 42-year-old female.'

'Can we find out if he actually placed a call?' Allen queried.

'Already have. It's right here,' Weaver reported. 'What the hell is this? I'll be damned. Says here the number called is 772-9377 . . . that's the number for dial-a-prayer.' Weaver looked up and shook his head in disbelief before standing and walking to the window. 'What's this bastard doing? Asking for absolution?'

'He's deliberately trying to taunt us, but he may be getting too cocky. When I was first assigned, weren't you considering the possibility he was a religious nut?' Allen asked.

'Yeah, maybe he just confirmed that for us. Make a note to have one of the detectives contact churches, especially Catholic, and alert them. And find out what outfit runs dial-a-prayer. Maybe he's confessed to someone. Plus, we'll have to review all suspects and victims for religious angles,' Weaver directed.

Allen nodded, realizing now, finally, maybe she could convince Weaver to consider Brock. She remembered Connors had said Brock was preaching in a church on the south side. She felt maybe there was hope with this new information. 'Any evidence of rape?' she continued.

Weaver flipped back several pages, 'Yeah, here it is,' He read directly from the report, 'Both victims show signs of vaginal trauma consistent with forced entry. The little girl was sodomized with an unknown object. Cause of death . . . loss of blood, due to knife wounds. Three wounds on mother and twenty six on the kid.'

'Yeah, I noticed the difference at the scene, but didn't know the number.'

'For some reason he really carved the kid,' Weaver summarized.

'No indication of bullet wounds?'

'No, looks like he just used a knife.' Weaver paused, then continued, 'But, here's something strange. You know all the victims have been skinny broads. That fits the mother, but the little girl, she was big, actually fat.'

'How old?'

'Fourteen.'

Weaver returned again to the lab report, 'Looks pretty routine. All blood to date matches only the two victims, same with hair samples. Nothing. Also fingerprint samples negative. Nothin' under either victim's fingernails,' Weaver paused, 'Be sure to make note of that. It's a major issue with Captain Phillips, I think he saw it in a movie once.'

Allen continued her efficient note taking, half listening to Weaver's ramblings. Her mind was fixated on Brock and the growing trail leading to this mysterious sexual offender with a prison record. She

257

wondered what Connors had unearthed in the past few hours.

'Here's something,' Weaver boomed, seated again and pouring over the report. 'This might be the break we've been lookin' for. They found a trace amount of AB blood on the girl. A rare type. We should be able to eliminate several suspects on this. Call . . .'

'Bud,' she interrupted, 'Earth to Detective Weaver.' she frowned and shook her head.

'What?' he looked up irritated.

'Let me help you review some details. Remember, most of the crime scenes have been tainted with foreign blood, true all common types, but different each time. The fact that we now have AB doesn't lead us anywhere except to the conclusion that this rapist is salting the crime scenes. Don't you see that?' she asked, exasperated.

Weaver slumped back in his chair, his steam gone, 'You're right, we tie these rapes together with the blood type and any attorney worth his salt will tear our case apart. Talk about reasonable doubt, we'd be talkin' total doubt.'

'Bud, what if he is baiting the crime scenes with other men's blood?'

'Another man's what? You're losing it Allen!'

'I'll explain it when I get back from the lab. You will have to handle the meeting with Phillips yourself.' She dropped the note pad down on the desk, 'Here are my notes; hope you can read them,' Allen said as she headed out the door.

Weaver sat with a confusing lab report before him and a whole set of new questions. But one thing he knew for sure, he couldn't lose control of Allen. 'Too much at stake,' he thought, 'It's past time to bring Stringer out of the shadows and put an end to this disaster.' He stood and went looking for Howell.

41

His night began much earlier than usual, but then this was an unusual mission. It was 11:25 p.m. when he walked out the back door of his house carrying only a flashlight. The night was clear and crisp and he drew a deep breath.

An exhilarating sense of anticipation filled his senses. Vaulting over his back yard fence, he moved quietly past his neighbor's house and out into the street. Three blocks later he was walking north on 65th Street. He moved along the sidewalk with long even strides, giving the appearance of being out for an evening stroll.

Pausing once and bending down, he pretended to retrieve something, using the maneuver to check back down the street. Several blocks back a car pulled abruptly against the curb and turned off its lights. He smiled and said to himself, 'good. I've got him hooked.' Reaching a weed covered lot he stepped off the sidewalk and moved quickly to a partially covered Dempsey dumpster. He found his bike and pushed it out to the street. In the bike's rearview mirror he could see the dark car, still parked. He continued north on 65th, alternating his speed from very slow to very fast.

'Come on big guy, just a little further and you're mine,' he thought. When he reached Folsom Blvd. he stopped briefly, then pedaled quickly across the four-lane street and into the parking lot of the old Farley Iron Works, faded and lonely, a symbol of an era gone by, used now only to store earth-moving equipment.

The wood building stretched two blocks, flanked by an old rail spur. Accessing the building was now routine, having been in and out several times in recent days. Tonight's entrance would buy him more freedom; for the big guy there would be no escape.

He dismounted his bike and leaned it against the back of the building, making sure it was in plain view. Once inside, he stopped long enough to secure the door with a rusty bar set into waist high brackets, his whisper fairly humming, 'Come into my lair, said the spider to the fly.'

Then, he turned on his pen light and guided the narrow beam over the ladder, pulley, steel cable and counterweight. Satisfied everything was in place, he turned off the light and began an ascent into the rafters.

Frank Graham was tenacious. He could tell Brock worked hard to avoid being followed. 'He's not doing a very good job,' Graham thought. 'The bastard is slick, but I'm on his ass.' He continued driving slowly down 65th Street, keeping a close eye on the bicyclist several blocks ahead.

When he reached Folsom Blvd., he pulled into the parking lot of a gas station on the southeast corner of 65th. He watched as Brock rode his bicycle into the parking lot of the Farley building. 'What'n the hells goin'on?' he thought. Brock disappeared behind the building. 'Gotta be where he hides the VW,' Graham muttered to himself, settling down to watch.

After almost thirty minutes, he grew restless. No sign of any VW, nor did Brock reappear. 'Got to find out what the bastards up to,' he muttered.

Graham drove across Folsom, past the Farley building and parked on 64th. Exiting the car, the detective began his approach to the back of the building. He moved slowly, deliberately, conscious of each step, diligent to minimize any sound and careful to avoid even the slightest misstep.

Old tires, wire and boards scattered randomly throughout the weeds challenged his progress. He saw the bicycle leaning against the back of the building, found a door and tested it. Locked.

Moving further along the building he spotted an open window. 'There's my entrance,' Graham thought as he looked up to a series of dirty windows. The PI turned and retraced his steps back to an old wood pallet and set it gently against the building. It made an adequate ladder, allowing him to climb high enough to reach the windowsill. He double-checked his shoulder holster, adjusted a flashlight clipped to his belt and then, with relative ease, pulled himself up.

Quietly, very quietly, he thrust his head and shoulders through the open window, balancing on his stomach, doing what he did best – watching, assessing his next move. Graham thought he heard something . . . below . . . above? The rousting of a bat . . . his imagination? In the darkness of the building's cavernous bays, the silent home of giant machines, he looked up to the rafters and witnessed only a lone shaft of moonlight shining through the windows on his left.

As his eyes adjusted to the darkness, he began to search for a safe way to the floor. Again he thought he heard a sound, a very slight sound. Scratching? 'A rat

262

maybe?' His nerves tingled as he waited, straining forward to listen, to hear.

'Ga – gaugh – ca – ca – ca . . .' Graham could hear himself gasping for air. The sudden pressure on his throat, claustrophobic. He clawed, unconscious of the effort, to free the steel cable around his neck. It took only seconds to jettison his body through the window, upwards in a flash, jammed against the ceiling, the cable ever tightening . . . five, ten, fifteen, twenty seconds. And then, nothing.

A dying man's choking gasps, the distinct voice of death echoing in the otherwise silent building, brought back memories of another time. This trap with its masterful clutch was familiar and he smiled, gazing up at the man dangling in the faint light. A nemesis no more. His soldier-trained mind returned to the missions, where he could still hear the gunfire, the mortar rounds pelting his senses.

Then, he disappeared into the night.

42

Card by card. Stack by stack, all in alphabetical order, sorted by last name. Six months of field interrogation cards, each bearing the names and description of a person or persons stopped and questioned by patrol officers between 11: 00 p.m. and 7:00 a.m. on the east side of town.

Allen and Weaver hunched over the conference table, reading and re-reading each one. The pair had already spent two hours looking for matches, anything that might provide a lead. 'Basics, basics, go back to basics,' Allen said to Weaver, reiterating the technique emphasized by her professor at Sac State during a course titled 'Investigative Strategies 330.'

She had been working on her Masters in Police Science one course at a time. This semester, however, she'd wisely put her studies on hold. Allen was a bright student and had no trouble maintaining a high grade point, but she could only squeeze so much out of a day. For the past several weeks, the rape investigation consumed all of her time.

Since her assignment to the case, she hadn't visited her mother, gone to the movies or read a book. The only diversion she'd found time for was to spend a few hours here and there with Scott. The thought of this brought a smile to her face and she realized she missed him.

'Somewhere in this mass of paper, we've overlooked something. The law of averages says he's somewhere in these stacks,' she intoned. It was difficult for her to understand how Brock had never been stopped during his nocturnal crawls. The fact they had no FI card on him seemed unbelievable.

Weaver did not look up and made no attempt to hide his distaste for this type of detail work, 'It's impossible to find anything of value in this pile of crap.' Suddenly, their work was interrupted by a detective who rushed into the room, puffing hard from his sprint up the stairs, eager with news. 'Guess who was found hanging from the rafters in the old Farley building?'

'Hopefully our rapist,' Weaver said, eyes still glued to the cards.

'No such luck. It was Frank Graham.'

'No shit!' Weaver exclaimed, losing all interest in the FI cards. 'What'n the hell was Frank doing in Sacramento?'

Allen sat frozen.

'Don't know. All I heard is it was Frank. They found him hanging with a steel cable around his neck. Nearly took off his head,' the detective described Graham's death- by- hanging.

'Musta' been related to a case he was working on . . . any indication it might have been suicide?' Weaver asked, then proceeded to answer his own question, 'No, Frank was too cocky to ever kill himself.'

'You're right there,' the detective agreed. 'He apparently climbed through a window right into a lasso. Damn thing jammed his head smack against the roof. Pretty ugly. Never seen anything like it in all my years. Hard way to go, that's for sure.'

'Anything at the scene to indicate who was responsible?' Weaver asked, oblivious of Allen's silence. 'Not that I saw. The ID guys were crawling all

265

over the rafters when I left, but I doubt if they'll find anything.'

Weaver stood and began pacing, something he often did when he felt nervous. 'Strange he was in Sacramento. When he left, he told everyone he didn't care if he ever saw this damn river town again.'

While the two veteran cops carried on about Graham's death, Allen sat mute, half listening. A deep feeling of disbelief threatened to send her running from the room, perhaps to the bathroom. Her insides were churning. The voice from within told her she must come forward, pony up. It was now or never, and so she jumped in, 'I know what he was doing here.'

Both men turned to stare at Allen, waiting for her to continue. Weaver broke the silence, 'How do you know that? You been datin' Frank on the sly?'

Allen shot a hard look back, 'Bud, this is no time for your sick humor. I did meet him for dinner, but it was a group affair, certainly not a date. He was in town to work with Scott Connors. Frank was probably following Tyrus Brock, the man you say can't be our rapist.'

Weaver frowned, 'That punk Connors still nosin' around?' He continued, ignoring her reference to the rapist, 'Sounds like Frank. Probably lookin' for the reward. But the EAR? And the Farley building? Hard to put those two pieces together. Ain't no one to rape in that old building.'

The room remained silent.

'Never liked Frank, but he was a god-damned good cop. Didn't deserve to die like that,' Weaver reflected.

266

Allen stood, 'Bud these FI cards can wait. I'm going to call Connors and see what he knows.'

As she left, Weaver yelled after her, 'Just a reminder, don't get yourself involved in anything else and keep that wanna-be professor out of our business.'

Allen ignored him.

'Scott, Susan here,' Allen said, trying to keep her voice calm, 'I'm glad I caught you still at home. Have you heard about Frank?'

'Sure, I talked to him last night. When he left, he said he was going to sit on Brock.'

'Scott, Frank's dead,' she half whispered.

'What?' Connors blurted.

He's dead,' she spoke now in a firm voice. 'He was found this morning hanging from the rafters in an old warehouse.'

'Hanging?'

'Yes, hanging. Did he follow Brock last night?'

'I . . . that's what he said, but I guess he might've been working on something else,' Connors answered, struggling to clear his head.

'I doubt that. No, I have this sick feeling this has everything to do with Brock.' Allen said.

'Why would he confront Brock by himself?'

'That's just who Frank is . . . was. Always playing the tough guy.'

Connors struggled with the news. He felt overwhelmed, but he knew he had to stay focused. 'Did you get a chance to talk with those women? It's imperative we talk with them.'

267

'Yes, all three called. They promised to not return home until they hear back from me.'

Connors returned to Graham and his activities, 'I know Frank's been following Brock since arriving in Sacramento. But why would he be careless and walk into a trap?'

'Scott, you've got to keep in mind Graham considered himself invincible. Apparently, he met his match and lost,' Allen said, trying to steer Connors away from blaming himself. 'We both kept trying to warn him. I don't know what more we could've done.'

'I know you're right, but God, this is horrible. Have you told Weaver?'

'Yes. I told him I'd given Graham's name to you. I also said I knew he was in town to follow Brock.'

'His response?'

'Discounted it entirely. He said there's no obvious connection between Brock, the rapes and the old warehouse. Same old story. Bud isn't going to change, even after what Graham found out. He's obviously under orders.'

'Have you heard back from the lab?' Connors asked.

'Nope. And I don't expect to today, either. The lab guys are snowed under. I probably won't get the results until tomorrow, maybe not until the next day. With Graham dead, the blood he collected will never be admissible in court.'

'By then it may be too late anyway. If Brock was busy killing Frank last night, then tonight is when he'll get back to his real business. So, we have to do something tonight. When do you plan to meet the three women?'

'Early afternoon, they all work near Sunrise Mall; we're meeting at a *Walgreen's* cosmetics counter.'

'See if you can figure which one he's most likely to attack. The two I saw don't fit his victims' profile,' Connors directed.

'I'll do my best. I should have more information by evening . . . we can decide what to do then.' Her voice trailed off as the reality of Brock's brutality took a firmer hold. 'Gotta go Scott. Talk to you later.' She hung up before losing her composure.

Connors sat at his kitchen table, clearly shaken by the news. More unnerving was the awareness that Susan, too, was sensing a new level of terror and evil at their doorstep. 'God,' he muttered, 'what have I done? Frank Graham would be alive if I hadn't brought him into this.' First Annie and now Graham.'

Allen returned to the squad room and found Weaver staring out the window. Turning he said, 'Before we do anything else, I've got to take a look at the place where Frank met his Waterloo.'

Allen concurred, although she knew her time would be better spent on the phone. She also realized it was time to confront Weaver's stubbornness, 'Bud, you need to take off the blinders and see Brock staring right at us.'

'Forget it Allen. The Farley warehouse has no connection to our rape series and further this rapist works alone. There's no way one man could take Frank out,' Weaver, said making no effort to hide his irritation. He continued, 'My guess is this is an organized crime hit. They're trying to send a message to someone.'

269

'Whatever.' Allen was the first out of the office. They drove to the warehouse in silence.

43

It was the need for a short break and a hot cup of tea that sent Darlene Grant in a new direction to learn more about Tyrus Brock. As she stood in the break room of her office building waiting for the tea water to heat, she came across a news article, now several days old, in the Metro section of the *Sacramento Bee*.

The short story gave cursory details of a fatal motorcycle accident involving a 25-year-old woman. Her name: Janet Brock. The parole agent double-checked the date of the story and for a moment stood stunned, clutching the paper, oblivious to the boiling water.

She rushed back to her office and scanned her appointment book until she found what she was looking for, an entry for Tyrus Brock. 'That bastard!' her words spilled out. 'His wife was dead and he lied straight through his teeth. He sat right here and said he was happily married with his wife's body hardly cold.' Grant began a hasty search through the stacks on her desk until she located Brock's file.

She quickly reviewed her last notes. 'Dr. McKinley hasn't returned my call,' she said aloud as she reached for her telephone. The telephone receptionist at Folsom Prison put her through directly to the staff psychiatrist and the affable man answered on the fourth ring.

'Dr. McKinley, I'm Darlene Grant, a parole officer in Sacramento and I've been trying to reach you for several days. I need some information on one of my parolees who spent three years at your institution, an ex-soldier who committed a rape shortly after returning to the states. His name is Tyrus Brock.'

'Oh yes, Mr. Brock, the charmer,' he laughed, 'How is he doing? Not well, I suppose, or you would not be inquiring.'

'According to him everything is great, but I have some serious concerns. There seems to be a very significant disconnect between what he says and the truth.'

'Precisely. You must have read my letter. I believe I said there is a significant variance between his rhetoric and reality.'

'What letter? I haven't found any letter from you in his file.' Could she have misplaced a letter she wondered, and then dismissed the notion, knowing how alert the staff secretary was to all letters, especially one from a prison psychiatrist.

'I certainly sent one. Actually, it went out three weeks before his parole date. One to your agency and a carbon copy to the Sacramento County Sheriff's Department.'

'Strange. Initially, I received only a partial file. Later I requested and received the full file, and it contains no such letter. Can you recall your observations?'

The doctor responded with a question, 'Are you having a specific problem with him?'

'Serious concerns. As you are aware, there have been a number of violent rapes and now murders here in Sacramento. The Sheriff's Department tells me Brock is not the rapist, however, I'm beginning to wonder. Dr. Bevins, his therapist, has him journaling and his reflections are quite disturbing. In addition, when I talked with Brock he lied about his past and told me everything was fine in his marriage. Just today, I learned his wife was killed in a motorcycle accident before our last session. Yet he said nothing about her death. Something is very wrong. I'm hopeful you might give me some insight,' Grant said, her frustration evident.

'Oh, I remember him very well. He has a propensity for mistruths. Unfortunately, I was never able to break through his carefully constructed defenses. My letter explained my reasons for opposing parole.'

'What were your concerns?' Grant pressed.

'Early on, Brock developed a reputation as dangerous. The inmate social structure evolves in such a way that the weak are preyed upon and dominated. Brock kept to himself. He was a loner. One day, soon after his arrival, there was a shower incident,' the doctor paused.

'What kind of incident?'

'From the correctional officer's report, Brock was being teased by several, shall we say, burly inmates, all with a history of violence. It had something to do with Brock's genitalia, which apparently is small. Brock had to be restrained, but no one was hurt and it was considered minor. However, several days later, the most vocal of the inmates was found dead with a lead pencil stuck in his carotid artery.'

'Was Brock the killer?' Grant asked.

'We never proved that. Nobody would talk and charges were never brought up on Brock, but the word around the yard was don't mess with him. The inmates simply avoided him, which told me he likely was guilty.'

'The letter. Did you specifically warn our agency and the Sheriff's Department that Brock should be considered dangerous?' Grant continued her questioning.

'Absolutely. Further, I indicated I was worried about a repeat of sexual offenses. The closest I got to a break with Brock was when I questioned him about his mother. He hated her. A carefully contained hatred. Not a good sign in a rapist. No, Mr. Brock is one inmate I will never forget.'

Grant sat stunned. The doctor's words were as heavy on her spirit as anything she could imagine. She realized Brock was playing his therapist and her for fools. In fact, he was playing the entire criminal justice system. Hanging up the phone, she sat for several minutes. Every angle was glaring, from ineptness to alarm. Mostly, she had grave concerns about the lack of communication from agency to agency.

Retrieving his phone number from his file, she dialed Brock's number, thinking the least she could do is call him in and have a talk. The parole agent let the phone ring fourteen times. There was no answer. Then she was struck by another recent occurrence. 'What had that young man, who had barged into her office and asked about Brock, meant when he said, Monday might be too late?' She quickly called DOJ. 'I need to speak with an intern named Connors.'

'Just a moment ma'am.'

As she waited, she started writing down notes from her conversation with Dr. McKinley.

'Ma'am, I find no record of any Connors.'

'He's an intern.'

'Who does he work for?'

'I'm not sure. He used his boss's name, but I don't recall.'

'Sorry, with interns it's often months before we get their names. Usually, by then they're already gone. If you remember who he worked for, call back.'

Grant hung up the phone, numb.

44

Let's go 'round back,' Weaver said to Allen as they approached the graying exterior of the massive Farley Iron Works. 'First we should check out the window Frank crawled through.' They proceeded to the back, traversing the weed-filled parking lot, passing a pile of discarded tires and wood pallets. Weaver chatted to hide his nervousness. 'Yeah . . . this place hasn't been active for years.'

Allen said nothing.

As they turned the corner and looked down the back of the long building, they spotted a row of windows. Weaver guessed them at fifteen feet above the ground. 'There doesn't appear to be any other way in except through that one open window,' Allen observed. 'Wait a minute . . . there's a door. Let's check it out'

'Forget it,' Weaver said, 'see that big, rusted padlock. That door hasn't been used in years.'

But Allen was already there. 'Not so quick. Take a look at this,' she said, pointing to the rusty padlock with her pen. 'Someone went to a lot of trouble to cut through the lock. This cut is fresh. Whoever did this lined the lock up so it would appear untouched.' Her mind immediately flashed back to similar cuts on the motorcycle handlebars.

She glanced at her feet, bent down and stirred fresh metal shavings with her pen. 'Bud, these filings are still bright. This was cut within the last few days.' She stood and removed the lock.

'Son-of-a-bitch. Wonder if those fuckin' kids from the crime lab even found this. Hang on to it, always good to embarrass them.' Weaver grabbed the doorknob and twisted. It opened easily. Looking closely at the hinges he could see evidence of fresh oil. 'Damned if someone didn't lube these hinges and not long ago,' he rubbed a clear drop between his thumb and index finger.

As they stepped through the door, Weaver stumbled momentarily over an iron bar lying on the concrete floor. Allen stopped, stooped down and ran her eyes left to right across the bar. 'Fresh scrapes here. See this end?' she pointed.

'Right . . . look . . . that bar was used and then dropped on the way out,' Weaver examined the brackets on either side of the doors interior.

'Your right, whoever killed Graham came through the door, and then secured it from the inside using the bar. That's why Graham came through the window.' Allen glanced around, her eyes resting on the open window, 'Pretty obvious someone set a trap for Frank. And he crawled right into it.'

'This is one clever set-up. Looks to me like there must've been several fuckers involved. Let's find Garcia and see if he's figured out how the rest of this worked.'

They found Garcia standing in front of a large, open overhead door talking with two crime lab technicians. When he saw Weaver and Allen, he broke away, joining them directly under the cable noose still hanging from the rafter. Allen showed Garcia the padlock. Together they returned to the door and examined the scrapes on the back door. Allen's sequence seemed the most plausible explanation. She couldn't help but note how slow Weaver had been to

277

make these observations. He really was slipping, she thought.

'But how'n the hell did they drag Frank through the window?' Weaver asked gazing up at the rafters.

'Not as hard as you think. It's a matter of physics. Whoever is responsible used this air compressor,' Garcia said, pointing to a large tank just a few feet from them. 'First, the compressor was hoisted up to the support beam, using that pulley wired to the roof rafters,' he pointed upward as he spoke.

'There are two boards nailed to the lower rafter with fresh scrapes made by the compressor. Once the cable was around Frank's neck, the compressor was pushed off and when the weight, probably at least six hundred pounds, hit the end of the cable, Graham jerked through the window like a shot. Left him hanging with his head jammed against the roof. He strangled quickly, but the poor bastard tore up his hands clawing at the cable.'

Weaver stood staring at the pulley apparatus, shaking his head. Allen felt sickened by the thought of the pain endured by Graham. No one deserved to die like this.

Garcia continued, 'He was probably most of the way through the window before he was snared. Whoever did it was standing on the rafter and dropped the loop over Graham's head. We're going to try to recreate the scene as soon as the technicians finish checking for prints. They're bringing a numb john over from the gym. The mechanics who found the body said no one from the company had been in the building for over a week, so the trap was set yesterday or sooner. We're checking that out of course.'

'That's quite a description. I've never heard of such a thing,' Weaver said, still shaking his head.

'Me neither,' Garcia agreed, 'in the states that is. When I was in Nam, the Viet Cong often set up this type of trap. Snares were fairly common both in the jungle and in buildings.'

Allen interrupted, 'Gentlemen we're wasting time. It's over. Graham is dead. How many people did it take to pull this off? That's what we need to find out. Once you recreate the event, would you let me know?'

'Wait a minute Allen,' Weaver interjected. 'This isn't our case.'

'Let's just say I'm curious and let it go at that,' Allen answered and turned to Garcia, 'You're checking to see where the cable and the pulleys came from?'

'Oh yeah,' Garcia replied, 'Lopez is working on it. Nothing yet, but we'll probably have to check local and the entire Bay Area, Graham being from Frisco.'

Allen motioned to Weaver her intention to leave. 'I've seen enough. This place gives me the creeps.'

279

45

It was 8:00 am when Sergeant Howell turned his unmarked patrol car onto the River Highway and headed south. He drove slowly, mindful of the light fog on a narrow road. Despite the morning's mission, he found some peace in the calm river view; two Canadian geese honked overhead.

The aging sergeant contemplated the man he was going to meet. It was a meeting he dreaded, just the thought of Stringer made his stomach queasy. 'Why didn't Brandt talk with Stringer himself?' Howell knew why: Albert Stringer carried the smell of death and Brandt feared the stench.

'Tell Albert it's his own fault. If he hadn't turned down a direct order, there wouldn't be a problem and it's on him to clean up the fuckin' mess. Tell him he does this and he can retire. He's a handy man to have around, but I gotta let him go.' The sergeant recalled his orders.

'Just like the old man,' Howell thought, 'having someone else do his dirty work and insulating himself from any blame. Seems the cash always flows to the top and the blame to the bottom.'

Howell knew Stringer owned an old abbey near Toulouse in Southern France and apparently he planned to retire there. 'At least I can give him that opportunity,' he thought, mentally prepping himself for their meeting.

Twelve miles later he turned into the long driveway leading up to Stringer's large brick house.

###

An alarm went off as soon as the car turned off the main road. Stringer, a 34 year veteran of the Sheriff's Department, who had not worn a uniform for 20 years, punched the off switch on the alarm and moved to his picture window. 'What the hell does Brandt want now?' he thought as he watched the unmarked sheriff's car approaching. Moving onto the front porch he was surprised to see Howell rather than Brandt get out of the car. 'George, you old bastard, what the hell are you doing here?'

Howell waited until he reached the bottom of the steps. 'Brandt couldn't make it so he sent me. Albert, we need to talk.'

'Thought you'd already be retired and living in Florida,' Stringer chuckled.

'No, I'm sitting, like you, waitin' on Brandt to let me go.'

'Don't know about you, but I told the old man I'm not hanging around much longer,' Stringer made his point firm.

'That's the good part of this visit. He's gonna let you move on,' Howell felt relieved to find a conversation opening.

'Spare the chatter. What's the bad part?' Stringer questioned.

'One little job.' Howell said.

'I don't do little jobs.'

'I know, I know. We need to take a walk and I'll fill you in. I doubt you'll talk in your house.'

Stringer responded, 'Nor near it. Let me get a coat,' he walked back inside.

Howell leaned against the car and waited.

In less than a minute, Stringer returned wearing an army style jacket, stopped at the foot of the stairs and directed with his right arm, 'Turn around and get your hands up.'

'This isn't necessary. We go way back,' Howell said as he turned and raised his arms.

'Don't mean you're not wired," Stringer came up behind Howell and ran his hands up and down Howell's stout body. 'Now take off your hat and jacket and unbutton your shirt.'

Howell did as he was told, carefully laying the items on the car hood.

'Now take off your shoes and drop your pants,' Stringer ordered.

Howell hesitated, 'This is going too far Albert. We're on the same side.'

'Like shit. I won't say anything to you until I know you're clean.'

Howell removed his shoes and dropped his pants. 'There, you satisfied?'

'Yeah. Get dressed. Let's walk down to the river.'

They walked in silence. Stringer spoke first, 'Okay what is it the old man wants?'

Howell kept his eyes focused on the water, 'You remember the Sawyer killing?'

'Sure, rode with him for almost two years. That's why I turned Brandt down cold.'

'Shouldn't have done that,' Howell admonished.

'Only job I ever turned down. Brandt knew why. Even I got limits. I should'a been allowed one turndown, especially Sawyer being a friend of mine.'

'Not when it causes a big problem.' Howell snapped.

'So . . . now what? Suppose Brandt wants me to bail him out of something.'

'Not just him. The whole fuckin' department.'

'Shit . . . what's this about? Stringer asked.

'Get revenge for Sawyer. Kill the fucker who shot him,' Howell said as they reached the bank of the river.

'If I'd wanted revenge for Sawyer, I'd killed that bastard Brandt long time ago. Who's on his hit list now, another deputy?' Stringer said, sarcasm rising.

'No, that's the problem. Brandt fucked up and had someone hire an ex-con. Damn stupid. I thought so at the time. Just askin' for trouble.'

'This fucker on parole?' Stringer spat the sharp tip of a toothpick to the ground.

'Yeah,' Howell said.

'Don't mind killing an ex-con, especially since he can't carry a gun. Makes my job easy.'

Howell turned to face Stringer, 'Don't be so sure. This guy is that crazy rapist we can't seem to catch, let alone kill. And he packs a gun when he's raping. You're getting a little long in the tooth. This won't be easy.'

'I got no worries.'

'One more thing. Orders are to get his done post haste. Brandt is absolute about this,' Howell reported and waited for the reaction.

Stringer frowned and turned toward the river. They walked in silence for several minutes. 'I won't have time to create any cover. Just be a dead man, maybe even on a public street. That's bound to raise questions.'

'Don't worry about that. Just make sure he's dead. Brandt will take care of the cover, probably say it was a drug hit. Not your problem.'

'I gotta have the guarantee from Brandt approving my retirement – in writing,' Stringer stopped walking.

Howell sighed, 'The retirement form is in my car, along with a file that will fill you in on this guy. You read it and you'll know all you need to know to kill him.'

They walked back to the house. When they reached the car, Howell broke the silence, opened the car door and handed the thick file to Stringer. "You'll find a bonus in there, I think the old man called it extra cash for takin' out another guy.' Howell reported, unsure of Stringer's reaction.

What's this about another hit?'

'Some nosey young guy. College kid. A nobody. It's all in the file. He'll be easy. Lives alone in South Sac.'

Stringer sighed as he took the file from Howell. 'It'll be done. And be sure to tell the old man *au revoir* from me.'

46

Tyrus Brock, in his white Ford van, left Sacramento, driving east on Highway 50. Ten miles past Placerville, he turned south onto a dirt access road into the El Dorado National Forest. The sun was barely upon the horizon when he killed the ignition and rolled down the driver window to smell the fresh, piney air. A chorus of bird calls echoed from the solid rock wall at the back of a quarry pit, a site he'd visited many times.

Opening the van's cargo doors he studied its fullness. Two trunks filled with books and shoes, sleeping bag, tent, grocery bag full of bread, jars of peanut butter, cans of tuna and instant coffee. And, a muddy pack holding a Colt .44 Magnum pistol and two bowie knives. The dirty pack irritated him. Last night he'd quickly unburied it from his yard and taken care to return the empty hole and dirt to proper order, but little thought to clean the pack. There had been no time. His mission in Sacramento was fast drawing to a close, and he needed to focus every task, every minute for his ultimate goal.

The Colt and the knives were his protection, as he would be driving south on I-5 and could not afford any contact with a traffic officer. If necessary, he knew the magnum had the power to go through most bullet proof vests. 'I can't be too careful,' he thought. Knife or gun, no police officer would be spared; this much he knew.

Target practice in the old rock quarry always settled his nerves. His practice style was methodical. First, he shot with his right hand, then with his left, altering body positions and target distances. He did not stop until he was satisfied. The drive back to Sacramento was slow as the morning commuters headed into the city. He noted the skyline, small as it was, and laughed aloud, 'This is one city I can call my own. The women here will never be comfortable again.'

'Should leave now for Los Angeles,' he told himself as he drove, but one remaining mission called to him. She was tall. Her hair dark and long. The details of her comings and goings, her friends and her lover could fill a page or two, but he was now growing tired of the surveillance. It was time to take her – tonight.

He had planned to stop by his empty house and rest, but as he approached the neighborhood, an old feeling, a sense of danger, surprised him. The feeling was both loathsome and welcome. It had saved his life several times in the jungle, so often he had given the foreboding a name: Ghost of the Viet Cong.

Suddenly, he felt very alive and within minutes he knew why. A white Lincoln had circled the block and was now behind him. 'I'm being followed,' he said aloud, taking the next few minutes to make several turns and verify his suspicion. The Lincoln remained on his tail. What to do, now?

He recalled a house prowled just last week in order to obtain documents for fake ID's. Bradford was their name and they both worked days. Two facts now drew him there: they wouldn't be home and their house had an enclosed chimney on the right side of a low roof line. He drove there and parked directly in front and then walked quickly to the back yard, entered and closed the gate behind him.

Stringer settled into the thick leather of his Lincoln Mark IV. City streets were not busy and his speed decidedly slow. He loved the car and appreciated its ease of handling, especially when checking the magazine of his revolver with his right hand. Surprisingly, he sensed his comfort shifting to confusion as he watched Brock pass his house, turn left on 43rd Street, make two more street turns, before stopping in front of a brick home on the corner.

Driving past Brock's van, he continued one block before parking. Then he walked back down the street to the brick house; as he approached the gate, he pulled his revolver, held it close to his thigh and used his left hand to open the latch.

Brock crouched, poised on the roof edge, his body invisible behind the chimney, bowie knife in his right hand. Then, in an instant: the jump, the contact and the jugular pierced. In less than 3 seconds, Stringer attacked and dismissed to slip into death.

Brock rose, leaving the knife imbedded deep in Stringer's throat, turned and returned to his van. He stripped off his bloody shirt and gloves, zipped on a clean jacket. Ten blocks and two turns later, safely behind a grocery store, Brock stopped by a stack of wood pallets, jumped out and switched license plates.

'That fucker. Now my entire day has me waiting. Wasting all day before my last zero hour,' Brock muttered. The murderer drove from the city, towards the Yolo causeway where he could burn the bloody clothes and dive into the water to rid himself of another man's blood.

47

It was well after seven by the time Allen finished her workday and drove toward Connors' apartment. She'd been on the go all day, fielding phone calls, meeting with the three women identified as possible rape targets, working on reports, and then ending the afternoon with another meeting in Phillips' office.

Feeling hungry, she pulled into a *McDonalds* drive thru, ordered her favorite, the Big Mac, with a small ice tea and continued on, eating as she drove. Driving through the quiet streets, she began to plan the approaching night's potential encounter with a killer.

The past couple of days had been jarring enough, but now she was preparing to take on a dangerous criminal with only her wits and the partnership of a man she'd known for a few, short weeks.

For an instant, it all seemed absurd and she wondered if she'd lost her senses in agreeing to align with Scott Connors. What stirred her on was a strong sense of justice and growing passion for women of Sacramento who were living in constant fear for their safety, for their very lives. And there was Scott. Somehow, she instinctively believed in him. Her decision was set. There was no turning back.

The unusually mild spring evening found children still playing outdoors, enjoying the ebbing sunlight well past the dinner hour. She watched a young couple with a small dog on a leash, walking hand-in-hand. 'God, what I wouldn't give to have their life,' she said aloud. Soon, she reached Connors' apartment.

He greeted her with a long hug but only a quick kiss. 'Can't let myself become distracted,' he smiled. 'We have to stay on task.'

Susan stepped back and offered him a dramatic pout, hoping he might lighten up for a moment. He barely noticed, so she taunted him, 'True, but a real kiss would be nice.'

Connors was already walking toward the living room, but he returned and brought Susan into his arms. She fit so well in his embrace and her eagerness delighted him. Here, now, in the comfort of Susan's softness, with the reality of a brutal rapist- turned-killer foremost on his mind, he was surprised to find himself thinking back to Laurie, intense Laurie.

By comparison, he couldn't recall ever feeling the comfort and completeness he felt with Susan. Laurie had rarely engendered warmth like this. Susan's kisses were so different and he was learning to savor them.

'That's better,' Susan smiled. 'Now we can settle down to business,' leading him into the kitchen. 'Start some coffee. This could be a long vigil.'

'The big question is: Will Brock strike tonight?' Connors asked as he went about the task of making coffee.

'Nothing is for certain as to when, but we know he will. The lab report came back on the Davis homicides, and the technicians found a very small amount of AB blood that didn't match either victim. Just before I left the office, the report on the handkerchief blood came back. Turned out Graham's wino also has type AB. Sure seems like the dots connect.'

Connors nodded, listening, as she continued. 'But Brock didn't plant much blood. I checked that out carefully with the lab guys.' Susan took a half teaspoon of sugar and stirred it into her coffee, before continuing, 'Graham said the wino told him Brock filled a syringe. That means he's holding and now it's Tuesday, his favorite night. He must have saved blood for a reason.'

'What if he doesn't hit tonight and stops? Graham's stalking may have spooked him,' Connors suggested.

Susan settled on Scott's couch, kicking off her shoes and curling her long legs back under her body, a position Scott loved to see. It showed Susan relaxed, something she desperately needed.

Tonight, especially, they both needed clear heads and minimal tension in order to make the right decisions. Scott went to his dining table, now a make-shift command post, searched for and found a copy of the internal memo from the Sheriff's Department forewarning the rapist's de-compensation. He found the memo's accuracy amazing. 'What about the woman on Carter Drive, the one I didn't see? Does she match the victim profile?" he asked.

'She does. Her name is Faye Collins. She's tall and slender with long dark hair. She'll be the one. Thankfully, she and her husband agreed to stay with her parents for as long as necessary. Now it's up to us to go to Carter Drive and wait for Brock.'

Connors walked toward the window as he ran his left hand through his dark, curly hair. It was a slight, nervous gesture Susan had grown to recognize as something he did to buy thinking time. She couldn't help but consider how attractive he looked, silhouetted against the window, pensive, one hand in his pocket. She also considered how different things would be had they met under more normal circumstances.

What was it her grandmother used to tell her? 'Your best work is accomplished by always being where you are when you're there.' She thought it odd that such a thought would rise up at a time like this. Well, she was here all right, with a man she trusted and a plan that had to work.

Connors turned to face her and broke the silence, 'I can't help thinking how difficult Weaver's attitude is. If only he had agreed to help us . . . .'

'That's wishful thinking,' Susan interrupted. 'He's more cynical than ever, even about the handkerchief. I remember his words exactly: "Don't care much about a bloody handkerchief taken from a wino by a dead man." No, Weaver is no help to us.'

'His loyalty to Brandt is shameful.' Connors offered.

'Well, we can't worry about him. By the way, I sent a memo to the graveyard lieutenant and asked for extra patrols in the area. They're usually pretty good about taking care of my requests; we can count on some nearby back-up.'

'I can't get Brock's MO off my mind. He's extremely smart, yet his pattern is established, a pattern we've discovered. You'd think he'd change his location or the type of woman he chooses, at least change something.' Scott continued.

'Didn't you learn that in your classes? All criminals, from the dumbest to the smartest, seem to follow established patterns. I guess if something works, it's difficult to change. Don't you have a special kind of woman who attracts you?' Allen asked, feeling the apt timing of a gentle tease, hoping to relax Scott.

Connors smiled, his disarming, youthful grin, 'I'll take the fifth on that one. Are you absolutely sure you want to go through with this? I'm still concerned about problems you'll run into with your brass.'

'I've given it a great deal of thought,' Susan answered slowly. 'If we're wrong and Brock is a no-show, no one from the department will ever know. If Brock shows and we arrest him, then all the risk is worth it.'

She paused to study Scott's reaction before continuing. 'Three weeks ago I started sending memos to Captain Phillips summarizing my conversations with Weaver as well as my meeting with Brandt concerning Brock. I've kept copies of the memos, a paper trail to prove I've tried to convince them of Brock's involvement. It's something at least.'

'So you are worried. Maybe you should let me handle this – alone,' Connors said.

'No, I can't do that. You're not a sworn officer, nor do you have the training. I took this job to protect lives and apprehend criminals. The only thing I'm doing wrong is not going through the chain of command; and, of course, I'm working with a civilian. According to regulations I should have briefed Weaver on our plan, but, I'm done trying to force him to consider Brock.'

'So this could get you fired?'

'Could. The point is Brock has to be stopped,' she spoke with authority. 'No, tonight we're going to

Carter Drive and set a trap. I'll deal with the department after we've put Brock away. Don't give it any more thought. Let's focus on how were going to arrest Brock.' Susan said, her tone resolute.

'You keep talking about arresting Brock. What if he doesn't submit? Remember: this is a highly trained Special Forces soldier, a soldier with a gun. If you try to arrest him aren't you giving him an opportunity to shoot you?'

'It's a chance I have to take. I can't just execute him. As a peace officer I can use deadly force only when necessary,' Susan replied.

'I still feel unsure. I know your mind is made up; let's get to what's next,' Connors was resigned.

Susan stood and walked towards the kitchen. 'First, we need to drink as much coffee as possible. Can't have you falling asleep,' she smiled and winked at Connors. 'Keep in mind we think he enters a house between two and three in the morning, but it would be just our luck to walk in and find him waiting to surprise us. He outsmarted Graham. Let's not let him do the same to us. We should stake out sometime before 11 p.m.'

'I'm also concerned that he might set a trap again. I don't think we should use the front door,' Connors suggested. 'I think I should enter through a window, first.'

' Right. The window in the dining room on the east side of the house?'

'That's very specific. Do you know something I don't?' Connors asked.

'Yes, I'm way ahead of you. I stopped by the house this afternoon and left a dining room window

294

unlocked for just that very reason. And, surprise, I found a rear bedroom window unlocked.' She paused, 'Honestly, finding the unlocked window gave me chills.'

It chilled Connors, too, but he didn't let on. For the past hour the couple's mood had jumped from playful to sober and back again. There was no need to linger on fear. For a while neither spoke, Scott's ticking cuckoo clock the only sound in the small apartment. When the little bird exited to announce his ten cuckoos, Scott looked at Susan. 'Let's get on the road. But first 'Another real kiss for the detective lady,' and he drew her into his arms.

48

The agony of indecision was unnerving and dangerous. He'd baited and killed the fucker. Good. Then the second guy popped up, the bastard that ate my knife. 'The fuckers had no business following me. Who the hell were they?' he muttered to himself.

The snare had been flawless and the ambush perfect. Had to be the Sheriff's Department. They're on to me, but so what. I'll be gone by morning. Let them sit on my house, I'll be half way to L.A. before they find it empty. I'll dump the van and switch cars in Stockton, pick up my new identification documents, and start a new life. He knew his enemy. Strike quick before they can plan. Tonight's mission: the house on Carter Drive.

He still had a syringe with blood and a picture of the woman. A picture he'd pilfered and studied for days. She taunted him, broadcasting her vulnerability. She stared up at him from the picture on the passenger seat, next to a candle, next to his devotional book. Her smile a summons.

Two thoughts pulled equally like a Chinese finger puzzle. First doubts, now hesitation. The angst was unbearable. Still, he wanted this mission. Focus on the mission. Take control. Take control. He burned the thought into his brain.

He'd have her alright. 'God damned bitch, I'm coming.' Finally, his thoughts were settled and he felt his control return. It was time to move on. Thoughts of Southern California were appealing to him more and more. It was time to relocate. He tucked the money he had withdrawn from his bank account into his back pack. He picked up the picture from the seat and stared at her smiling face. 'Tonight I own you,' he said aloud.

Allen parked her car two blocks over and one down from 11375 Carter Drive. It was 10:24 p.m. 'Weapons check,' Allen said while they were still seated. 'Make sure your revolver is loaded. Double check your flashlight.'

'Yes ma'am,' Connors quipped, trying to mask his mounting tension.

'You did say you could hit a running rabbit at twenty yards?'

'I did, but that was more than ten years ago. And to be honest, I didn't hit them every time.'

'Now you tell me,' she sighed, and then with a zesty resolve, 'Let's go.'

They walked three blocks to the house. Heavy clouds blocked out the moon, intensifying the darkness.

Allen was pleased to see the Collins' car left in the driveway, just as she'd requested. Everything appeared normal. 'Let's circle the house before we go in. You go to the right, I'll take left. Meet me in the back yard. Look everything over with the flashlight. Have your gun ready and, remember, every time you push the button on your flashlight, hold it out at full arm's length, just like I showed you. Oh, one last thing. Before you turn on your flashlight close your right eye. Keep it closed until you turn the light off. This keeps your night vision intact, at least in one eye.'

297

'I'd never considered that,' Connors absorbed Allen's directions.

'Little things can save your life. Don't forget: I will be coming towards you in the back yard.'

'Got it.'

When they joined in the back yard, Allen motioned for Connors to continue on, 'Meet me back in front,' she whispered.

They met in front. 'No problem so far,' Connors said. 'Which window is the dining room? I'll enter and check the interior.' He felt his confidence as a stealth artist taking hold.

'Okay. But once inside, go to the front door immediately and let me in. We check out the interior together. Inside, I go first. You follow seven or eight steps behind. Step only when I do. If he's hiding and listening, we may be able to fool him into thinking there's only one person,' Allen continued to instruct. Connors nodded in agreement.

After maneuvering through the window, Connors walked silently to the front door where he threw the deadlock, allowing Allen to enter. They moved slowly through the house checking every possible hiding place. When they were satisfied the house was empty, Allen said, 'We can talk now.'

Turning on the living room light, they sat, away from the window, talking in quiet tones. 'If he's watching the house, we have to make things look normal,' Allen said.

Connors nodded, 'This sneaking around in the dark, thinking there might be someone ready to kill you, sure gives a person an adrenaline rush.'

'You mean you're scared to death?'

'Something like that,' Connors replied.

Allen smiled, 'Well, this might be for nothing. He may be a no show.'

'He'll show,' Connors declared. 'The memo from the psychologist said that once the escalation sets in, the perpetrator's urge control is unstoppable. I believe this is the level Brock has reached.'

'It's a horrible thought,' Allen responded.

'Horrible and real. One of my biggest frustrations with this case is not being able to convince anyone in authority, to consider the psychological and social clues this guy is sending.' Connors said.

Susan nodded, realizing he had more to add.

Connors continued, 'In order to change criminals we need to understand what drives them. Brock spent three years in prison. Taxpayers spent more than one hundred thousand dollars on him and it was wasted. Nothing was done to or with him while he was in prison to address his problem, his twisted sex drive.'

'I can't imagine how that could ever be accomplished short of castration. But, I'm just a cop and my job tonight, and yours, is to stop a criminal, not treat him.' Susan responded.

'But think about it. Not only did taxpayers pay to train Brock how to kill people during his army service, but then they paid to teach him how to avoid being caught.' Connors caught himself. Time to stop talking he thought. He had fallen in love with a cop and she was right. All the theory in the world wouldn't help them now. It was down to basics. 'What's our next step?'

'Where to position you. When he comes in the back bedroom window, my guess is he'll check out the rest of the house, cut the telephone cord in the kitchen and then come to the master bedroom. So where you hide is critical.'

'What about you?'

'I'll be in the master bedroom. We'll put pillows under the covers, mess up the bed so it looks like two people sleeping. I picked up a hairpiece to stage a sleeping body.' She pulled a thick brunette fall from her jacket pocket. 'I'll hide in the closet with the door open. Once he enters the bedroom, he's going to focus on the bed.'

'Wait a minute. Shouldn't we both be in the bedroom?'

'No, not enough room. If there's shooting, we might hit each other. Plus, we can't predict his reaction. No, it has to be me. I'm the deputy. You're my backup.'

Connors started to protest. Allen cut him off, 'This is no time for male ego. I'm the senior person here. I want you in the laundry room. Once you hear me yell or shots fired, then cover the retreat.'   Scott shook his head, considering again whether or not they should continue.

Susan pressed on, 'Probably he'll try to exit the way he came in, but we've got no guarantees, so memorize the layout of the rooms and all the doors. At that point it's about reaction, period.' She looked deeply into his eyes to determine his readiness, found it and waited for Connors to speak.

'Okay, you're the boss on this, but I, for the record, want it known I would prefer being the one to initially confront him.'

300

'I would suggest we take our positions around midnight,' she looked at her watch.

'That means we have to stay in hiding for up to three hours,' Connors calculated.

'Right. My guess is he won't show until around three, but we can't risk him changing his timing. Welcome to the world of police work. I once spent seven straight days on a stakeout and the guy never did show. It takes skill and patience to be ready for the short episodes of intense action. And if the coffee gets to you, use the laundry room sink. Which is a better option than I have. And don't ask. I am going to handle that problem. Sure you're up to it?'

'I am. We're a team and you can count on me.' Connors said.

'I know,' Allen answered.

49

He drove very carefully. Parked four blocks from the river adjacent to the bike trail which meandered along the American River. Removing the bike from the rack on the back of his van he began pedaling east, just as a cool breeze rose from the river.

For a few brief moments he felt normal, just a regular guy on a late night bike ride. He rode slowly, allowing the rhythm of the ride to settle the tension in his body. It was 2:05 a.m. when he positioned himself behind some overgrown shrubbery in the back yard of the target, having checked and found the couples' car in the driveway.

For several minutes he sat and waited, allowing his mind to embrace the challenge. He savored this time, especially the anticipation. He thought of his van packed and ready. Once this mission was finished he was free to leave for Los Angeles. He had prepared well.

At 2:30 a.m. he stood, removed his clothes, folded them neatly, placed them behind a bush, threw the backpack over his left shoulder, and began the approach. Two steps into the yard, he froze at the sound of a nearby siren wailing. He felt his body quiver as he sought refuge behind a large camellia bush. Again, he waited. Still as a statue, his naked body pumped with adrenaline, his eyes searching for any sign of danger. Just like in the jungle.

Checking his watch, he read 2:56 a.m. four more minutes . . . then the faint, distant train whistle commanded: *Advance.* Moving silently to the window, he stopped again and listened. Then he crouched, pulled on his ski mask, adjusted the eye holes, pulled surgical gloves onto his hands and re-shouldered the backpack. He was ready. Zero hour.

The window opened easily, silently. He pulled himself up to the sill, bumping his right knee, the impact slight. Through the window he snaked, slinking to the floor, standing and listening. He heard nothing. Next, he pulled the revolver and flashlight from the backpack and started his prowl through the house. As always, earlier memorization of the floor plan guided him, and he found assistance from the streetlamp's reflected light through the windows. When he reached the kitchen, he used his knife to sever the telephone cord. There was a soft snap as the blade cut through the sheath and wires.

He looked around slowly, focusing for a moment on the half-opened laundry room door. He paused. Something didn't feel right. His head cocked like a lizard on heightened alert. Standing still for several seconds, time seemed to stop. The silence satisfied him. He continued to the hall, towards the sleeping couple.

Once again, he fought back images of naked, olive-skinned women. 'Stay alert, focus,' he reproached himself mentally. Strong, silent commands and admonishments always kept him on course.

Connors stood stiff, his back pressed against the wall behind the laundry room door. Despite his best control, he needed to extend his legs, one at a time, every ten or fifteen minutes. Twelve inches to the right, twelve inches to the left, his legs ached and so did his neck. He slowly readjusted from the shoulders up, forty-five degrees to the right, forty-five to the left, hoping to prevent a kink or worse a cramp. At first he stole frequent glances at the luminous dial on his watch, but the time passed too slowly and he stopped looking.

Standing still was proving to be the hardest work he'd ever done. After a wait that felt like an eternity, he heard a soft bump from the rear of the house. He froze. A sound so minimal he would not have heard it except for tonight's acute vigilance.

He pulled the door toward him another few inches and stood rigid, his back against the wall. The cocked revolver in his right hand and a flashlight in his left, he waited. No more sounds. Breathing silently but deeply, he struggled to suppress anxiety, anxiety defying his will. Then he heard something, something ever so faint. The telephone cord, he thought. The rapist was in the kitchen, now, not twelve feet from him. 'He's too quiet, like a phantom,' Connors thought. He forced himself not to move.

'Annie, this is for you,' he thought. Then he heard a soft brushing noise. Something had moved past his hiding place. His mind screamed . . . he remained frozen.

Allen was positioned in the closet, the door two-thirds open with a line of vision to the bedroom doorway. Blackness enveloped her territory. A long silk dress and cotton pants suit hung directly in front of her. Stacked boxes of shoes hid her feet. It was the best she could do. Straining to see between the garments she waited patiently, trying to maintain poise.

Any panic could prove fatal. She filled the time with thoughts of her father and how she missed him. Then, she flashed on her mother. If she died tonight, how would her mother handle the loss? Would it re-ignite her drinking? Can't go there. Negative thinking, she forced the thoughts from her mind.

Scott Connors. How did she really feel about him? Was it love or just tension release? Can't go there either. She changed her thinking to his support, his back up. Could she count on him? Yes, she knew she could.

She willed herself to return to the here and now, to focus on the present, the waiting . . . the doorway. Would Brock walk in and look only at the bed? She would wait until he turned on the flashlight and then make her move. If she kept her revolver aimed at him as he entered the room, she could easily shoot him in the chest. That would be the safest.

But, as a peace officer, she knew she couldn't shoot until it was absolutely necessary to save her life. Would she be able to maintain that integrity? Could she kill in cold blood?

She had to give him an opportunity to surrender, even though it could prove fatal to her. She said a silent prayer imploring God, her dad and his beloved Catholic saints to be with her. She wondered what Brock's reaction would be. Would he realize there was no breathing coming from the bed? Would he freeze and drop his gun when ordered?

The questions, especially about Brock, swirled through her mind. He was not a normal criminal and

305

she shouldn't expect predictable responses. This was Brock, an ex-Special Forces soldier. If he turned, swinging his revolver toward her, then shoot him she would. But in the dark she might not know where his pistol was pointing. If he turned and ran, she could justify shooting right into the center of the doorway. What else might he do? Maybe drop to the floor? The time moved painfully slow. Allen heard nothing.

Then fear flooded her senses as she realized she was no longer alone. She could not see him, but instinct told her the rapist was in the room. Straining, she was sure she could hear him breathing. Did he know? Could he sense the bed was empty?

Suddenly, there was blinding light, burning directly into her eyes. She shouted, 'Police, you're under . . . .' Then an explosion. The bullet hit the closet cross rod, not an inch from her head. Twice she fired at the flash. Turning on her flashlight, she saw movement at the door and fired again. She dove for cover just as a bullet passed over her left shoulder.

Connors heard the shots. He raced out of the laundry room and sprinted toward the bedroom. All he could think of was Susan. Bam! Collision. He and another man, one coming, one going, both down in a tangle of arms and legs. Strange how the events seemed to move in slow motion. He could smell the assailant, the faint, distinct smell of *English Leather*. Connors tried to roll clear, but was struck with a glancing blow to the side of his head and he fell back on the floor, stunned momentarily with pain. He struggled to stay conscious.

'Die fucker,' the enemy commanded as Scott rolled to his right. A gun exploded; he could smell the

306

burned powder and feel the impact of the bullet as it pierced the floor. Instinctively, he swung his gun toward the figure running for the front door and fired twice. Connors heard a yelp and saw him stumble, a naked silhouette floundering momentarily. Then silence. Connors struggled to his feet as Allen raced past. Her form framed in the open front door. She fired once. 'Damn, he's gone,' she cursed into the night.

Shock and pain. He felt both as the bullet struck his right side. He flinched, staggered and struggled against the urge to collapse. Only a weak soldier yields. Then his right arm exploded and dropped weakly to his side, warm blood spreading over his chest, running down his back. His revolver clattered as it hit the porch floor. Escape. Run and keep running. Think only of escape.

To the river, run to the river. Despite the pain and the blood, he could still sprint. No stopping for clothes. He painfully, willfully, climbed the back fence, leaving large blotches of blood behind. The dry brush ripped at his naked skin as he ran straight toward the American River.

Fear blocked out pain as he raced headlong. He could hear sirens in the distance. Sliding down the steep bank of the river, he jumped feet first into the dark swirling water. He floundered against the current, his right arm useless. Downstream he bobbed, bloody water swirling around him. His backpack, still looped around his left shoulder now acting as a drag. Still free. Naked and alone. His body slipped slowly under the dark swirling water.

###

Susan could not control her shaking. She stood on the porch, flashlight in hand, her right arm at her side still clutching her revolver. Scott put his left arm around her shoulder and pulled her close. Slowly, he could feel her composure return.

A bloody doorjamb and front steps broadcast reminders of the burst of terror the two had just experienced. 'The bastard got away. I can't believe he got away,' Scott was the first to speak.

'But he's wounded. Badly, I think,' Susan turned now to face her partner, 'and you did it Scott. You did it.'

'What did I do? We . . .'

'You hit the running rabbit,' Susan interrupted. Immediately, Scott began to refute his act, but Susan lifted two fingers to his lips, 'Shhh, own it. It's yours. Take this, too.' She reached up with her left hand and gently brought his lips to her.

The sound of approaching sirens broke the silence. 'Somebody must've heard the shots and called the police,' Susan said. 'Wait here and show the deputies the blood trail. With the amount of blood on the ground, he won't get far. I'm going next door to call Bud. Better he hears about this from me directly. And lay your revolver down. We don't want the deputies thinking you're the bad guy.' It was clear, Susan was back in charge.

Scott watched Allen walk toward the neighbor's porch light as he noted the near full moon peeking out from a bank of clouds. In the distance a dog barked. He glanced at his watch: 3:20 a.m. 'It's finally over,' he announced to the night air.

As the flashing lights approached, he thought back to his first introduction to the rapist, given by a professor who had called it correctly, 'This is a terrorist. One who plans his violent attacks. Someone who has been trained.'

Tyrus Brock had proven to be that and more.

Epilogue

Allen arrived at work at 6:15 a.m. She had slept fitfully for weeks. The stress of her suspension had drained her energy and her spirit. For nearly three weeks she had waited for the department review of the shooting incident.

During the wait she had felt like a Girl Friday. Restricted to in-house paperwork and answering the phone. She was beginning to resent police work, in fact the whole criminal justice system. She realized how bureaucracy and corruption had resulted in deaths and destroyed lives of many women and even of the men they loved during the rapists' reign of terror.

Weaver had told her to expect the report from internal affairs at any time. 'This week for sure,' he had said, so she wasn't surprised when she found a sealed envelope marked *Confidential* in her mailbox.

Allen took the envelope to the conference room where she could sit with privacy behind a closed door to digest the report. Policewoman or not she knew a wave of tears might hit and she certainly did not want the openness and vulnerability at her desk should that happen.

She wondered if she should call Scott to tell him the verdict on her future lay before her in an unopened envelope. She had found his support helpful, but this was her life. She decided against the call.

Opening the envelope, she scanned the first two pages. As she read she kept muttering, 'This is unbelievable,' but thankfully no tears, just anger. The verdict: *Recommend a 30 day suspension without pay. No loss of rank.* The brass was slapping her hand, lauding some of her actions and ultimately killing her career all in the same document.

They did write: Detective Allen showed great courage in encountering a dangerous criminal who had committed a series of rapes and murders. Then for two pages she read of her failure to comply with department regulations, initiating a police action without advising her superior officer, and involving a citizen in a police action without proper clearance.

The report was technical and cold, just as she had expected. And, her original trepidation turned to anger. Howell had been right. She had ruined her career with the department. Allen stood and walked slowly back to her desk to call Scott.

Thanks for coming, Susan said, 'It looks like I have some time on my hands.' The couple sat in the Mediterranean Café, coffee cups between them, early morning traffic noise swirling around.

Connors slowly sipped his coffee as Susan read her suspension notice in a low voice. He could see she was close to tears despite her stoic posture.

'Susan your suspension probably will not hold up. When the press gets this information you will be a hero. You stopped a serial killer. Brock is at the bottom of the river, and we can now focus on our relationship. Which is all the reward I need.'

'Agreed,' Susan said, reaching for his hand.

Appendix

The following is a confidential memo issued by the Sacramento County Sheriff's Department to their deputies during the crime series which was used as the inspiration for this novel. The names have been changed.

COUNTY OF SACRAMENTO
SHERIFF WILLIAM BRANDT

Inter-Department

TO: ALL PERSONNEL
FROM: Captain Phillips
          Homicide/Sex Crimes Detail

STATUS: CONFIDENTIAL: Not to be shared with press or public

SUBJECT: EAST AREA RAPE INVESTIGATION – CONFIDENTIAL
At this writing there have been 19 rapes attributed to the East Area Rapist (E.A.R.). These crimes were compiled into a series, using the description of the rapist, similarities of victims, and M.O. factors. This series has been given such wide publicity that most of the M.O. factors have been reported. There are, however, some specific behaviors peculiar to this rapist and they clearly indicate all the rapes have been committed by the same man.

POTENTIAL FOR DANGER

Due to the findings of profilers who have studied the majority of the rapes in this series and the resulting danger they believe exists for any law enforcement officer approaching this suspect, all officers are required to read this report. For this reason we have included a summary of the findings of the profilers in unusual detail. *Personnel are ordered NOT to share any part of this report with the general public or the press.*

THE SUSPECT

All that is known about the suspect at this time is that he is a white, male, adult, 20- to 30-years-old, 5'8' to 6'0 tall, with dirty blond to medium brown, collar length hair, bright blue or hazel eyes. His build is muscular, not fat. He wears size 9 or 10 tennis shoes. We believe he has type A blood. He often enters the home naked, but when clothed he wears dark clothing, with a preference for army green. He always wears a mask and gloves during the commission of the crimes.

FINDINGS OF THE PROFILERS

Professional profilers, after studying the first fifteen crime reports and interviewing the victims, list the following observations:

- At this time it does not seem probable that he is married, but if so, it would be a relatively new relationship rapidly deteriorating due to infrequent sexual performance bordering upon impotency,

313

because of the violence necessary for the perpetrator to become aroused.

- It is thought that the suspect is unable to maintain any normal heterosexual relationship with a female. As a consequence, he is capable of harboring deeply rooted feelings of inadequacy, which manifest themselves in the rape crimes. It is through the crime of rape
That he is finally able to establish dominance over the female, asserting his masculinity and perhaps *repaying* all of womanhood for causing him such anxiety.

- It is thought that any past involvement with the authorities would be in the area of indecent exposure and peeping Tom. The indecent exposure aspect is considered in view of the suspect removing his clothes, on many occasions, prior to his entering a victim's
home.

- It is further felt that the suspect is not addicted to any hard narcotic, but is probably a pill popper. The reviewers also feel that the suspect neither smokes nor drinks. They also believe there may be a strong religious tie inherent in his childhood. In this respect, the fact that several victims themselves are active in their churches could prove slightly more than coincidental in their selection.

- It is felt that he comes from a middle-class family environment. This is based upon his apparent change of attire – including shoes and various shapes and color of masks. The basic theory is that an individual in a lower-income bracket would have the tendency to wear the same clothing. In the cases where the rapist entered wearing clothes, the attire has varied considerably.

- The suspect also acquires familiarity for the areas in which the crimes occur. It is possible that he either lives in, or has lived in the immediate areas of the offenses. The days in which he attacks suggest he is probably a student or is drawing unemployment.

- There is a *definite increasing aggressiveness* in the suspect's method of attack. This is indicative of what is termed 'de-compensation.' This would indicate the rapist is a dangerous individual who would kill himself and/or any law enforcement officer (or person) attempting to take him into custody. Following the commission of the rape the suspect harbors extreme guilt feelings from his acts, and any thought of public exposure or attending ridicule would fully justify his self-destruction. When the subject is planning his crime is when he feels like a whole human being. As a consequence the overall planning and preparation are the main impetus sustaining his personality with the actual assault on the victim probable secondary.

FIELD INTERROGATION
Any officer approaching this suspect for a field interrogation must be aware of the rapist's state of mind. Given his psychological profile, the suspect's reaction to any field contacts with law enforcement personnel will be dependent on when the interception takes place.

If the contact is made before he enters the house his demeanor will be cool, calm, cunning and cooperative. He will also be extremely alert.

If the contact is made when the suspect is leaving the scene of a rape, explosive resistance will be immediately encountered.

Officers must be aware that any approach to this suspect must be done with extreme caution.

Anyone with information or tips about the East Area Rapist should contact the Sacramento County Sheriff's Department via Tip Line 916-874-TIPS (8477)

Look for the sequel to
TERROR AT 3 AM

By Duane D. Wilson
duanedwilson.com